BLOOD STORM

A Random House book
Published by Random House Australia Pty Ltd
Level 3, 100 Pacific Highway, North Sydney NSW 2060
www.randomhouse.com.au

First published by Random House Australia in 2012

National Library of Australia
Cataloguing-in-Publication Entry

Author: Hart, Rhiannon
Title: Blood Storm / Rhiannon Hart
ISBN: 978 1 74275 478 9 (pbk.)
Series: Hart, Rhiannon. Lharmell; bk 2
Target audience: For young adults
Dewey number: A823.4

Photograph of girl by Ana Gremard
Other images © iStockphoto/DavidMSchrader;
MO:SES/Shutterstock.com; Nadya Korobkova/Shutterstock.com and
Kiselev Andrey Valerevich/Shutterstock.com
Cover design by Design Cherry
Internal design by Midland Typesetters, Australia
Typeset in 12.5/17 pt Garamond by Midland Typesetters, Australia
Printed in Australia by Griffin Press, an accredited ISO AS/NZS
14001:2004 Environmental Management System printer

Random House Australia uses papers that are natural, renewable and
recyclable products and made from wood grown in sustainable forests.
The logging and manufacturing processes are expected to conform to the
environmental regulations of the country of origin.

BLOOD STORM

THE SECOND BOOK OF LHARMELL

Rhiannon Hart

RANDOM HOUSE AUSTRALIA

ONE

I spied the harming from two hundred yards off. A hooded cloak concealed its features, but I could picture its black hair, its icy blue eyes – eyes that mirrored my own. I am a harming, but I am un-Turned. With great hardship and pain I have resisted the pull of the tors, the chanting that calls those with Lharmellin blood northwards, home to Lharmell.

I raised the crossbow with my right hand and dug my heels into the horse's sides. 'Yah!' I cried, leaning forward, eager for the kill. We galloped across the dusty expanse of ground. I gripped the horse with my knees, steadying myself for the shot. I wasn't adept at firing a crossbow. My weapon of choice is a traditional bow but that has its disadvantages.

To start, you can't fire one-handed, so it's difficult to make a kill while on the move.

I aimed at the harming's chest, the expanse between us closing fast. At thirty yards I fired. The bolt thudded into a tree, yards wide of its mark. 'Blast!' I pulled my horse around and reached for another bolt.

The thunder of hooves bearing down on us made my horse scream in panic. Rodden was hot on our heels. He aimed his crossbow and fired, severing the rope that suspended the dummy from the tree branch. It landed on the ground with a thump and straw fell out from inside the cloak. Rodden wheeled his horse to face me. His white-blue eyes flashed. 'Lucky I'm here, or else you'd be dead.'

I swiped sweat from my upper lip with the back of my hand. 'Thank you, Rodden. Thank you for saving me from the nasty bundle of straw. How will I ever repay you?'

The sarcasm was completely lost on him. 'You can repay me by learning to fire your weapon. You're an absolutely terrible shot.'

That was rubbish and he knew it. 'Who wiped the floor with you at an *archery* tournament five months ago? In front of the whole court? Oh, that's right. It was me.' There was no way I would have lost that tournament, not when losing meant that I would've had to marry him, the stuck-up, arrogant jerk. I'd rather be Turned.

'By the barest fraction of an inch, Zeraphina. And clearly your skill doesn't go far. It's all very well firing at a stationary plank of wood at twenty paces, but how useful will that be when we're being ambushed by harmings? And if you can't fire from horseback, how will you manage from a brant?'

I turned my horse and trotted back to the other end of the field. 'Do you have to lecture me?' I called over my shoulder.

The sun was blazing overheard and my feet felt like they were cooking inside my dusty riding boots. Goodness knows why we had to train right in the heat of the day. It was particularly sadistic of him. My skin was becoming tanned and freckled in the Pergamian summer sun. Coming from the southern queendom of Amentia, where in places the ice never thaws, I wasn't used to such heat. I was thankful for the airy trousers and shirt that had become my uniform of late. If my mother, Queen Renata, could see me now she'd have an apoplexy. Even she wouldn't wear corsets in this heat, but she would be firmly against a princess of Amentia wearing trousers, and would be wild with rage at the sight of me straddling a horse. Young ladies, I could hear her saying, ride side-saddle *only*. Thank goodness she was safely in Amentia and I could get on with things.

At the edge of the field I turned and watched Rodden string up the harming dummy. Then he rode away with a flourish of his arm, giving the dummy a wide berth – too wide, in fact. I wasn't that bad a shot. It was testament to our partnership that he could needle me at two hundred paces and without saying a word.

Concentrate, came his thought-pattern, more feeling than word, but I caught the sentiment. I flung up my wall to block him out.

Not far off, Leap lay beneath a tree, watching us with half-closed eyes. Leap was my cat, and a very clever one. He came from the sewers of Verapine and his silvery fur was slick like an otter's. With his luminous green eyes he could see even better in the dark than me. Griffin was circling overhead in thermals rising from the heated ground, her eagle-eyes scanning the landscape for furry morsels. These two were the only creatures in the world who knew the real me, had seen my darkest moments, and still loved me unconditionally. Rodden knew my true nature, and I his, but all that was between us was a grudging respect. Once I had wondered if there could be something more, but I had been mistaking the intimacy of thought-patterns for true intimacy. I knew better now. Plus, the danger we were in was hardly conducive to romance. We lived in constant dread of the Lharmellins just across the Straits of Unctium, not to mention our own volatile natures. It was difficult to trust another when you could barely trust yourself. I had succumbed to the pull of the tors of Lharmell once and nearly paid the price with my life.

I galloped at the stuffed harming. This time my bolt stuck in the thing's arm – not a fatal shot with regular arrows, but if this had been a real harming and the bolt was tipped with yelbar, an alloy poisonous to those with Lharmellin blood, it would eventually cause death.

Rodden gave me a curt nod and said, 'Let's call it a day.' We turned our horses towards the stables and let them set their own pace back. On my wrist was a leather gauntlet, and I held my arm aloft as I called Griffin down with my mind. She alighted in a flash of golden feathers, her sharp talons digging into the leather. Griffin was not only a deadly hunter and a sharp lookout, she'd been known to attack harmings with her razor-sharp beak and claws. Leap followed behind us.

As I dismantled my crossbow and put away the bolts, I considered what Rodden had said about firing from brant-back. Neither of us had talked about what would happen next. I had spent the whole spring at the palace. A long time, it was true, but not so surprising considering my sister Lilith was newly married to Prince Amis and my home was so far away. But I hadn't been idle. I'd been reading everything I could on Lharmell, and quizzing Rodden too. He was generous with his knowledge, but as soon as I asked details about himself, especially his past, he clammed up. I'd been hesitant to speculate out loud about the future, lest he suggest I was better off at my own palace, but I'd been thinking hard. I suspected he had been too, but he wasn't the most forthcoming of men. He'd never even told me how he became a harming.

I felt a tightness in my chest, a smarting that radiated down my arms and up the back of my throat: I was thirsty. I thought of the rabbits Rodden kept in his room, and my mouth watered. Blood was life and ambrosia to harmings. It made us hum with vibrancy and power, gave our bodies unnatural strength and honed our senses like a knife edge. I would die without blood, but for me the act of feeding was laced with guilt and revulsion – afterwards at least.

The moment the liquid life touched my tongue, I felt drinking it to be the purest, most candid deed in the world.

But I wanted to be free of the tors and the blood-hunger. I was kept going by the hope that one day I would be – as well as an iron resolve to maintain whatever humanity I had left. But there's little to feel human about when your body craves blood.

I'd seldom heard the Lharmellins' chanting of late and it was rare to see brants swirling in the night sky since we'd returned from Lharmell several months ago. But whether we had dealt our enemies a serious blow or merely slowed them down, we were yet to discover. Killing the Lharmellin leader and disrupting the Turning ceremony wouldn't have finished them; it may have prevented new harmings from being made, or it may have done nothing. We just didn't know yet.

At the stables a footman approached with a letter for me. I looked at the seal and felt a twinge of annoyance. The mark was a griffin rampant, the Amentine standard. Which could only mean the letter was from my mother. They were becoming increasingly frequent and tiresomely similar.

I tucked it into my pocket and helped Rodden unsaddle the horses and brush them down. While he was occupied trying to dislodge a stone from his horse's shoe, I wandered out to find shade under a large oak, and opened my letter. In Renata's firm, black strokes I read:

Darling,

What a warm summer we are having! The mornings are quite clear and we can see all the way to the Teripsiin Mountains. I hope you are keeping out of the sun and applying the lotion I sent you. Lilith tells me it's scorching hot but there are all sorts of things to do, such as sea-bathing. What fun you must be having on your little holiday. Has anyone interesting turned up at court? I did hear a whisper that Prince Folsum might be there with his sister, Penritha. What a dear thing she was as a baby. And I'm sure I don't need to remind you that he is a first son and will be King of Ansengaad one day.

Do send my love to your sister and tell her from me that nothing will secure her place at court better than giving her husband an heir. And please encourage her to make it a son. Not only will daughters drive her mad and send her broke, but Pergamians are very fond of a home-born king.

Lastly — and I should have said this first — I needn't

remind you that it is your birthday in a few months.
I would like you home by then to discuss certain matters
of your coming of age, and I fear you are trespassing
too long on King Askar's hospitality. The whole spring
you've been absent! I'm sure you've never been so fond
of your sister. And it is very selfish to leave me all on my
own. I am quite bored to tears. Do come home.

R

I folded up the letter. I kept on folding until it was the tiniest square I could manage, trying to obliterate the thing. How could she write such stupid sentiments? I wasn't on holiday. She knew very well why I had to 'trespass' on King Askar's hospitality. Un-Turned harmings were compelled north by the tors, and travelling south meant excruciating pain. Besides, I didn't *want* to go home. As frustrating as I found him, being with Rodden and learning about Lharmell was far more exciting and fulfilling. Renata would want to fill my days with dress fittings, letter writing and visits from exceedingly dull people. She would drive me batty with talk of husbands.

I ground the letter in my hands until the parchment began to crumble and let the pieces blow away on the breeze.

I had seen this Prince Folsum at the stables one day earlier in the summer. He possessed some very fine black horses. I had taken an immediate dislike to him when he'd shoved one of his horses rather savagely for treading on his toe. He'd then bellowed at it for several minutes, upsetting all the horses in the stable. The footmen had raised their eyebrows, but could do nothing. He was a prince.

I paused for a moment, wondering what it would be like to be married to such a man. Then I shuddered. Undoubtedly it would be dreadful.

As I entered the bailey, I spied Rodden crossing the flagstones with Hoggit, the paunchy, pock-marked captain of the guard. Their expressions were grave and they were consulting a piece of parchment. Rodden was King Askar's right-hand man, his advisor in all things pertaining to the Lharmellins. He was a tall man, and black-haired as all harmings are, and walked with a confident stride. Some might say he had fine cheekbones and broad shoulders, and a pleasantly foreign aspect. His figure was lithe and athletic, so different from Prince Folsum's over-muscled frame. I suppose you could say Rodden was handsome, though I would never care to. On those rare occasions when he smiled it could quite take your breath away. So I'd been told.

Hoggit departed, and Rodden looked up at my approach. 'Bad news?'

'Just my mother. You?'

'Yes. Dead bodies.'

'Regular dead bodies or bloodless ones?'

'Bloodless.'

I felt a stab of alarm. 'It's starting again, isn't it?'

He regarded the parchment and sighed. 'I don't think it ever stopped.'

'You mean there have been more? Why didn't you tell me?'

Without looking up, he said automatically, 'Mortality reports are my affair, Zeraphina. The captain of the guard reports to me.'

I gritted my teeth. He was twenty-three years old – his birthday having been in spring – to my sixteen but sometimes he behaved as if the gap was decades. 'Not when they're killed because of Lharmellins. Then it's my affair, too.' I thought he had stopped keeping me in the dark. Alarm made my voice shrill. 'You can't go on keeping things from me.'

'I haven't kept anything from you. I didn't know until now about the destitutes. I suspected, but I wasn't certain.'

'You should have told me what you suspected. It's my right to know. We're partners, aren't we?'

Rodden raised an eyebrow at me. 'You're royalty. You have a responsibility to your people. It's my job to worry about the dead bodies.'

I bristled. 'May I remind you that *we* didn't kill the Lharmellin leader. I did.' I stalked across the bailey.

'Zeraphina, wait!' He jogged to catch up with me. 'I'm sorry. It's my habit to be private. Here.' He held the report out to me. 'I should have given you the others, too. Until now, though, I wasn't sure that the bodies had anything to do with the Lharmellins. Look here,' he said, pointing a finger at a column of figures. 'There has been a spike in the number of beggars and cripples found dead. No one bothers much to investigate how they die, but a fortnight ago I ordered that all bodies be checked for exsanguination. Do you see what it says?'

Next to a list of destitutes was the notation 'EXS': exsanguinated. 'All of them?'

Rodden nodded. 'They've been put back on the streets and arranged to look as if they died in their sleep.'

'I thought harmings just dumped bodies when they were finished with them.'

'They used to. But it seems they're getting smarter.'

'That can't be. We killed their leader only a few

months ago. They're supposed to be disorganised and weak. Renata says they're having a warm summer in Amentia.' Our queendom had been blighted by ice for decades, something we Amentines had attributed to a natural but unfortunate change in the weather patterns. But Rodden suspected there was more to it. The Teripsiin Mountains of Amentia were rich in metals, including yelinate, which was used to create the alloy yelbar. Yelinate was all but useless to humans, but yelbar was fatal to Lharmellins and harmings. Even un-Turned ones like us. Rodden believed the Lharmellins had learnt of Amentia's yelinate and had been trying to freeze out potential mine-works. A temperate summer might indicate that our enemies' power had waned. 'Do you think it's just a coincidence or a trick to put us off our guard?'

Rodden raked a hand through his black hair. 'I don't know. I don't understand it either. I have been uncertain how to proceed. The thaw in Amentia suggested that the harmings and Lharmellins had grown weaker, but this report seems to indicate otherwise.'

'I've been thinking a lot about it, too,' I admitted. 'What we might do next. It's not right they go on killing people. When will it stop?'

'It won't stop.'

'Not unless we do something.'

He met my gaze, hesitating.

'Tell me,' I urged.

'Not here.'

We climbed the stone steps to the battlements and made our way along the parapet, heading for his quarters in the northernmost turret of the palace. From this height, under a vaulted blue sky, we could see over all of Xallentaria, the capital city of Pergamia. I saw the tree-lined boulevard that led from the palace to the city, the spires and domed roofs in the distance. In the east were the wilds of the king's hunting grounds, home to deer and tusked boars. To the south, beyond the city walls, were heat-shimmered olive groves and farmhouses; to the north-west were the docks. Xallentaria was a major trading port and hundreds of ships were in the harbour. The sight of a full sail bearing a ship out to sea could make my heart contract with longing. I ached to be on deck, free from the tors at last and heading away, anywhere, without fear of pain.

I avoided looking northwards as I knew what I would see: a vast, empty ocean stretching all the way to the horizon. The tors of Lharmell weren't visible from this distance, but I knew they were there.

I could feel them calling to me, tugging at the cord between us.

When Rodden and I reached the top of the spiral staircase, I saw that the place was a mess of papers and books as usual, and only thin rays of sunlight filtered through the arrow slots. Griffin flew from my wrist to perch high up in the rafters. Leap crouched by the rabbit hutch, his tail undulating with curiosity. Inside, brown rabbits hopped about on straw. I felt my pupils dilate at the sight. I would have to feed soon.

Most of the books were familiar to me now, and I'd spent many hours poring over them as well as Rodden's maps and other charts. I'd learned, for instance, that bennium, one of the components of yelbar, the metal poisonous to those with Lharmellin blood, could be found deep in the desert of Verapine. I also knew that there wasn't any bennium at the palace, and Rodden had barely any yelbar.

I spread a map over the books and general litter on his desk. Near the top was Pergamia, a sausage-shaped country painted in brilliant, lush green, which stretched east to west across the northern part of Brivora, the great continent on which we lived. Far to the south was Amentia, my tiny, landlocked home. The artist had painted mountains and fir trees and intricate snowflakes. Directly north of Pergamia lay the Straits of Unctium, the sea that separated Brivora from Lharmell. Lharmell was a small island, dominated by a ring of tors surrounding a bowl-shaped valley. The Lharmellins' lair. I had been there: it was an ancient spent volcano, a crater of basalt and black volcanic glass. Just seeing it on a map was enough to tighten the tor-line connected to my body. Much of the island was blackened, dead forest. The dirt and skeletal trees were poisonous to humans. Because we were part-human, the toxins had burned Rodden and me, but the Lharmellin blood in our veins prevented us from being poisoned to death. Humans, on the other hand, would die quickly if they stepped into the forest. I remembered the acid rain, and shuddered.

'Here,' I said, moving my attention from Lharmell and pointing to Verapine. It was on the continent of Ossiria, an hourglass-shaped landmass west of Brivora, the Osseran Sea in between. It was a large country, made up mostly of desert. The first time I'd looked at the map I'd not been able to believe such a huge, barren expanse existed. 'Verapine. That's where Leap's from, but it's also the only place in the world where bennium occurs naturally, is that right?'

Leap looked around at the sound of his name, his tail curling into a question mark.

'Yes.'

'Would an alchemist have any bennium?'

Rodden shook his head. 'No, it doesn't have a great many uses, so unfortunately no one trades in it.'

'How long would it take to send someone for it?'

'Weeks. Months. It's funny you should mention bennium, though. It's been on my mind too.' He cocked a dark eyebrow at me. 'I was thinking we could go and get some.'

I looked again at the map. 'Wouldn't that take a lot of time?'

'Yes, but it would be well spent. There are things we could learn while we travelled.'

I gripped his arm. 'I've been thinking that too. We don't know how many harmings are out there or what they're saying to one another. About us. About the Turning we disrupted.'

'Exactly. And there are people we could talk to in the Pergamian cities. The captains of the guard know to look for exsanguination, but they might have left details out of their monthly reports that could be useful to us.'

We. Us. His words made excitement bubble up inside me. Our journey into Lharmell had shown how well we worked together. And the idea of travel was thrilling. I wouldn't have to go home, at least for now. It seemed almost shameful to consider an expedition across Pergamia, the Osseran Sea and deep into the desert an adventure when so many people were dying every day and even more lives were at stake, but it was an adventure just the same.

'We could travel by land across Pergamia,' he said, and his finger ran across the names of cities: Rendine, Ercan, Jefsgord. 'Then by boat to Verapine. Here's the capital, Pol.' He tapped the map. 'It's a slum city. Some of the poorest people in the world live there. Brivorans would think it an ugly, dirty place, but it's not.' He smiled. 'It's quite beautiful when you look past the patched houses and dirty streets. The people are proud, and very talented. They're happy, too – there's such a great sense of community. You don't get that here as much, where most people have plenty.'

'Have you been there?' I asked.

'You could say that,' he said, frowning down at the map. 'The desert sands are used to make a very special kind of glass. That's another reason we should go ourselves – the glass could prove very useful. And then through the desert for the bennium.' He looked up, his eyes challenging me. 'If you think you can handle it. I could always go alone. In fact, I should. It's hardly right for me to travel with you unchaperoned.'

I jutted my chin. 'Nonsense. Who'll watch your back and keep you from walking into an ambush if Leap and Griffin and I aren't there?'

He looked down at the map, a smile tugging at his mouth. If I didn't know better I would say he was pleased at my insistence. 'And we will have to go to Amentia.'

I groaned. 'Really? Renata will never let me leave. She'll have me married the instant I step foot in the castle.'

'We don't have to go to the capital. Remember the mines that were set up after Lilith and Amis's wedding?'

I nodded. Ostensibly they were to mine copper and tin, but the vital activity was the mining of yelinate.

'We should inspect progress and collect the yelinate we'll need. But do you really want your mother to discover you went all the way to Amentia without seeing her?'

'Yes.'

Rodden rolled up the map. 'You say you want to retain your humanity. Well, human girls like to visit their mothers. You should be thankful you have a mother.'

He turned to put the map away and I gave him a sharp look. His mother was dead? I tucked that little bit of information away in a corner of my mind. I was gathering intelligence on him: one day I would be able to piece all the morsels together and he would find that, despite the secrets he kept from me, I would know everything. At the rate I was going it would only take me, say, eight hundred years.

'Fine, fine,' I muttered. 'But we're leaving before she has me walking up the aisle.'

TWO

I'd promised Lilith I'd have dinner in the great hall that night as I hadn't been present in weeks. I didn't so much avoid court as forget about it. There were so many better things to do, like training or practising control of my thought-patterns, reading in the palace gardens in the long evenings or riding down to the ocean with Rodden to exercise horses on the beach. The climate in Pergamia made me yearn to be outdoors. Growing up in Amentia had meant howling winds, ice and sleet, and numbed fingers clutching a bow-string on gloomy afternoons. The days were short and the cold nights long. Here in Pergamia I spent every chance I could out under the open sky, wearing breeches and letting my long black hair hang as it would down my back. I saw little need to keep up appearances. For our journey to Pergamia, Renata had spent lavishly on silks and velvets, insisting we look our very best in an attempt to fool the king and queen into believing we weren't as poor as was rumoured. But the Pergamians weren't interested in our coffers. Once Rodden had discovered we had yelinate in our mountains, a quiet word in the king's ear had secured the union between my sister Lilith and Prince Amis.

I pulled on one of the sleeveless silk gowns that were the fashion in Pergamia. I had to admit, the dress was lovely. And functional in its own way, being loose and cool, though I had worn nothing but trousers for weeks and they were infinitely more practical. I belted the dress with some braid, ran a comb through my hair and was done. The only jewellery I wore these days was a single silver ring on my thumb. It was one of a pair. Rodden wore the other on his right hand. Originally he'd stolen it from me so that he could track me on my journey from Amentia to Pergamia. He wore it now so we would always have a way of finding each other if something happened, although in truth the mind-thread between us seemed more than sufficient. Testing it gently, I could feel him now in his turret room, poring over his books. I tried to ignore the thread most of the time, as drawing his attention to it seemed to annoy him. But it was always a comfort to feel it there, humming away.

I could hear voices emanating from the great hall as I padded down the corridor on sandalled feet. Pergamians love to entertain and throw parties. The court was full the year round, and below the dais, trestles were set up to accommodate the hundreds of nobles who visited. Daughters were debuted and alliances were forged, all under the high ceiling of this hall.

Dusk had fallen and the candles were lit in the chandeliers. The air was thick with humidity and cast a soporific pall over the guests. Girls lounged, chins in their palms, picking at plates of fruit and conducting conversations with lowered lashes. Men flashed rakish smiles and strong white teeth, banging tankards of ale together and roaring with laughter.

Being sister to the future queen, I sat at the high table. As the king's right-hand man, Rodden would sit at the high table, too, if he was there. But he avoided these occasions even more than I did. Queen Ulah sat on her throne, fanning herself and sipping cordials. King Askar was drinking with some heavily armoured men at a lower table, protocol relaxed for the sake of the heat. I sat beside Carmelina, Amis's sister. She was an engaging, cheerful blonde thing, and I found that whenever I was with her she could draw me out of the deepest reverie.

'Don't look now,' she murmured, the moment I sat down, 'but Prince Folsum is looking right at you.'

I felt a prickle of unease. My attention drawn to the prince twice in one day: I didn't like it.

'Rubbish, he's looking at you,' I murmured. Taking a sip from my water glass I looked surreptitiously around. There he was, seated below at a trestle, staring up at me from beneath thick brown brows. The young prince smirked and raised his goblet to me. I hastily put mine down and looked away, but not before I'd caught the baleful stares of a handful of barons' daughters.

Carmelina had noticed, too. 'Don't worry about those harpies,' she muttered. 'They're just jealous.'

'Of what? I've been here all of a moment.' I helped myself to a dish of yoghurt and wild honey.

'They've seen you riding with Rodden.'

'So?' I took a mouthful of yoghurt. It was so thick and rich it was like eating cream.

'So, they've got a crush on him. Haven't you noticed that the spoiled daughters of stuffy barons and earls always do? They're so used to limp-wristed, slope-shouldered inbreeds that they're dying for someone halfway rugged to run away with. It would so annoy *Daddy*.'

I thought of the way Rodden's shoulders looked clad in his shirt as he grappled with the reins of his horse; his large brown hands that could draw the stiffest bow. The delicate silver band he wore only made them seem stronger and more capable. I felt heat rise in my cheeks and squashed the thoughts down. What if he *heard*?

To distract myself I sneaked another look at Prince Folsum. He was as tall as Rodden, but where Rodden was lithe, this man was uncomfortably muscular. His hands were like sides of bacon. Some would call him handsome, but his face was too broad and fleshy for my liking and there was something not right about his flinty grey eyes and the set of his mouth. He was listening to the discussion going on at the table but I could swear that it was only a superficial interest. His mind was elsewhere, and by the expression in his eyes I suspected it was a murky, unpleasant place.

I shifted my attention back to Carmelina. 'You can tell all this from seeing them glare at me once?'

'It's obvious. You should see the husbands they really end up with. Quite tragic. It would make me want to run off with the hired help.'

I felt a flash of annoyance at her snobbish tone. Rodden was doing far more for this country than she ever would, no matter how well she married. 'Do you think me tragic, too?'

She coloured. 'No! I didn't mean you were anything like them, Zeraphina. If you and Rodden –'

'Me and Rodden nothing. I'm marrying a limp-wristed inbreed and I can't wait.'

There was a pointed cough from Carmelina's other side. 'Nice of you to join us,' said Lilith, leaning forward. She wore a shimmering gown shot with gold thread, and was dripping with diamonds. She would be queen one day, and a beautiful one at that.

Renata had never told her that I was a harming, and I didn't intend to either. For some reason the thought of her knowing what I was vexed me greatly. I recalled the looks she would give Leap and Griffin whenever they crossed her path, one of wrinkle-nosed disgust. What if she gave me that look?

'Mother sends her love and encourages you to have a son,' I told Lilith.

Her green eyes flashed. 'You had a letter too? I do wish she'd stop harping on about it. I'll have children in my own time.'

I looked down my nose and affected Renata's

imperious tone. 'Do try, darling. It would be quite charming if you could oblige me.'

Lilith laughed. 'Shall we visit the markets next week? I need some cooler fabrics or I'll just expire in this heat. Do you suppose I'll ever get used to it?'

I played with the yoghurt in my dish. 'Well –'

'Actually, I'm taking Zeraphina on a little trip.'

I looked up, startled, as Rodden slid into the empty chair beside me. He'd changed from his grubby training gear into a crisp white shirt. He smiled at Lilith. 'You don't mind, do you?'

A liquid look came into Lilith's eyes. I'd seen it happen to other women when he flashed one of his rare smiles. Then she frowned. 'I'm not sure that's very proper,' she said, fingering the diamonds at her throat. 'Where are you going on this trip?'

I hesitated, glancing at Rodden.

'We're taking Leap to Verapine and then we're visiting your mother,' Rodden told her.

Put like that it sounded rather genteel.

Lilith looked startled. 'How . . . pleasant.'

Rodden poured himself a goblet of wine and when no one was looking, pulled a little bottle from inside his jacket, popped its cork and poured the contents in. I smelled blood. It would be invisible in the redness of the wine.

Where the hell was mine?

'Thirsty?' he murmured in my ear.

I nodded. He took a mouthful and surreptitiously switched glasses with me. I took a sip from the goblet and then sat back to savour the rest of it, the food in front of me forgotten. The tightness that had been gathering in my chest eased. I took a deep breath, and gazed around the table with renewed vigour.

Amis, who had been listening to our conversation from the other side of Lilith, wasn't fooled. At the mention of Verapine he had given Rodden a sharp look. 'Will you be going into the desert at all?' he asked lightly.

Rodden nodded.

'I see,' he said. 'And you're taking Princess Zeraphina?' He frowned just like Lilith had.

I began to wish Rodden had never spoken of our plans. Perhaps it would have been easier to have slipped away. All this protocol and decency. It was such a bother.

Then Amis said, 'My father is waving to us, Rodden. Shall we?'

It was my turn to frown as Amis led Rodden away. I wondered if he was going to try to change Rodden's mind.

As soon as the men had left us, Carmelina leaned

forward. 'You're taking him to see your mother?' she hissed.

'Hmm? Oh, nothing's definite.'

'But you *are* going to Amentia?' Lilith asked.

Reluctantly, I nodded.

'Just visiting?' Lilith asked. 'You're coming back?'

Again, I nodded. This was awkward. As far as she was aware I had no legitimate reason for spending so much time in Pergamia – especially as I spent so little of it with her. Sooner or later I was going to have to come up with a better excuse than being on holiday. If only she would get pregnant; then I could flutter around her belly like a broody hen.

'She'll never let you marry him, you know,' Lilith murmured.

I opened my mouth to state that Rodden was definitely *not* the reason I was still in Pergamia, at least not in the way she thought, but then shut it again. He was as good an excuse as any.

Carmelina leaned towards us. 'I heard,' she said in a whisper, 'that one of my great-great-great-grandmothers ran off with the captain of the guard. It upset everyone for a time, but they got over it. And she was a second daughter, too,' she said, wagging her fork at me.

I thought of Hoggit, the present captain of the guard. He was an exceedingly capable man but one in possession of a face that only a mother could love. I drained my glass of blood and wine and set it on the table. 'Carmelina, if I decide to run off with Hoggit, I promise that you will be the first to know about it.'

———

That night I wrote my mother a letter. It was a task I usually shirked until the very last moment but tonight I couldn't wait to put pen to paper.

Dear Mother,

I have good news! I'll be with you in Amentia soon. I'm afraid I shan't be able to stay long as there are all manner of princes here at court. Don't bother to write back as I shall be leaving for Verapine shortly. Expect me at the palace by autumn at the latest.

I stopped writing. Autumn. My birthday was late in the summer; I would be seventeen, and of marriageable age by the time we reached Amentia. That could give my mother ideas. Bad ideas. But there was nothing to be done about that. I would just have to be firm with her when the time came: I wasn't ready for a husband.

Unable to resist goading her, I finished the letter:

Oh yes, Rodden Lothskorn will be with me. You remember him? He's the commoner I almost married.

Your obedient daughter,
Zeraphina

P.S. Still no sign of a son from Lilith. I'll check again in the morning.

———

'Feeling okay?'

I took another swig of blood and nodded. 'Yes. Just.' Sweat was running down my temples and I was biting down hard on the insides of my cheeks.

Rodden and I were on horseback, twenty miles south of the palace. It was the furthest I had been from Lharmell since travelling to Pergamia. The tor-line felt like metal hooks in my skin. The hooks were attached to cables reaching all the way to the tors and they were stretched taut. I imagined it was a similar sensation to being flayed alive.

'Don't you feel it?' I asked Rodden. He seemed unaffected, his hands loosely holding the reins as he glanced around at the birdlife in the trees. Griffin was perched on the back of his saddle, and I could sense she found it amusing to be bobbing up and down with the stride of the horse. Leap sat in front of me on the saddle blanket, looking up at me with big worried eyes. I patted his head. 'I'm okay,' I muttered.

'Of course,' Rodden replied, watching the trees. 'I'm just blocking it out. There,' he whispered, reaching over his left shoulder for the crossbow he had strapped to his back. 'Squirrel.' He looked at me. 'Your shot. You need the practice.'

Reluctantly, I reached for my crossbow and notched up a bolt. It hurt even to move, and my hands shook. The grey squirrel was sitting on an oak branch up ahead: an easy shot. Or it should be. As I aimed, sweat ran into my eyes. I wished I could halt my mount but that would defeat the purpose. I had to learn to shoot on the move. I made my shoulders unclench, let out the breath I was holding, and fired. The squirrel plunged from the tree, the bolt through its body.

Rodden grinned at me. 'That's more like it.'

I dismounted and collected the kill. 'Halvsies?' I asked, holding the dead squirrel up by its fluffy tail.

'Don't mind if I do.' Rodden swung off his horse and we sat in the shade of a tree. I yanked the arrow out of the small creature. 'After you,' I said, passing it to him.

I cleaned the bolt on some grass as he drank. After a moment he passed the squirrel back to me. I fastened my lips onto the wound and drained it dry. The pain ebbed from my back slightly. Then I cut a hind leg off with my knife and threw it to Griffin and gave the rest of the carcass to Leap.

Today was a test: how far can Zeraphina get from the tors before she passes out? Not much further, it seemed. I arched my aching back, trying to rid myself of the feeling of being clawed by wild animals.

'You're doing well, you know,' Rodden said.

I snorted. He'd not even broken a sweat and I was about to become the first girl to drown on dry land.

'You're not fainting, or dead.'

'I could *die*?'

'Some do, if they're forced south against their will. Or they go mad. We're not going directly south on our journey, at least not at first. Tomorrow we'll take the Drissian Way overland to Jefsgord, the closest Pergamian city to Pol. It's almost directly west of here. The roads are very well paved and the going is flat, so if we change horses at every city it should take us a week and a half. Then we'll take a ship to Pol. That will be a little harder as it's south-west. And if you get seasick it will be worse for you. The trek across the desert is directly west again, but it's not an easy journey for anyone, especially this time of year. You'd better hope that you acclimatise to heat quickly.'

I dabbed at the sweat that was trickling down my neck. I sincerely hoped so too.

'But it's the journey to Amentia that I'm worried about,' he told me.

'You mean it gets worse?'

'Amentia is south-east of Pol. Quite a bit south.'

I grimaced.

'It will be painful. And don't even think about asking me for laudanum.'

'Why not?' Laudanum was oblivion in a bottle. A few mouthfuls and I wouldn't even remember my own name.

'Because it's poison,' he snapped. 'It can turn you into the living dead. I won't see that happen to you.'

'All right, be calm. I'll manage.' Shoot. Secretly

I'd been counting on a little apothecarial help to get me through the worst part of the journey.

Rodden must have seen me blanch. 'You don't have to do this, you know.'

There he went again.

I leaned my head back against the tree trunk and stared at the canopy above. Very slowly, I said, 'Let's get one thing clear. I am in this until the end. I want to do this with you. But more than that. I *have* to do this. I can't sit in a palace wearing a pretty dress and doing nothing. Not while people are dying. I won't. It isn't right.' I rolled my head to the side and glared at him. 'Okay?'

Rodden was twisting my ring on his finger and didn't reply for a moment. When he spoke his voice was quiet. 'If you get killed, or worse, it will be my fault.'

'No, it won't. It'll just be an unlucky coincidence. I am perfectly capable of dying or getting Turned without your help, thank you very much.' It was meant to be a joke, but he wasn't laughing. There was something weighing on his mind. I tested the thread between us, trying to discern his true feelings. He spoke the truth: he was worried about seeing me die. That was no surprise – I didn't fancy it either. But there was something else. Guilt.

There was a whole miserable lake of it lapping at his insides.

What did Rodden have to feel so guilty about?

Leap butted his head against Rodden's arm. He clamped down on the thought-thread between us and the connection was severed. Getting up to mount his horse, he said, 'Gallop. Ten minutes south, no stopping. Then we'll head for home.'

I struggled to my feet, relieved that today's ordeal was nearly over. Home meant north, towards the palace – but also towards Lharmell. Home indeed.

———

Lilith intercepted me at the door to my bed-chamber. I was still light-headed, sweaty and anxious for a bath.

'I've been worrying about this journey, Fina,' she said. 'You aren't intending to make it alone, are you?'

I swiped perspiration from my upper lip. 'Of course not. I'll be with Rodden.'

She pursed her lips. 'Don't be pert. You know that's what I mean. The two of you travelling alone together ... it's not proper.' She hesitated a moment before saying, 'I – I can't allow it.'

'You sound just like Mother.'

'In her absence I *am* in charge,' she blustered.

'Since when?'

'Since ... since ... Oh, come on, Fina. You know she'd refuse to let you go. So I have to refuse too.' She squared her shoulders. 'I forbid you to travel alone with that man.'

I drew myself up to my full height, which was an inch shorter than hers. 'And how do you propose to stop me?'

'I'll tell the stewards not to give you horses. I'll send Rodden on a tour of duty. I'll make you one of my ladies-in-waiting.'

Drat. She could do those things, too. 'All right,' I growled.

Lilith looked startled. 'Really? But your fights with Mother usually go on for hours.'

'I believe you're thinking of *your* fights with Mother.'

Lilith considered this. 'Oh. Yes. Well, then ... go to your room.'

I swept an exaggerated curtsey. 'Yes, Your Highness.' And I slammed the door on her nose.

I fumed. Who did Lilith think she was? How many times had she moaned to me because Renata wouldn't let her do such-and-such, or Renata expected her to marry so-and-so? And now suddenly she was doing what she thought Renata would want. Well, I wasn't just going to lie down and take it. She would be angry, and she would be annoyed, but that couldn't be helped. I was in the right, after all. There were lives at stake, and why should a notion like propriety stand in my way? Impropriety never killed anyone. Impropriety didn't drain anyone's blood.

I went straight to my writing desk and scribbled a note. Handing it to Griffin, I said, 'Northern turret, please. No need to wait for a reply.'

I watched from the balcony as my eagle winged her way to Rodden's turret room against a brilliant, rose-streaked sky, my note clutched firmly in her beak.

THREE

I packed lightly. All my necessities could fit in a small saddlebag: two spare shirts and pairs of trousers, soap, dry rations, bandages and salve, a water skin and a comb. I hesitated over my harming cloak. The long, hooded garments were the garb of those with Lharmellin blood and would be necessary once we were in Lharmell. Harmings favoured them as they disguised their tell-tale black hair and unsettling pale eyes, and the grey puffiness of their skin once they'd been Turned. The eyes of a Turned harming were even icier than our own, and their veins tended to pop out in their necks and on the backs of their hands. Lharmellins, on the other hand, could never pass as humans. They were something else entirely, a strange species that, with a combination of blood and ritual, turn humans into harmings. Harmings and Lharmellins shared many characteristics, like the glowing eyes and craving for blood. But Lharmellins couldn't walk among us. That's why they needed harmings to do their bidding. They were constrained to Lharmell by the air temperature, needing the cold to function. I had seen a Lharmellin with its hood thrown back and it was a grisly sight. It had been hairless, its skin grey and mottled by a network of swollen veins. A lipless mouth had revealed dozens of sharp, pointed teeth. But when it sang, a sound of the purest beauty filled the air that could transfix even the most reluctant harming such as me. I shuddered at the memory. I had worked hard on strengthening my mind over the spring since I'd returned from Lharmell. I wouldn't let myself be overcome like I had been at the last Turning.

But did we wish to be identifiable to our own kind? The cloak was warm, and the only suitable garment of its kind that I owned. I would take it, but be wary when I wore it.

I would also take my bows. The crossbow and bolts I would use the most, but nothing would be more soothing than firing a few slick arrows once in a while. Between us, Rodden and I had a few dozen arrows and bolts tipped with yelbar, as well as some regular points for hunting. The yelbar-tipped points we had to be extremely careful with, wearing gloves when handling them as the tiniest nick could make us ill for days. If enough got into our bloodstream we would die – even just from a foot wound. I carried my yelbar points in a metal-reinforced quiver.

When I was done I sat on my balcony to wait. I wished there were more things to pack, to organise. It would give me something to do instead of just sitting and worrying. What if Lilith had already told the steward not to give Rodden horses? What if there was a guard outside my room right now to prevent me from sneaking away? What if this was a huge mistake and Rodden and I were going to be ambushed by harmings as soon as we stepped beyond the palace gates? We didn't know how many were out there.

But that was the whole point: to discover such things as how many harmings had infiltrated Pergamian cities, and what they were doing now that we'd killed their leader. They must have a new one by now. But would they have rallied round that Lharmellin? Would the Turnings be occurring every full moon like they should? And what was the best way for us to sneak into Lharmell again and disrupt the harmings and Lharmellins even more?

I took a deep breath and gazed out over the city, trying to calm my thoughts. I had an excellent view. The streets were lit by lamps and the western sky was filled with stars. It was also very hot, and I pulled at the neck of the plain shirt I wore. Not even the feeblest puff of wind stirred my hair. This long after sunset the temperature still hadn't dropped. Leap lay on the cool stone, indolent with heat. If only there was a breeze it wouldn't be so stifling.

Distractedly, I tested the atmosphere with my mind, attempting to detect any movement at all. In frustration I grasped at it with clutching thought-fingers, trying to drag a stubborn wind towards me. I felt the air give like a rope being tugged loose, and a soft gust fanned my face. I looked around, surprised. Where had that come from? I cast my mind out again, and pulled. Cool wind lifted my hair from my shoulders. I laughed in delight, and directed a gust down at Leap. He bared his belly to the breeze.

A dull hammer-blow squashed my good mood as I realised what was happening. Lharmellins could control the weather. They could draw down ice and acid storms that brought misery and death. I remembered reading that some harmings could manage to influence the weather in a small way as well. The reminder was unwelcome: no matter how despicable

I found them, how much I clung to my human side, I was still a harming. Un-Turned, but a harming just the same. I stalked inside and flung myself on my bed. I didn't want any part of it, heat or not.

I checked the time candle. Hours until midnight. I began pacing the room, too anxious to be still.

———

I started seething over Lilith's words again as I waited at the north-west gate. Creeping away like a common criminal, I thought with a snort. Like I had something to be ashamed of. Renata was hundreds of miles away, and yet her influence seemed to extend all over.

I heard the clip-clop of hooves on cobbles, and Rodden emerged out of the darkness, leading two horses.

'This is rather dramatic, wouldn't you say?' he drawled. 'Creeping away in the dead of night?' I saw the flash of his teeth as he grinned in the darkness. He hailed the guards, asking them to open the gates for us.

'I read it in a book once,' I said sourly. 'Thought it sounded like fun.' I mounted my horse, and Leap jumped up to sit on the saddle blanket before me.

Griffin was already settled on the horse's rump, her head nodding.

My grouchiness began to dissipate and I felt a little thrill as we trotted out the palace gates onto a wide gravel thoroughfare. These were the times I liked best, when it was just the four of us. My skin prickled with excitement.

We reached the main boulevard and broke into a canter. Few were abroad. We slowed to a walk as we rode through the city, passing patrols and one or two staggering drunks. Darkened townhouses gave way to black paddocks, dotted with farmhouses, and then we were on the open road, flanked by fields. This was the Drissian Way, the highway that connected the four major Pergamian cities, from Xallentaria in the east to Jefsgord in the west. The road was smooth and flat, and during the day it was populated with traders from all over Brivora. Everyone came to Pergamia to sell their wares. It was the richest country on the continent.

An hour or so before dawn we napped under a copse of pines, the needles springy and fragrant beneath us. Blazing sunshine woke us, and we were back in the saddles, sharing an oatcake and a water skin as our horses walked side by side. I couldn't help but be reminded of the time we'd spent living and sleeping rough in Lharmell. It had been a terrifying, thrilling time, and a totally alien experience to me then. I felt proud I could slip back into the simple, meagre way of life as if I'd been born to it.

We alternated trotting and walking, and around early afternoon I felt the pain begin. We'd been travelling parallel to the tors but our distance from them must have begun to lengthen. It wasn't the clawing pain I had felt the previous day, but a dull throbbing, enough to make me shift uncomfortably in the saddle.

To distract myself I looked at the countryside. The year was creeping towards high summer and the hay stood tall and golden in the fields, alive with chirping grasshoppers and delicate blue-and-white butterflies. I had a switch of willow leaves in one hand that I waved in front of my face, shooing the flies. Our horses were continually flicking their tails to discourage the insects.

Rendine was our first stop and we were to reach the city the day after tomorrow. After the sun had gone down we settled ourselves some distance from the highway, making camp under the spreading branches of a sycamore to avoid the falling dew. I lay on my cloak, with my saddlebags acting as a pillow, and chewed bread and cheese and a few dried figs. Griffin was nodding off in the tree and Leap lay curled beside me. I fed him morsels of cheese which he licked from my fingers with a rasping pink tongue. The horses were tethered nearby, noses in bags of oats.

It was growing dark and Rodden's eyes began to glow faintly. That was one of the side-effects of having Lharmellin blood and he seemed to be able to turn it on and off on a whim. Right now he was using the light to clean his crossbow.

I pictured the world map in my head, using the tor-line as a compass and measure of distance. The thread was quite useful that way: its tautness and angle told me just how far we'd travelled from Xallentaria, and in which direction.

'What will you ask the captain of the guard when we reach Rendine?'

Rodden didn't look up. 'I want the most up-to-date reports on missing persons and dead bodies. He might reveal other things as well, things that are playing on his mind but seem too inconsequential to put in a report. It's the little things that will help us now. But we should get some sleep. Good night.' He wrapped his cloak around himself and lay with his back to me.

I watched the stars appear through the branches of

the tree above, enjoying the drowsiness a day in the saddle had caused. It wasn't long until I fell asleep.

———

We reached Rendine in the mid-afternoon two days later. It was located inland on the River Frix and was small and sleepy, more like my home city of Prestoral than Xallentaria. Rodden booked us into a tavern and then we went straight to see the captain of the guard.

The guardhouse was right in the centre of town. From its front door I could see the market square, a smithy, a millwheel turning on the river. Outside, a knot of soldiers sat on benches.

'I'm looking for Captain Tibble,' Rodden told them.

A balding man with a heavy black moustache looked up. ''At'd be me. Who's askin'?'

'Rodden Lothskorn.'

The man's bushy eyebrows crept up his forehead. He stood up, offering his hand. The two men shook firmly.

'It's an honour to 'ave you in Rendine, sir. Where y'staying?'

'The Pig and Gristle.'

'Aye,' said Tibble approvingly. 'Gobbin there'll see y'right.'

What charming names these country folk had.

'Is there somewhere we can talk?' asked Rodden.

Tibble stood back to allow us into the guardhouse and seemed to notice me for the first time. 'Who be this?' he asked, eyeing me up and down.

I stood up straight, resting my hand on the knife at my belt. 'Zeraphina Herm –'

'My sister,' interrupted Rodden.

Tibble regarded us, his moustache twitching. Then he held out his arm, indicating we should go inside. Despite the fact that we both had black hair and icy blue eyes, I could tell he didn't believe that we were siblings, and I swept inside with all the dignity I could muster in trousers and travel-grime.

'Your latest report didn't say much,' Rodden said, as soon as we were seated.

''At's because I din't have much to say.' Then as an afterthought he added, 'Sir.'

'You've been checking for exsanguination, as ordered?'

'Aye.'

'You reported none.'

''At's because we've had naught. T'only dead body we've had this month be old Bobby Jopper.'

'And what was the cause of death?'

'He got drunk, fell in t'river and was dragged under t'millwheel.' Tibble tutted and shook his head.

'I see,' said Rodden. 'And have there been any strange occurrences since?'

'Nay. T'millwheel be right as rain now, y'can see for y'self.'

Rodden looked at me. 'Was there anything you'd like to ask, Sister?'

I racked my brains for something intelligent to ask, but the image of the poor drunk under the millwheel was still stuck in my mind. I shook my head.

Rodden stood. 'Thank you for your time, Captain Tibble. You know where we are if you think of anything else.'

As we walked back to the tavern Rodden looked gloomy.

'I remember a time,' I mused, 'when a lack of dead, bloodless bodies was a good thing. Such happy days they were.'

'This is not a case of no news is good news. It would be helpful to discover something.'

'Does the discovery have to be dead?'

'When it involves harmings, yes.'

'Could Rendine be harming-free?'

'You mean apart from you and me?'

We looked around at the town, with its thatched roofs and flowering window boxes; a place where nothing more unpleasant occurred than the town drunk being dragged under the millwheel on his unsteady way home.

Rodden sighed. 'I suppose. Come on, I need a drink.'

———

Two days later, on the road to Ercan, we got our lead. Griffin had been hunting up ahead but came swooping back to me with an *alert!* that nearly knocked me out of the saddle. Harmings. We'd been bound to pass some sooner or later. But would they know who we were? I pulled my horse alongside Rodden's.

'You've got your mind shielded?' he murmured. His eyes were scanning the road ahead.

'Yes.'

He nodded. 'Good. Just act natural. We're travellers like anyone else.'

With their safety in mind, I urged Leap and Griffin to make themselves scarce. Then I concentrated on keeping my thought-wall impenetrable.

I watched the flow of traffic: a farmer with a cart full of squash; a wagonload of children with a dark-haired man at the reins; a young boy leading a milking cow with a big clanging bell around its neck. Then I noticed something peculiar about the children in the wagon. They were young and scrappy, the eldest about fourteen, and they all wore the same pale blue shirt. But what raised the hairs on the back of my neck was their uncanny silence. Two dozen pairs of icy blue eyes stared at us as their wagon trundled by. I turned and saw the wagon pulling off the main road onto a dirt track. When they'd disappeared we pulled our horses over.

'Those children were all harmings, weren't they?' I rubbed my forearms, suddenly chilled to the bone. Children. It had never occurred to me that they'd take children.

Rodden had one hand on the strap of his crossbow and his eyes on the turn-off. He nodded. 'Did you see the shirt they wore? It looked like an orphanage uniform. That road they turned off on leads to Yib. It's a farming district, and a pretty lonely one.'

'What do you think it means?'

'Enclaves. I haven't seen them in Pergamia before. My guess is they were stolen from an orphanage in Ercan and are being taken to a training enclave.'

'They were so young,' I said wistfully.

'The harmings are taking the destitutes off the streets and the unwanted from the orphanages; people no one will ever miss. Some for blood and some to swell the harming ranks, I'd wager.'

'Should we do anything?'

Reluctantly, Rodden shook his head. 'There's not much we can do for them now. Except . . .' He trailed off.

I winced. Except kill them, he meant. 'It's such a waste. Their lives are over before they've begun.'

He looked at me with worried eyes. 'Stay close, all right?'

I nodded. Leap and Griffin returned, and I clutched my cat against my body as we broke into a canter.

FOUR

The blinding sun did little to dispel our grim mood as we rode into Ercan the next morning. I had slept badly, partly because I had been thinking of the harming children. I couldn't help but wonder if they'd been afraid when the harmings had come for them; if they'd cried out for their mothers, even though they were orphans and their mothers were dead. It was awful to contemplate. For the first time I was glad that I'd been infected as a baby – if it'd had to happen at all – and not when I was old enough to remember it.

But mostly I slept badly because of Rodden. I didn't think he had slept at all. Instead, by the light of his glowing eyes he had sharpened all our weapons. First his knife, then my knife, then the arrow tips – both the yelbar and ordinary ones – and even the crossbow bolts. The rasping of whetstone on metal had been incessant. It had been on the tip of my tongue to tell him to knock it *off*, but I sensed that my protestations would be ignored. At first light he had been up and away and I had managed to drop off for a moment, but all too soon a fresh rabbit carcass had been dumped on my cloak. Rodden had looked pale and cheerless in the wan morning light and I didn't bother to make conversation over our meal. It seemed the sight of the harming children had upset him as badly as it had me.

The set of his shoulders was murderous as we rode into Ercan. I hoped the captain of the guard had his reports in order, or heads were about to roll.

Ercan was another land-locked city but large and bustling compared to Rendine. It was just the sort of place where the homeless and orphaned could go missing with no one any the wiser.

We rode straight to the guardhouse and Rodden shouldered the door open without a word. I thought we might have spruced ourselves up a bit first: after nearly a week in the saddle we looked rather scruffy, hardly the ideal look for the king's envoy.

Captain Verlin sat behind his desk, legs splayed, a churlish expression on his features as Rodden questioned him.

'Nup. Nothin' strange.'

The muscles in Rodden's jaw bunched. 'It says here in your latest report that thirteen people died from miscellaneous causes.'

'S'right.'

'Would you care to elaborate?'

Verlin shrugged, his eyes wandering around the room. 'Old age.'

The tension in the room, obvious to myself but clearly not to Verlin, was making me nervous. My nails were making crescent-marks in my palms.

'Twelve were under twenty.'

'Folks don't live long round these parts. It's the pollution. No sea air. Not like you fancy folk in the capital.'

Rodden started taking off his gloves, one finger at a time. 'Captain Vermin –'

'Verlin.'

'– I put it to you that you are a lazy, imbecilic, corrupt individual who is wasting my time and the king's money.'

Verlin ignored Rodden, his wandering eyes wandering over to me. He winked. 'Such a pretty sister. Wouldn't mind one of 'em of me own.' He laughed as if it was the funniest thing he'd ever heard.

Rodden's patience snapped and he reached over the desk and grabbed the captain by the scruff of his jacket.

'Oi!'

He marched Verlin out of the guardhouse past his guards, across the square and over to the stocks. I followed, fascinated and horrified at the same time. Surely he wouldn't put the man in his own restraints?

'Last chance, Vermin,' Rodden said, the man still dangling by his uniform. 'Any idea how those people died?'

The captain said something rather uncomplimentary about donkeys and Rodden's mother, and a few seconds later he found himself clapped in the stocks. He struggled as Rodden stripped the badges from his uniform. As Rodden strode away Verlin yelled, 'Y'can't do this! I'm the bleedin' captain! Come back here, ya goat-swivin' son of a donkey's turd!'

Rodden ignored the demoted captain. We approached the knot of guards that had gathered outside their headquarters, struck dumb by the sight of Verlin struggling in the stocks.

'Question time, gentlemen. Who can tell me which orphanage in Ercan dresses its children in pale blue shirts?'

After a moment, a young, sandy-haired soldier cautiously raised his hand. 'Fallowood Home for Unfortunates.'

Rodden tossed the soldier the captain's badges. 'Congratulations …?'

'Sergeant Milson, sir.'

'Milson. You're the new captain. Take me to Fallowood, and bring two of your guards.'

Milson looked rather startled at his sudden promotion, but did what he was told.

———

Fallowood was in a seedy part of town, a dank, grey building nestled among the brothels and the less sanitary butchers' shops. We picked our way down the narrow street, avoiding puddles of filth in the middle of the road. Toddlers ran about without their napkins, dirty marks down their legs. On their backs were pale blue shirts, just like the ones we'd seen on the harming children. This place was a far cry from the 'glorious' nation of Pergamia I'd heard so much about. It seemed there were cracks to slip through, and we were in one of them.

The new captain knocked on a door and a dour, middle-aged woman opened it. When she saw the guards she stepped back to let us inside. She gave Rodden a once-over, taking in his scruffy beard and dusty travelling clothes. 'I'm fresh out of wenches,' she told him. 'Hafta come back next week if ye want one over eleven. I'll call the ones I 'ave, if ye like. You can have one cheap. But they're a stringy bunch.' She nodded at me. 'Hafta make do with this one for now.'

'You beastly woman,' I growled. This had to be the place the harmings had taken the children from – or bought, it seemed. Had she so little compassion that she could sell someone in her charge to just anyone who came asking?

Rodden placed a hand on my shoulder. 'Now, here's something we *can* fix,' he murmured.

Before he could speak, Milson coughed apologetically. 'This is the Honourable Rodden Lothskorn, ma'am.'

'Who?' She peered at Rodden afresh, but the name clearly didn't mean anything to her.

Rodden addressed the soldier. 'Milson, was Captain Verlin in the habit of allowing slaves to be peddled out of orphanages?'

Milson shifted his shoulders uncomfortably. 'Yes.'

'Thank you for your honesty. The selling of children won't happen in the future, I'm sure.' He turned to the matron. 'Are you missing a quantity of children as of yesterday?'

The woman spat on the ground, barely missing Rodden's boots. 'Not missing. Fostered.'

'Two dozen at once?'

She looked quite pleased with herself. 'Aye.'

'Milson,' said Rodden. 'Have this woman suitably fined, flogged, or jailed. I don't care which.'

Milson nodded to his men. The matron began to scream in protest as the two guards hitched her up by her armpits and hauled her away. Two dirty children, barely four and five, watched her go. They looked like they were infested with lice and hadn't seen the bristly end of a comb in a long time.

It angered me that King Askar could let this sort of thing go on. It didn't happen in Amentia, did it? I thought of the capital, Prestoral, small but neat. It had seen desperate times, but surely Renata had kept a close eye on greed and corruption. I had to assume so, but I didn't know. I'd never bothered to concern myself with such things.

If I ever married and became queen, I decided, I would take an interest in everyone, rich and poor. I would go into the cities myself and speak with the people who were doing things in my name and under my pay. Or my husband's, as the case may be.

But not yet, I thought silently to Renata. I'm not ready to be married yet.

All the way back to the guardhouse, Rodden lectured Milson on his new captaincy. 'Your first duty is to rehouse the remaining children from Fallowood in reputable establishments. Orphanage inspections are to happen monthly, and you are to see to it that only trustworthy individuals are in charge of and allowed to foster children. Disappearances and deaths in this city are to be treated with the utmost seriousness. A coroner is to determine cause of death and reports are to be made to me. I am sending ten of my own guards from Xallentaria to work under you and by the time they arrive I am sure there won't be even a whiff of corruption among the king's guards of Ercan. Right, Captain Milson?'

'Yessir.'

'Good. Any questions?'

'Yes. What's a coroner, sir?'

———

Rodden ran his hands down the legs of two fresh horses, checking for lameness. I held their bridles and thought fondly of bathwater and bed sheets.

'Do you really think "a doctor for dead bodies" is

a good explanation of what a coroner is?' I asked.

Rodden lifted the horse's foot and inspected it. It seemed he didn't trust anything in Ercan. 'I don't care. I just want to get out of this stinking cesspit of a city.'

I patted one of the horses on the nose. 'Nothing personal,' I told it. I peered at the horizon. 'It's getting late. And it looks like rain,' I added hopefully.

'No, it doesn't.'

I scowled. 'Snow then. Can't we stay? I'm out of clean clothes.'

'This place gives me the gripes.' He stood up and regarded me, smiling. 'But you do look a sight. Maybe I will trade you in at Fallowood.'

'Go swive a goat.'

He dug out some coins to pay for the horses. 'Princesses shouldn't know such language.'

'It must be the company I keep.'

He paid the stable keeper and we led the horses outside. 'All right. Which flea-bitten inn do you fancy then?' he asked.

We found one on the western side of town close to the road to Jefsgord. 'For quick and easy departure,' Rodden muttered as we crossed the threshold.

As the sun set I stood out the back with my sleeves rolled up, giving my two spare outfits the scrubbing of their short lives. I felt an odd sort of accomplishment as I did it. There were worse things I could be doing; sucking on dead squirrels and rats did tend to put things in perspective.

With pruned fingers I joined Rodden in the tavern. He was staring into a flagon of ale, the very picture of dejection.

'Hungry?' I asked.

He shook his head.

I sat down. 'Rodden, are you an orphan?'

'My parents died when I was sixteen,' he said, his voice flat. 'Does that count?'

A serving maid came over and I asked for a cider. I sipped the dry, fruity ale in silence for a moment. Then I asked, 'Are you from Verapine?' Rodden had told me once that he wasn't Pergamian, and with his olive skin, dark brows and stern features, he didn't look like any Brivoran I had seen.

Rodden looked at me from beneath his lashes. 'Yes.'

'Do you want to ...?'

'Talk about it?'

'Yes.'

'Do I ever?'

I shrugged. 'No skin off my nose. Brood all you like. The aunts find it sexy.'

'The who?'

'Amis's aunts. They're quite taken with you.' I'd had tea with Amis's aunts before Lilith's wedding, and Rodden had featured high on their list of favoured men at the palace. I smiled at the memory.

He thought for a moment, and then looked horrified. 'Not those tarty middle-aged hags who are incessantly shoving cakes in their faces?'

'That's them.'

He made a face. 'I wondered why they were always badgering me to come to their parties.' He took a sip of ale and looked at me over the rim of the cup. 'And what about you?'

'What about me?' But my face was already flaming. Curse my good circulation.

'Do you find it sexy? My brooding.' When he grinned like that he looked like a Hallow's Eve pumpkin.

I coughed and looked away. 'I find it exceedingly dull. Excuse me, I'm hungry.' Face aflame, I went to study the menu, which was a piece of slate with some chicken scratchings in chalk on it. My spine prickled and I was certain Rodden was watching me with that wicked grin on his face. I didn't find his brooding sexy, I decided. I liked it better when he smiled. He had a disarming smile, crooked, with dimples in just one cheek …

Shut up.

'Meat Stu,' the menu read. What sort of meat, I wondered. 'Taters. Cheppers Py.'

'Excuse me,' I said to the bar-keep, who was polishing glasses with a dirty apron. 'What is "cheppers py"?'

'Cheppers py is cheppers py,' he said gruffly. 'Where you from?'

I wondered if I should say Prestoral, but he probably wouldn't have heard of it. 'Xallentaria.'

'Oh,' he said, as if that explained a lot. 'Cheppers py is ground meat wiv taters on top.'

'What sort of meat?'

He widened his eyes and snorted as if I were being particularly bothersome. 'Goat. Sheep. Bit o' cow, maybe. If you're lucky.' He laughed and I saw blackened teeth in his mouth.

I said I would try it. He disappeared for a moment and came back with some grey slop topped with some white slop. 'Five coppers,' he said, setting it on the counter.

I paid him and took the steaming monstrosity back to where Rodden sat. 'Dare me to eat it?' I asked.

He tasted a forkful. 'That's good shepherd's pie,' he said.

'Shepherd's pie? I couldn't make out what the idiot was saying,' I muttered.

Rodden lapsed into silence as I ate. When I finished I decided to try one last time to draw him out. I picked something safe, something that he might want to talk about. 'Tell me about Verapine?' I asked. When he'd talked of it that day in his turret room he'd seemed almost happy.

'You'll see it for yourself soon.'

'I know. But tell me anyway.'

Leap was crouched under the table, no doubt hoping somebody would be clumsy with their dinner. Rodden pulled my cat onto his lap and stroked his silvery fur.

'Well, there're lots of these little buggers running around, in Pol at least. No one keeps them as pets in Verapine but they are respected and loved. They keep the city rat-free and we would all have died of plague without them. Even though it's in the desert, there are sewers to cope with the monsoon rains. The cats spend long periods down there in the dark.'

Leap, sensing he was being talked about, went all boneless and purry in Rodden's arms.

'It's all slums, Pol. It's not a rich place. It doesn't have the agricultural power that Pergamia has because most of the land is desert. But the tribespeople and city crafters make beautiful carpets and silks. All those floaty dresses you girls wear, the fabric comes from Verapine.' He smiled as he rubbed Leap behind the ears. 'I grew up in the western fringes, right where the slums meet the desert. At dusk the last of the sun's rays would stretch across the sands and turn the whole city golden. Sometimes it felt like the twilight would go on forever, just like the desert.' His eyes hardened. 'So you see, Your Highness, I'm as common as the bar-keep. A slum-dweller.'

I felt my face burn again. 'I'm not a snob.'

'We can't help our upbringing.' He stood, tipping Leap onto the floor. 'Which makes me wonder why I bother,' he muttered under his breath. Without another word he stalked up the stairs to his room.

I'm not a snob, I fumed. I'd done my own washing, hadn't I?

There was a man with a leather cap pulled low over his eyes watching me from the other side of the tavern, so I got up and went to my room. I didn't feel like being taken for a prostitute a second time that day. Leap followed Griffin out the window to hunt and I lay on my bed. What had he meant, 'he wondered why he bothered'? Was he referring to me? No, that didn't seem right. He'd been referring to himself, but the comment was too cryptic.

I fell asleep, angry and frustrated but too tired to think on the matter any longer.

———

A flash of light woke me. I didn't know how long I'd been asleep. It was dark now, but I thought I could hear something moving. 'Leap?' I called. But he hadn't returned from hunting. I reached out with my mind but Griffin wasn't nearby either.

Something clamped over my mouth, and I screamed silently against the obstruction. I struggled, trying to fend off whoever it was, but I was pinned, as if a dozen hands were holding me down. Except I couldn't feel any hands. There was no one there. Only this oppressive weight, everywhere at once.

Twin points of blazing blue light appeared over my head and bored into my eyes. A harming! But not here in the room. It had sent its presence, just like Rodden could. Terrified, I flung up my mind-wall and immediately felt black tentacles probe against my barrier. They began to jab as if trying to punch through. I floundered around in my mind, searching for Rodden's thread, Leap's or Griffin's, but came up with nothing. I couldn't even feel the tor-line and that really terrified me. I could always feel the tor-line; I dreamed about it. I was trapped and at any second the harming was about to worm its way inside my head.

I heard a bang and weak yellow light from the hall spilled into the room. Rodden stood in the doorway. I could finally see the shimmering dark form hovering over me.

Rodden cried out and ran forward. The dark presence whirled, knocking him backwards, but it still kept its pressure on my body. Rodden reeled back, hitting the wall and holding a hand to his face. I thought I saw blood.

Then he crumpled to the ground.

I panicked. I couldn't get enough air into my lungs because of the force on my chest. The harder I fought the more quickly I tired. Black spots began to dance in my vision.

Then suddenly the weight was gone. I sucked in air and sat up. Rodden was still on the floor, out cold. But now there were two shimmering forms in the room, one dark and murky, and the other blazing with white-blue light. I recognised it instantly: Rodden in his phantom form. They struggled frantically, flickering like candles caught in the wind. I tried to get up and find a weapon, but the moment I stood their whirling forms knocked me back down again. The darker one seemed to be losing ground. Rodden's form blazed brighter and brighter. And then with a drone like a swarm of bees, the darker one seemed to pull itself together, shove Rodden off and then zip out the window.

Rodden's phantom form hovered in the air for a moment, as if waiting to see if the other would return, and then sank back into his body. Several silent, agonising seconds passed, and then his eyes flickered open.

I was off the bed in a second. 'Rodden!' My hands felt all over his body, reassuring myself that he was solid once more and all in once piece.

He groaned and sat up. His nose was bleeding and he swiped at it with the back of his hand.

'Are you all right?'

His eyes focused. 'Are *you*?'

I nodded. 'He was trying to punch his way through to my mind. A few more seconds and he would have succeeded.'

'He?'

I paused. 'Yes. I'm sure it was a he. Even though I couldn't see him, I could feel him. I think I saw him downstairs, right before I went to bed.'

'And you didn't tell me? Why not?'

'Because,' I said, giving him a little shove, 'I'm

not flipping perfect. You and your mood swings distracted me, and it didn't occur to me at the time that it was a harming.'

He sighed. 'I think I know who you mean. In a leather cap in the corner?'

I nodded. 'He did something to my mind. I couldn't move because he was holding me down, but I couldn't find you, either, or Leap or Griffin. I couldn't even feel the tors.'

Before I could say anything more he put his arms around me and gathered me close to him. His heart beat a solid rhythm against my cheek. I loved the way he felt. I wanted to stay like that all night, but he released me.

I blushed and dropped my eyes to the ground, not knowing why him being close should make the heat rise to my face, but sure that it wasn't something I wanted him to know. Was Carmelina right after all? Did I have a crush on Rodden? I bit my lip, suddenly feeling guilty about the way I'd spoken to Lilith. If I did have feelings for Rodden, didn't that make her right about the impropriety of us travelling alone together? But of course, it didn't necessarily follow that Rodden had feelings for me. Did it?

Oh, *stop it*, I chastised myself. It was just a hug, for goodness' sake.

Griffin came hurtling through the window and perched on my bedhead, hackles raised. She made clicks of concern in the back of her throat. I could hear Leap clawing his way up to the first floor and a second later he appeared at the window and jumped into my lap. I hugged him gratefully.

'What do you think he wanted?' I asked Rodden.

'I think he knows who we are. Or at least suspects.'

I felt a stab of alarm. 'Then we have to leave, now. He could come back any second.'

Rodden stood. 'I'll go back and get my things. I'll just be a few doors away. Promise you'll call out if you see anything.'

I nodded, and he dashed back to his room. I began to collect my gear, and met him in the hall a few minutes later.

We crept down the back stairway and out to the stable. In silence we saddled our horses and led them out into the rear lane. The sound of their clopping hooves was shockingly loud in the still night air. Why was it that everything seemed louder in the dark? Every deep shadow was the harming about to leap out at us. I took a tighter grip on my crossbow.

Once we'd skirted the block and found the main

thoroughfare we mounted our horses and beat a hasty retreat from Ercan, probably the most horrid place in all Pergamia.

I steeled myself for another sleepless night.

FIVE

Five hours later I was nearly falling out of the saddle with fatigue, but we didn't dare stop. If Rodden was right and the harming had guessed who I was, then others might be after us, too. The thought of what would happen to me if I was captured kept me awake. Publicly executed in Lharmell, no doubt, at some grisly ceremony, with assorted tortures visited on myself, Rodden, Leap and Griffin immediately preceding.

Just before dawn, Rodden dismounted and we led the horses off the road and into some dense scrub. I sat on the leaf litter and stretched out my sore legs. Rodden fell into a cross-legged position beside me, hands over his face. The fight had taken its toll on him, and he looked pale and exhausted.

'Does doing your out-of-body thing usually make you this tired?' I asked.

He shook his head. 'I'm fine.'

But I didn't believe him. 'That harming might have been following us all the way from Xallentaria,' I said.

'I shouldn't think so. He would have made a move before now. We must have picked him up somewhere in Ercan. That town is infested with rotten creatures. I wouldn't be surprised if Captain Vermin let the harmings have the run of the place.'

I played the events of the night over in my head: being pinned to the bed, then the sudden shaft of light illuminating the room. 'How did you know? I couldn't even get a scream out.'

Rodden glanced at me, his eyes grey in the dim pre-dawn light. 'I wasn't asleep. All of a sudden I couldn't feel you any more, and I knew something was wrong.' He was silent for a moment before adding, 'Sorry I was such an ass over dinner.'

I raised my eyebrows. An apology? I wondered if he could be running a temperature. 'It's all right. I'm used to it by now.' I saw that blood had dripped from his nose all the way down his chin. 'You've got blood on your face.' I scrabbled in my pack for something to clean him up with. 'Did you manage to injure the harming?' I asked.

'No. It wasn't much of a fight, really. He was more shocked than anything else, and that's why he left so quickly. He was much stronger than me.'

My pack seemed strangely empty. Then I remembered why and I flung my bag away from me. 'Damn and blast and pox! I left my spare clothes at the inn. I washed them myself, you know.' See? Princess washing her own clothes. Not a snob after all.

'We'll buy you some new ones in Jefsgord.'

'How far away is it?'

'A day and a half.'

'What's between here and there?'

'Not a lot. Wilderness mostly.'

'Oh, terrific.' Empty wilderness. I had hoped we would be on the boat later in the day. I pictured harmings behind every bush, us being ambushed on a lonely road. My eyes were gritty and sore from exhaustion; I wouldn't be much good at fighting off an attack if it came to it. But I didn't want to sleep. What if the harmings found us?

'We should get some sleep. It's been too long,' Rodden said.

I must have looked stricken, as he said, 'You sleep. I'll stay awake.'

We'd always left Leap and Griffin on guard while we slept, but that didn't feel safe enough right now. 'Really? You haven't rested either.'

He reached for my hand and squeezed it. 'Go to sleep.'

I wrapped my cloak around my body and lay down, my head pillowed against my bags. I felt for Rodden's mind-thread, his sweet familiarity. I couldn't get the harming out of my head. The way his presence had held me down, and the desolate sense of being disconnected from everyone and everything as he had plundered my mind.

For once, Rodden let me keep the thread in my grasp and I fell asleep holding on for dear life.

———

It was late morning when I woke. I wouldn't say I was refreshed, but I was no longer one of the walking dead. Rodden was sitting up and staring out over the scrubby plain, loaded crossbow in his hands. It was notched with a yelbar tip: he'd been on the lookout for harmings, not rabbits. His eyes were tired, but stubbornly vigilant.

'Your turn,' I muttered, sitting up and reaching for the water skin.

He shook his head. 'I'm fine. Let's get moving.'

I protested, saying he needed to rest, but he ignored me. Once we were on horseback I strung my bow and took out a few regular arrows, fletched with Griffin's moulted feathers. My crossbow was perched in front of me, yelbar bolts at the ready. But we needed blood and I still didn't trust my aim with that contraption. Rodden was slumped in his saddle and barely in a fit state to ride, let alone to hunt. I aimed my bow into the scrub on my left.

And waited.

My arms grew tired, but I kept the bow up. After ten minutes Griffin came swooping back with a swamp rat for us, and I told her to give it to Rodden. She dropped it in his lap, and, bleary-eyed, he cut its neck and began drinking the meagre blood.

Afterwards he perked up, and together we brought down a rabbit and then a seagull. My heart gladdened at the sight of the bird. We were nearing the coast.

After our meal, with my crossbow in one hand and reins in the other, I urged my horse into a canter. I heard Rodden follow and, side by side, we ate up the lonely road to Jefsgord, alternately cantering and trotting for several hours. Every time we slowed to give the horses a rest I felt those black tentacles jabbing at my mind. I knew it was just my imagination but I couldn't keep myself from peering over my shoulder.

In the evening we roasted the rabbit carcass. Rodden fell asleep while he was eating, something that I'd thought was impossible to do. I tucked his cloak about him and reluctantly put the fire out. A harming would spot it from miles off.

I settled myself against a tree to keep watch. The sky darkened into full night and a half-moon rose. I kept myself occupied by making up names for the constellations, as I didn't know the real ones. I had just finished naming the Hunting Eagle and the Rude Bar-keep when I saw a bat pass over us.

No, not a bat. A brant.

I clamped down on my mind and was just about to kick Rodden awake when I saw the giant bird fly away. I watched closely, wondering if the rider had detected us and was winging its way back to its friends. By the way the brant was circling over the countryside it still seemed to be looking for something, so it probably hadn't spotted us.

I gave up naming constellations after that. Around two hours after midnight I couldn't keep my eyes open any longer and shook Rodden awake. 'Just two hours,' I whispered to him, 'and then I'll take watch again.'

But when I awoke it was morning. Rodden was attempting to shave with his knife, a bit of soap, and no mirror. I scowled at him. 'You were supposed to wake me up hours ago.'

The soap slipped from his fingers into his lap. 'Oh, damn. Hmm? What's wrong?' He began scraping at his cheek with the knife.

'Did you see any brants?'

He shook his head and then hissed in pain. Blood welled from a tiny cut on his jaw.

'Give me that,' I said, holding out my hand for the knife. 'You're making a mess.'

I knelt in front of him and took the knife. The blood was beading up like rubies and I dabbed at it with my finger.

I don't know what made me do it. An impulse, or curiosity. I put the finger in my mouth. His blood tasted like he smelled, like distilled Rodden.

His eyes widened. 'What the hell? Why did you do that?'

My face flamed as I realised what I'd done. I let my hair fall in front of my eyes as I tested the sharpness of the blade. Scraping it across his check, I avoided his incredulous look. I tried to concentrate but the taste of his blood was heavy on my tongue. Was I getting a taste for human blood? But it wasn't thirst that made me lick my finger. It was curiosity. A Rodden-specific curiosity. I wondered what it would be like to bite him. Not in a killing way – more like the way Leap sometimes bit me when he got playful. Testing my reaction, my ability to fight back. Horrified by the image that was forming in my mind, I squashed my thoughts before he could overhear them.

But I couldn't suppress one thought: that I liked the way he tasted.

I hadn't had much practice at shaving so Rodden's face ended up looking rather scrappy. I gave him back the knife without a word and found I couldn't look him in the eye as we packed up camp and mounted our horses. Once we were on the open road I was glad to ride behind him, out of his sight.

By midday the hot sun had burnt away my embarrassment and most of the strange, fluttery feeling I got whenever the image of grappling with Rodden entered my mind. We began the descent into Jefsgord. The city sat on the curving coastline, fortified by wooden palisades. There was very little farmland, the scrub extending right up to the defences in places. The dock, even seen from the far side, was prodigious. Ships' masts sprouted from the water like a forest of masts and ropes. Clouds of gulls wheeled over the boats though we couldn't yet hear their screaming cries.

I pulled up next to Rodden. 'Is it safe, do you think? What if that harming got ahead of us and warned all his buddies in the town?'

'Jefsgord isn't like Ercan. I know the captain of the guard here. He's good at his job and the harming presence will have been kept to a minimum. We'll go straight to him, and then down to the dock to find a trade-ship for the crossing to Pol.'

I was relieved to see archers atop the city gate, attentive as those in the capital.

Inside the guardhouse, Captain Helmsrid greeted Rodden like an old friend and they shook hands warmly. I waited to be introduced as his sister, but to my surprise Rodden said, 'This is Princess Lilith's younger sister, Zeraphina of the House of Amentia.'

The captain took in my black hair and icy eyes. Griffin was perched on my arm and Leap was already sniffing under the man's desk. 'I see,' he said, and I rather thought he did. He bowed. 'Your Highness.'

I bobbed, feeling odd acting so formally after spending the night lying on dirt. I sat down, hoping they would get things over with quickly so we could get down to the dock. We'd be safe once we were on board, I was sure.

But Rodden launched into an explanation of what had happened in Ercan.

'Why didn't it kill you outright?' the captain asked, turning to me.

'I think it wanted to make certain who I was first.' I remembered the jabbing black tentacles and shuddered.

Helmsrid looked grim. 'We'll post extra guards. My men reported brants in the sky last night, something we haven't seen in months. Here's the body count from the last report.' He passed a sheet of paper to Rodden. 'Three exsanguinations: two terminal cases in a hospice and one destitute, made to look as if they had died in their sleep.'

'Anything else to report?'

Helmsrid shook his head. 'Where are you going from here; back to Xallentaria?'

'No, by trade-ship to Pol.'

Helmsrid frowned. 'Then there is something I should mention. It could be nothing, but ... I was drinking with a sea captain last night and he mentioned the inordinate number of ships missing in action of late. It's something I'd heard about, of course, but until now I've dismissed it as pirates, or wrecks. Some of the boats that dock here are floating deathtraps with only their barnacles holding them together. But this captain was telling me that good sturdy ships are disappearing and the crew never heard from again. He agreed it could be pirates after the cargo, too, but the last two ships to vanish have been empty. Pirates aren't fools. They can tell which ships are loaded up by how low they sit in the water. These two would have been sitting very high indeed, and obviously empty, so it doesn't make a lot of sense. Unless …' He trailed off, looking between us.

Rodden nodded. 'Thank you, Captain. I'll keep that in mind.'

As we made our way down to the docks I asked, 'Harming attacks?'

'It would seem so.'

I sighed. I had assumed we would be safe on open water, but apparently not.

Down on the dock, it was dark among the bellies of the enormous vessels. Fat, shiny seals lay on the crossbeams beneath the boardwalk, barking at each other and slapping their sides with their flippers. Leap peered through the planks at them, his tail lashing. He didn't seem to be disturbed by all the water – but he was a drain-cat, after all. Griffin, who couldn't help looking fierce all the time, was glaring more than usual and digging her claws into my gauntlet. I wondered what could have got into her until I saw her murderous looks at the seagulls screeching and wheeling overhead. Their cries were hurting her sensitive ears. The gulls followed us in a cacophonous cloud, alarmed by the bird of prey in their midst.

The air was pungent with damp seaweed and rotting wood. I could see what Captain Helmsrid meant about floating deathtraps; we passed some very sick-looking vessels. Rodden dismissed ship after ship, some that looked quite acceptable to me, and I feared we wouldn't find even one that met his exacting standards. But at last he called to a sailor carrying a calico bale up the loading plank of the *Jessamine*.

'Who captains this ship?' he asked.

'Cap'n Krig,' the sailor replied. He was heavily tanned, the skin around his eyes prematurely wrinkled by the sun. Faded blue tattoos of anchors and mermaids decorated his wiry forearms.

'Where would we find him?'

'O'er there, at the Krill 'n' Mermaid.' The sailor pointed at a lean-to on the far side of the docks. We thanked the sailor and struggled over to it, the way mostly blocked by rigging and crayfish pots.

A white-haired man in a threadbare blazer sat blinking in the sun, a pint of ale and a bottle of dark rum at his elbow. It was barely two in the afternoon, but maybe there were such things as sea-time and land-time and it was quite acceptable for him to be drinking hard spirits at this hour. Or maybe he was a sot.

'Captain Krig?' asked Rodden.

The man nodded.

'We're after passage to Pol. Is the *Jessamine* heading on there?'

'Aye,' the man said. 'For t'bird and moggy, too?' he asked.

I nodded. Leap had his head inside a crayfish pot and was sniffing with interest.

'We've already got a ship's cat. Don't think my Smokey'd like 'im,' he said.

'He's very friendly,' I insisted, as Leap tried to back out of the trap. It was rather one-way and he had his big silly ears stuck.

'Oh, aye.' The captain downed a slug of rum from a sea-green tumbler. He eyed our crossbows. 'Can ye shoot those contraptions?'

'Certainly can,' said Rodden, bending down to extricate Leap.

'Oh, aye.' The captain took a moment to squint up at us. 'We don't up anchor until tomorrow evening. Goin' with the tide. Y'in a hurry?'

'Well, yes. But we can wait, for the right price.'

The captain 'hmphed' at that. 'Ten pieces each. Bird and cat free. Now, if that ain't a bargain, I know not what is.'

He and Rodden shook on it and we made our way back into town. A whole day and a half in Jefsgord. I hoped Captain Helmsrid was doing as good a job as he said and we weren't about to run into any old friends.

We needed supplies, especially clothes for me, but the market was already closing. We checked into an inn with a view of the sea from the first floor. I asked the keeper for a bath in my room, intending to soak myself into a pleasantly pruned state. Before I got into the steaming tub I locked my door and gave it a rattle to test its strength. Not totally harming-proof, but it would do.

I could see the ocean from where I bathed and watched the ships slipping over the horizon. I was looking forward to this journey, though my excitement was tempered by Helmsrid's story of missing ships. I hoped the *Jessamine* had a good lookout.

SIX

Rodden was bashing on my door at dawn, telling me to get up.

'Don't you ever sleep in?' I called through two inches of wood. I had hoped we would lie around for a while on our last morning on dry land. I threw the blankets off in a huff and climbed once more into my filthy clothes.

The humidity of the air in Jefsgord, even at this early hour, was playing havoc with my hair. As we walked along the street I tamed it into a braid. 'Are we going to the market?' I asked, nodding at our horses, which he was leading.

'Yes. We'll sell our horses and pick up some gear for Verapine.'

We stopped at a stall selling heavy winter clothes and Rodden began searching through a stack of coats.

'I thought it was hot in Verapine.'

'It is. But at night the temperature plummets to just above freezing. There's never any cloud cover so the heat of the day escapes back into the sky.'

I pulled on a woven poncho and a heavy pair of trousers over my clothes. They were very warm, so I took them off again quickly and bought them. From another stall we picked up pairs of plain breeches and shirts.

'Do you want any dresses?' Rodden asked.

I shook my head. As I was going to be on a ship full of men I wanted to look as sexless as possible. Coarse shirts and badly cut breeches were prudent choices.

The horses we sold to a dealer and then, tucking our parcels of clothes under the table, we sat at a tea shack for some breakfast.

'Are we going to have enough yelbar points if we're attacked?' I asked.

Rodden swirled his mug of milky *camai*, an import from Pol. It was spicy black tea, brewed with milk and sweetened with honey. He broke a small loaf of currant bread in half.

'I don't know,' he muttered. 'I'm beginning to think this mightn't be a good idea.'

'But we need the bennium.'

He watched me for a moment. 'Even after what happened to you in Ercan, you're not afraid?'

A shiver went up my spine. I *did* find my mind returning to that moment, reliving the harming's attack. 'Of course I am. But that fear seems to be buried so deep, under layers and layers of other fears. Do you know what I mean?'

He nodded slowly, looking at his *camai*. 'You're more afraid of other things. Like what might happen if we do nothing.'

'Yes, that's exactly it. What about you – are you afraid?'

He looked at me, the sunlight making his white-blue eyes sparkle. 'Who, me? I know no fear, princess.' The words were said lightly, but without humour. Looking in the other direction, his fingers brushed mine, and then held. I could feel his heart beating in the veins of his hand.

There was something I hungered for that wasn't blood, nor water, nor food. I felt it keenly when he was close, when he let down his guard. When he touched me as he was doing now. I didn't know how to satisfy the hunger, or even if I should want to.

'Why do you think the harmings have started attacking ships?' My voice sounded hoarse, and I coughed to clear it.

'I suppose because there aren't any witnesses on the open sea, not if you kill everyone or take them prisoner. Sailors are tough. They'd make good attack harmings. The children they took from Ercan, on the other hand, some they'll train to fight, but most they'll train to be spies and infectors.'

The general picture of harmings I'd had in my head diversified into three sub-categories: attack harmings, spies and infectors. Then another category occurred to me: rebel harmings. Rarely seen in the wild, these harmings enjoyed throwing themselves into the path of danger and certain death. They were stubborn, cranky creatures, chronically under-slept and easily identifiable by the haunted look in their eyes.

'How long will it take to sail to Pol?'

'A week. Maybe a week and a half. It's not the best time of year for the crossing as the winds are weak. At the peak of the season you can do it in four days with a good ship like the *Jessamine*.'

A week and a half was a long time to be without anything to do. I would have liked to browse for books to read on our journey across the ocean, but

Rodden had other ideas. 'One more job. Remember what the captain said? He's got a ship's cat. That means no rats for us, and I was counting on them for our blood supply.'

'Oh, of course. So now what do we do?'

'Rabbits. We'll say they're meat for Griffin and Leap, which will explain why they'll be disappearing one by one.'

The only rabbits we could find in the marketplace were children's pets. They were fluffy and white with big floppy ears, and much fatter than wild rabbits. Rodden counted them. 'Fifteen. We'll just have to ration them. One between us every day.'

The stallholder overheard and widened her eyes, but the coins he slapped in her hand kept her mouth shut. We lugged the hutch of rabbits back to the inn with our parcels.

'We'll have to be discreet about feeding,' he cautioned as we laid the hutch in his room. 'Sailors are a superstitious bunch and I think blood-drinking would make them nervous.'

'That's all right. I'll just do it in my room.'

'Room? You don't get a room. You get a patch of deck to lie down on. This is a trade-ship, not a passenger boat. We eat, sleep and wash on deck.'

'I see,' I said, my voice tight. 'You didn't think that

as probably the only female on board I might like a little privacy?' I was beginning to get the impression that Rodden enjoyed putting me in situations that tested my limits of being filthy and uncomfortable.

He shrugged. 'Can't be helped. No passenger ships between here and Pol, Your Highness,' he added.

I rankled at the use of my royal address. He only said it when he wanted to annoy me. I put down the other parcels and stalked back to the market.

'Back by four,' he called after me.

I ignored him and kept walking. The rest of the day I spent browsing the bookstalls and sitting in tea shacks with more mugs of *camai*, and I only returned to the inn at the very last minute.

Rodden was standing outside. 'You're late,' he snapped.

I shrugged. 'Can't be helped,' I said, mimicking his words from earlier. We walked to the dock in silence, me carrying our bags and weapons and Rodden with the rabbits.

The ship wasn't quite ready for us to board, so we sat with the captain at the Krill 'n' Mermaid. Rodden was fidgety and drank an excessive amount of rum and I got the feeling he was nervous about something. The seagulls were annoying Griffin again and she sat on the back of my chair, hackles raised. Leap was preoccupied by the crayfish pots, peering at them suspiciously as though they were about to swallow him whole. I was still sulking and the captain was drunk, so there was very little conversation at our table.

At last a sailor waved to us from the deck.

'That'ssusss,' the captain slurred, getting unsteadily to his feet.

I cast a baleful look at Rodden. He'd checked that the boat was sound but had neglected to do the same for the captain. But Rodden was ignoring me, his face pale and clammy. As he stepped up to board he went green and vomited off the dock. Wiping his mouth he muttered about something he ate. A handful of sailors sniggered from the rigging.

We found a spot on deck that seemed to be out of everyone's way and sat down. Leap's ears were flat, and he had his paws splayed to steady himself against the rocking of the boat. Griffin was in the rigging, hunched up with slitted eyes as several gulls swooped around her. Rodden was still an unnatural colour. He slumped against the rabbit hutch and put a hand over his eyes.

Several sailors grinned at me as they passed and gave me cheery hellos, clearly pleased to have a female on board. I helloed back, and shielded my eyes from the sun to watch them shimmy up the rigging. Rodden managed to open his eyes long enough to glare at them. Turning to me he said, 'Stop distracting them from their work.'

'I'm not. Don't puke on the rabbits.'

From the helm the captain gave the call to cast off, rather too loudly and with lots of flinging of his arms. All manner of garbled instructions poured from his mouth but the sailors seemed to understand well enough. The sails filled, the ship gave a lurch and we were away. There was a bit of tricky manoeuvring to be done to get past the other ships but the captain seemed to be managing it well enough, though his tongue was poking out the corner of his mouth as he spun the wheel to and fro.

We'd been going less than a minute when Rodden leaned over the side and threw up again.

'Do you get seasick?' I asked, passing him the water skin.

'Yes,' he said thickly. 'I thought I might have grown out of it by now but apparently not.' He rinsed his mouth and spat into the sea.

I, on the other hand, felt perfectly fine. I wasn't quite ready to feel sorry for him so I left him where he was. His moans and retching followed me all the way to the prow of the ship. We were sailing west, straight into the setting sun. The tor-line tugged at me as we pulled out of port, but I felt strong enough to ignore the pain.

Leap jumped up onto a crate next to me and peered over the railing. He gave the sea a long, hard, distrustful glare. Then, apparently deciding that was enough to keep the sea down there and him up here where it was dry, he looked up into my face and purred.

I wondered if he knew he was going home, if he would remember Pol. His history was unknown to me and I didn't even know if he had been born there. It occurred to me that, once we arrived, he might even want to stay. Patting his sleek fur, I knew the noble part of me would be happy for Leap if that was what he decided. But the rest of me would be terribly sad without him.

———

I woke the next morning to screaming gulls and the smell of porridge and seawater. I'd spent the night stretched on my cloak with Leap's warm body curled against me and my new poncho covering both of us. By midnight Rodden had thoroughly expelled the contents of his stomach and managed to fall asleep. He awoke looking very drawn and unhappy and refused water, breakfast or blood. I left him dozing in the shade and went to get some porridge.

The sailors were excessively polite, urging me to the front of the line and fetching a bowl and spoon for me. The cook was a tall, thin man with auburn hair and wide-set eyes. There was something familiar about his aspect. I realised when I turned away what it was – he reminded me of home. He was Amentine. Before I could go back and say hello properly, the first mate, Orrik Lobsen, introduced himself.

'Best ship on the Osseran, the *Jessamine*,' he said proudly. He was about Rodden's age, and sandy-haired and robust. 'It'll be a smooth passage to Pol, mark my words.'

We sat on a bench near the captain's cabin with our breakfast. Loud snores emanated from within; the captain was still abed.

'He was up most of the night,' Orrik explained. 'Right now it ain't safe when the sun goes down. Been attacks. He likes to stay up and keep an eye on things.'

I wondered if it also might have something to do with all the rum, but I kept that to myself. 'How many of you can shoot?'

Orrik shook his head. 'Not a one. But we're all

deadly with a cutlass. Sailors fight hand to hand, where we can see the whites of our enemies' eyes.' He made it sound as if this was the only honourable way to fight. No wonder they were dying like flies. If it came to an attack there would just be Rodden and me to defend the ship – if he got over his seasickness.

'What's wrong with your man? He got no sea legs?' Orrik asked.

'He's not my man, he's my friend.' Even that was a stretch right now.

Orrik perked up. 'Oh, really? That so?' He flashed a smile at me. 'Get him some root ginger tea from the galley. Sometimes helps.'

'I will, thank you.' I put my porridge down half-eaten and chewed a thumbnail. I was thirsty. What with all the sulking I had done the previous day I had forgotten to drink. 'Orrik, say I wanted to wash up and do some ...' I waved my hands vaguely. '... women's things. Where could I find some privacy?'

'The hold,' he said. 'Just cargo down there. And Smokey. Anyone stops you, you tell 'em Orrik said it was okay.'

I thanked him, and then chewed my nail some more. That solved one problem, but not the other. I had been counting on Rodden to do the unpleasant business of slaughtering the rabbits, but clearly that wasn't going to happen. If he tried to move he would probably start retching again. I'd killed plenty of rabbits with a bow and arrow but never with a knife. I didn't have the faintest idea how to do it, but with a sharp blade in my hands it wasn't as if the bunny was going to come out the victor. Still, the idea was exceedingly distasteful. Orrik was right. There certainly was a difference in killing up close and killing from afar, and I knew which I preferred: the cowardly, far-off way.

But I couldn't sit there all day. I was thirsty and the rabbits weren't going to exsanguinate themselves. I bid Orrik goodbye and went to see the cook. He was eating his breakfast, his lean body propped up against a narrow counter when I tapped on the wall outside the galley and asked for some root ginger steeped in hot water. I couldn't resist asking as he picked through a cupboard, 'You're from Amentia, aren't you?'

He looked at me with green eyes, the kind I had seen looking back at me many times before. My mother's eyes. The eyes of the people of Prestoral. They held the echo of home. 'Yes,' he said, surprised.

'Which part?'

'Zantha,' he said. 'It's –'

'On the south-eastern border, at the foot of Mount Campion,' I interrupted.

He looked even more surprised and examined my colouring. 'Where are you from?'

'Prestoral.'

'You're never,' he said. 'I heard we were taking on passengers from Pergamia.' He still studied my face. 'But you don't have the Pergamian look about you either. You look Amentine, but that hair … We have a princess whose hair is that colour and her eyes are blue like –' He cut himself off, staring.

I smiled. 'Is that the ginger?' I asked, looking at the root in his hand.

Sneaking looks at me, he chopped a little and put it in a mug with hot water. 'You need any more, you just come and ask,' he insisted. 'My name's Lisson.'

I took the cup he offered. 'Thank you, Lisson.'

He gave an awkward little bow, his cheeks flushing pink. I went back to Rodden, smiling to myself.

'Here,' I said, handing him the tea. Rodden still lay on the decking. 'The first mate said I could get some privacy in the hold.' I put a rabbit and a flask in a saddlebag, hoping no one was watching me. The rabbit squirmed suspiciously inside the canvas.

Rodden answered with a groan, which could have meant anything from 'Oh that's nice' to 'Kill me, please'.

To lend authenticity to the story of rabbits being

cat and eagle food, I called Griffin onto my wrist. Her normally sharp and clear mind felt like it had a thunderstorm brewing inside it. The gulls were still with us and she was not a happy raptor.

Inside the damp, cool hold and away from the gulls, she calmed somewhat. Now it was my stomach that was churning. I could feel the rabbit flopping around in the bag. I crouched behind a large crate and wondered how best to go about my task. I could drink straight from the rabbit down here but Rodden could hardly do that on deck. The neck of the flask was wide and I thought that if I got the angle right I could drain the blood out of the rabbit and directly into it. I considered letting the rabbit out in the hold and hunting them down with my bow and arrow. Then I saw Smokey atop a barrel, glaring down at us with amber eyes. Smokey was a big white tom with a piratical patch of black fur over one eye, and with his ragged ears and scarred nose, he looked more than capable of taking apart my fluffy white rabbit. Well, it wasn't for him.

I held the rabbit up by its ears and unsheathed my knife. It hung limply in my hands, not even bothering to struggle. We regarded each other silently. I imagined that it had led a reprehensible life of womanising and child-beating.

It twitched its nose. I took this as a confession.

I flipped the rabbit so it was hanging upside down by its back legs and its throat was exposed. I placed the knife tip against the creature's neck, and then paused to steady my hand and squeeze my eyes shut. I couldn't bear the thought of sucking on its carcass in the dark. Under my breath I counted to three ... and then plunged the point in and jerked it across and out, severing all the arteries and probably its windpipe too. There was a light spray of blood and the rabbit twitched. Then dark red liquid began to trickle over its chin and into the flask. I let myself relax a little while it drained, glad that the worst was over.

Back up on deck, Rodden seemed to have rejoined the land of the living. I'd saved a haunch for Leap but asked him to eat it elsewhere. I didn't relish the sight of him chewing on the bloodied white fur. Griffin got a piece too and I turfed the rest of the carcass overboard when no one was looking. I avoided the accusing gazes of the fourteen remaining rabbits.

'Are you okay?' Rodden asked, noticing my guilty expression. He was sitting up, pale but composed for the moment.

'Peachy,' I muttered.

We shared the flask in silence. I licked my lips

when I was done, careful that no trace of blood be left on my mouth. 'Feeling better?'

'A little. Thank you for the blood.'

'You've been keeping me fed for the last five months. It was about my turn.'

'Use a knife?'

I nodded, looking away.

'It's not the same as hunting, is it?' He sounded as if he knew what he was talking about. I had no doubt he did, what with all the rabbits he'd done in over the years. 'I'm sorry you had to do it,' he said.

I shrugged, wanting to forget the whole thing. 'It's fine. If you can do it, I can.'

He sighed and lay down again, covering his eyes with the crook of his elbow. 'I'm still sorry.'

'Shh. Be still or you'll be sick again.'

But he muttered on, and I didn't know if his words were directed at me or the blue sky above.

'Deeds like that stay with you. No matter how remorseful you are or even if you have no choice in the matter, you'll always be that person. The one holding the knife, with blood on their hands.'

'Don't worry about me, I'm fine.' But I knew he wasn't talking about me. He was talking about himself. I had felt the great lake of guilt inside him open up as he spoke.

I stayed by his side until he fell asleep, wondering who it was he had killed.

———

Our days on board were monotonous: hot sun and fitful dozing punctuated by mealtimes and rabbit murdering. Rodden seemed better by day three, but on the fourth day, after a flask of blood, he turned green again.

I was standing nearby talking to Orrik as he explained how a sextant worked. 'This here instrument,' he said, holding up a hand-sized brass object, 'we use for navigation. As long as the sky is clear we can use it, day or night. You look through this eyepiece at a celestial body, like the sun or the moon, and calculate its angle to the horizon. This gives us our line of position on a map, and if we're stationary it's accurate to about four hundred yards.' He grinned and held it out to me.

'Gosh, really?' I said, trying to sound impressed as I turned the object over in my hands. I couldn't help feeling smug that my own internal navigation could be used day or night, cloudy or clear, and with my eyes closed.

Rodden suddenly scrambled to his feet and

vomited over the side. Orrik happened to be looking in his direction and saw that Rodden's puke was stained red.

'Is he all right? He's vomiting blood!'

'No, no,' I said. 'We had some raspberry cordial and I thought it might make him feel better. I won't give it to him again.' I felt my face redden as I lied.

Orrik frowned at me.

'Tell me some more about the sextant,' I said.

He shook his head. 'I'd better get back to work.' He cast a curious look at Rodden before walking away.

I slid down next to Rodden. 'Wonderful timing,' I hissed. 'You couldn't have held on another minute?'

'No. When it happens it happens. Get me more ginger.'

'Get it yourself.' I searched the eyes of the other crew members. 'I think they're getting suspicious. Have you noticed how they're always watching us?'

Rodden was slumped against the rabbit hutch and didn't answer. Griffin's performance the previous day hadn't done us any favours either. Tired of the taunting gulls, she'd launched herself at one in the middle of lunch. Horrified, the sailors watched as Griffin pinned the gull to the deck and proceeded to shred the bird to pieces, all the while screaming in anger and throwing feathers into the air. It was a grisly demonstration to the other gulls of just what would happen to them if they came near her again. It didn't endear her any to the crew.

Leap wasn't behaving much better. He and Smokey staged showdowns every few hours, pacing in circles and glaring at each other from either ends of the ship. Leap had claimed the quarterdeck as his own and Smokey stood firm over the bow. They hadn't crossed claws yet but trouble was definitely brewing.

'The captain might be drunk constantly but Orrik isn't stupid,' I continued. 'I'm sure he's heard of harmings and might even have guessed that they're behind the ship attacks.'

Rodden cracked open an eye and peered at me. 'Orrik,' he sneered. 'You're not actually impressed by him and his brass toys, are you? Fancy teaching a harming how to navigate.'

I rolled my eyes. 'Try not to throw your breakfast up where others can see you, okay?'

Later that afternoon, the wind died.

SEVEN

T he sailors stopped what they were doing and
stared about looking spooked. I found Orrik
and asked him what was wrong.

'This ain't right,' he told me, a haunted look
on his face. 'I've heard talk from other sailors of
the Osseran that on the nights when ships disappear it's like the wind has been magicked from the
air – on purpose like, to leave them stranded and
vulnerable.'

I nodded. 'We're armed,' I told him. 'We'll help
you fight if it comes to that.'

As the sun went down I got more ginger tea from
Lisson for Rodden, though the calmness of the sea
was doing wonders on its own. I strung my bow,
donned my gloves and strapped a quiver of yelbar

points to my back. The sailors were sharpening their cutlasses. The rasp of whetstones on metal was the only sound.

When it was full dark Rodden struggled up and notched a bolt to his crossbow. We stood together, watching the northern horizon. Out here, without the lights of nearby cities, the sky was like black velvet scattered with diamonds. The crew had extinguished all the lanterns on board but we knew it wouldn't make any difference. The harmings would find us.

Griffin was patrolling the area, doing wide circuits of the boat. Shortly before midnight she sounded the alarm, blasting a thought-picture into our heads so deafening I was sure even the sailors would pick it up.

'They're coming from the east!' I shouted, shattering the silence. Rodden and I sprinted to the stern. A second later Griffin blasted me again – there were more brants flying up from the south.

'I'll take the south,' Rodden said. 'You stay here.'

I drew my bow and aimed at the stars. Griffin tracked the brants' distance from the ship. One mile. Half a mile. Two hundred yards. I flexed my gloved fingers on the bow, willing myself to see through the darkness. Another picture from Griffin told me the harmings were travelling close to the water and very fast. I adjusted my aim just in time to see the moon reflected off an enormous shiny black beak. I fired.

Then they were on us from all sides.

My arrow hit the harming full in the chest and it toppled from the saddle. The brant screamed, its wings beating against the side of the ship before it turned back into the night. I had another arrow notched in a second but I wasn't fast enough. A nearby sailor was snatched up by a harming and hauled across the saddle of a brant. The man yelled in terror as the giant bird flew off. There were no screams of pain. Only fear. It seemed we were to be taken alive.

The sailors slashed at the brants with their swords. They were huge birds but quite nimble and the harmings were careful to hold them back.

In the dim light, and with the harmings dressed in black, it was easier to aim for the brants, but I realised my mistake when a harming toppled from its dying mount to land on the deck. Righting itself with alacrity, it dropped into a defensive stance as it was surrounded by sailors with drawn swords. The thing's hood fell back and I saw long black hair.

'Keep away from her!' I yelled, my fingers fumbling for another arrow. But before I could draw, a sailor lunged with his cutlass. The female was agile and had her blade out and stuck in the man's belly before he could even bring his down. In the next second she had my yelbar point sprouting from her temple.

I heard the scream of a harming behind me and knew Rodden had found his mark too. There was another just about to snatch Orrik up and I fired, catching it in the neck. The harming crumpled, flickers of orange fire running through its veins. The brant, suddenly released from its rider's mind-control, flapped wildly, its talons shredding a sail before it took wing.

The remaining harmings made a grab for sailors before turning their mounts and fleeing. I found Rodden's thread and yanked it, hoping fervently that he hadn't been snatched.

'I'm here,' he called. I caught sight of him as someone relit the lamps. He had a large, bloodied rip in his sleeve. I ran to him.

'Blasted thing's talon caught me after I killed its rider,' he muttered. 'Just a scratch.' He caught my wrist in his hand and said in a low voice, 'Never mind that. You and I are in big trouble. We need to get out of here.'

'But we can't – there's no wind.'

'Hence the big trouble.'

The captain stepped into the light. 'How many taken?'

Orrik did a head count. 'Five, cap'n.'

I heard the sailors muttering about demons from the north and blood-drinking monsters. It might have been my imagination, but some of their glares seemed to stray to us.

After he'd reported to the captain, Orrik came over to where Rodden and I stood. 'I heard you yell that they were coming from the east a full minute before any of us saw anything,' he said to me, eyes narrowed. 'And you,' he said to Rodden. 'You said, "I'll take the south".' He looked between us and I could see the distrust in his eyes. When we didn't offer any sort of explanation he said, 'I've got my eye on both of you,' and then turned and walked away.

I could see the annoyance on Rodden's face, but we had bigger things to worry about. He steered me out of earshot of the others. 'One of those harmings, if not all of them, is going to realise who we are, and we're stuck on this tub in the middle of the ocean. We're sitting ducks. They're not going to let an opportunity like this slip away.' I'd never seen Rodden panic but right then there was a definite glint of alarm in his eyes.

Something had been in the back of my mind ever

since the wind died. 'Rodden, harmings can control the weather, can't they?'

'No. Oh, possibly.' He looked puzzled. 'I'm not sure.'

'I only ask because I think I can. Well, I can draw a breeze at least. Once. The night before we left Xallentaria –'

Rodden gripped my arms. 'Can you summon a wind?'

'I don't know.'

'Can you try?'

I nodded.

He glanced at the rigging. 'One of the sails is shredded but it shouldn't matter. You try for some wind and I'll keep my crossbow handy in case the harmings come back.'

I looked around for the best position. The ship was pointed west towards Pol, so we wanted an easterly. I stood in the stern and faced the sails. Rodden gave me an encouraging nod. He still looked worried, but the fear had gone from his eyes.

I realised with a strange beating of my heart that he trusted me. He had faith that I could do this.

I launched thought-fingers into the atmosphere. I curled them like hooks around the air and began dragging them towards me. Then I sent out another set of hooks, and another and another, casting out afresh before the previous ones could get back to me.

I felt a breeze fan my face and the realisation that it was working spurred me on. The sails fluttered, and then I heard the ship creak. In another minute we were moving. I was doing it! We were going to –

A blow to my face knocked me sideways and I hit the deck hard. Pain bloomed in my cheek but I made myself look for my attacker. Orrik. My hand went to my belt but I'd left my knife with my bags. I groaned.

'Monster!' A fist reached back to strike me again but Rodden went crashing into Orrik, sending them both flying.

I sat up, gingerly feeling my face. My left cheek throbbed and I would have a black eye, but I didn't think he had broken anything. I struggled to my feet as Orrik screamed abuse at me. Rodden had his arm around the man's throat and a knife pressed into his kidneys.

'She's a demon! She summoned the others! We'll all die if we let her live. You saw the light in her eyes. She's not hu–'

Rodden must have pressed the blade harder against Orrik's back as the man cut off what he was about to say with a strangled cry.

All on deck were staring at me.

'Captain Krig,' Rodden called in a clear voice.

'Aye,' came the reply. The captain appeared out of the darkness. 'That's my first mate you're leaning your pig-sticker into.'

'I'll let him go in just a minute. Can you tell me if you felt a wind a moment ago?'

'Aye.'

'And did the wind die when your first mate punched my friend in the face?'

'Aye.'

'If you want to get off this ship alive you might want to let her go about her business, regardless of her glowing eyes. That's not a threat, it's a piece of advice. And may I remind you that she shot down two of your enemies just a short time ago.'

My eyes had been glowing? That was new.

The captain looked around at his crew. 'Boys, I believe it may be the time for a stocktake in the hold.'

I held my breath, wondering if the captain was about to have a mutiny on his hands. But one by one the sailors turned away.

'Thank you, captain,' Rodden said. He watched the deck clear before finally releasing Orrik and giving him a shove. The mate spat at Rodden's feet and shot me a look of pure hate before following the others into the hold. Captain Krig nodded to us and then strolled after his men, hands behind his back. I was beginning to see that little ruffled him.

Rodden turned to me and asked, 'Are you all right? Any dizziness?'

I shook my head, then regretted the action. 'Ow. No. Just a headache. I can still call the wind, I think.'

He sheathed his knife and reached again for his crossbow. 'Whenever you're ready.'

It took longer this time, owing to the pounding in my head, but I knew it was working when I heard Rodden puking over the side. Griffin was doing circuits of the ship again and so far there was no sign of harmings. After a quarter of an hour I felt us move into the path of a north-easterly. I got my hooks into this natural wind and pulled it towards us. The ship surged forwards.

'Is that you? It's as strong as a trade wind,' Rodden called.

I laughed. 'It's me, of sorts! I found us a real wind. You'd better get the captain before we're blown off course.'

I kept the wind blowing hard all night. It was a lot easier going than whipping up a breeze out of nothing. Sailors replaced the torn sail and the captain stood at the helm, the wheel in one hand and a bottle of rum in the other. Rodden stayed close by but Orrik didn't reappear.

Around dawn I swayed on my feet and had to let the wind go. We slowed, but the natural north-easterly kept the ship moving. Rodden, despite his nausea, got up from where he was slumped and helped me back to our sleeping place. I didn't need much encouragement to collapse onto my cloak.

Rodden sat next to me and smoothed the hair from my face, checking my swollen cheek. 'Well, aren't you full of surprises. Anything else I should know about you?'

'My face hurts.'

His eyes darkened. 'I could kill Orrik.'

'Did my eyes really light up?'

'Yes.'

'I feel oddly proud.'

'As you should. You saved us all.'

I awoke a few hours later to blinding white sunlight and a pounding headache. My mouth was dry and tasted like I'd hit the bottle along with the captain.

With careful fingers, I tested the puffiness of my left cheek. The skin was stretched and firm like a tomato, and was probably as red as one, too. Rodden was still sleeping, his skin sickly pallid against the black stubble on his chin.

I eased open the rabbit hutch and stuffed one of the unfortunate creatures into my saddlebag. The poor things didn't like the sea voyage any more than Rodden: they were getting decidedly skinny.

I made my way to the hold, but before I could enter its dark and cool interior, a figure blocked my path.

'What's in your bag?' It was Orrik. His face was hard and mean.

I clutched the strap higher on my shoulder. 'Nothing.'

But the squirming of the rabbit gave me away. Orrik snatched the bag from my shoulder and held it aloft like a prize.

'You lot!' he called, and the crew turned to look. 'What do you reckon the demon has here? Have you seen how those rabbits have been disappearing, day by day?' He fumbled around in my bag.

'They're meat for Leap and Griffin,' I insisted, trying to take the bag from him. Orrik gave me a shove that sent me reeling backwards.

He pulled the rabbit out of the bag by its ears. 'Have you seen her sneaking away to gut these creatures at her leisure? To feast on their blood? She feeds her demon lover too! I seen 'im, puking blood. They need to be got rid of. They need to be tossed overboard before they summon more of their kind to kill us all! Haven't they been nothin' but trouble since they were brought aboard?'

I searched the eyes of the crew, and I could tell from their glares and nods that they agreed.

'Captain Krig!' I called, desperate for his calming presence.

Orrik rounded on me, his eyes wild, the whites showing all around. 'That fat bastard's sleeping it off. I'm in charge now,' he hissed.

'What the hell is going on?' Rodden had awoken at last and was struggling to his feet.

'Boys!' Orrik shouted, spittle flying from his lips. 'Throw him overboard before we're all murdered or taken in the night.'

Four sailors descended on Rodden. I ran to help him fight them off but Orrik grabbed a fistful of my hair and stopped me with a cruel yank.

'We're on your side, you idiots,' Rodden was saying as he struggled. 'Let her go! Let me go or you'll bloody regret this.'

'Get off me,' I shrieked, kicking at the sailor's shins. I heard an almighty splash. '*Rodden!*'

'Your turn,' said Orrik, as he began forcing me to the side. More pairs of hands grabbed me and I was lifted into the air.

'One,' they chanted, swinging me forward.

'Stop it! Put me down. Are you all mad?'

'Two.' I was swung again.

'No! Orrik, you flipping numbskull, you'll all die if –'

'Three!'

I was hurled like a sack of dirty linen over the side and down, down into the dark blue water. I plunged several yards beneath the surface, my eyes wide with shock. I saw a blue-black abyss below me, an awful bottomless nothing. It was the most terrifying thing I'd ever laid eyes on. More terrifying than traipsing alone through the burnt forest in Lharmell; more, even, than being pinned by the harming as it ransacked my mind. It was, I thought, in the split seconds that I hung at the nadir of my submergence, uncanny how quickly the sunlight disappeared just a few yards down. Then the air in my lungs and the frantic kicking of my legs brought me spluttering to the surface, just in time to see Leap hurtling overboard. I made a grab for my cat and, claws out, he climbed up my body and onto my shoulder, clinging to me like a limpet to a rock. A soggy, unhappy *not like* thought-pattern emanated from him. Drain-cats, it seemed, did not like the ocean. Between his considerable weight and my sodden clothing I was finding it hard to keep my head above water. Rodden was close by, treading water.

I began to yell with all my might, begging Orrik to throw us a rope, anyone to do *something*.

'Look out!' Rodden's words were garbled with seawater but I looked around just in time to see the rabbit hutch being thrown into the sea. It hit the water not far from me and sank like a stone, taking the remaining rabbits with it. Next were our bags. Rodden dived beneath the waves and managed to come up with one, but the rest were lost, sinking slowly into the watery abyss beneath our feet. I tried not to imagine how many miles they would fall, how dark it would be down there on the ocean floor, what sort of creatures –

Rodden saw the look on my face and swam over. 'Stop it. Calm down.'

In a panic I grabbed a fistful of his shirt and made both of us go under briefly. My legs were tiring already. 'I c-can't help it.' I was shaking with fear and cold. Despite the heat of the day the water was freezing. The *Jessamine* was twenty yards away and moving fast. 'We won't – catch them up – we're going to – drown.'

I saw Griffin above us, flying in frantic circles. I told her to go back to the ship – ordered her, but she refused.

'She won't go back,' I cried. 'She'll just drown with the rest of us.'

'Ask her if she can see any brants in the sky.'

Griffin widened the circumference of her flight, searching this way and that. But she could see nothing. No brants. And no other ships.

Leap tried to climb higher on my shoulder and his hind claws scratched ragged stripes down my chest. I screamed in pain but the sound was muffled by seawater. The taste was foul, and I coughed and spat to rid myself of it.

The ship was now fifty yards away and beginning to look frighteningly small. There was panic in Rodden's eyes. I could see how pale he was; how days of illness had weakened him.

'Give me that bag,' I said, wanting to relieve him of the weight he carried. I would not see him slip beneath the surface first. I would not.

'No.'

'Are you going to argue with me right to the

end? Give me that bag you stubborn, arrogant, obstinate –'

Griffin screamed in triumph and hurtled towards the *Jessamine*. Were they turning? No – but someone had dropped the ship's boat. Leap screwed up his face in disgust and launched himself towards the vessel, his body slipping otter-like through the water.

'Oh, praise for blood,' Rodden groaned, muttering the harming oath.

We swam the seventy yards, our eyes rooted to the bobbing boat, frightened that it might slip from our reach if we looked away even for an instant. Griffin sat on the stern, shuffling left and right as she watched our slow progress.

Leap reached it and struggled up over the side, his ears flat to his skull. I reached it next, groaning with relief as I hung from the bow, my body still in the water. I found the strength to pull myself up and over and then haul Rodden up too. He lay in the bottom of the boat, gasping like a landed fish.

I scrabbled around, hoping to find emergency supplies. Strapped beneath a seat were a packet of ship's biscuits and two flasks of water.

Rodden lifted his head. 'Is there a mast and sail?'

I felt about in the bow, and let out a sigh of relief as my fingers touched canvas. Rodden fought down his nausea just long enough to raise the mast and rig the sail before collapsing in a fit of puking.

'Angle the rudder right to go left, and left to go right,' he gasped. 'Keep the sail about forty-five degrees perpendicular to the wind.'

I angled the sail and made a grab for the tiller, turning the rudder so we were headed towards the *Jessamine*. By now it was a mere speck. Soon it would disappear over the rim of the horizon and we would be alone.

I wondered who had dropped the boat. Not Orrik, that was for certain. It must have been Lisson, the red-headed Amentine cook. He'd been so friendly every time I'd gone to him for ginger, an amused, secretive smile playing on his lips.

Whoever it was had saved our lives, but whether it was only so that we might die a thirsty, sun-burnt death on a tiny craft in the middle of the ocean instead of sinking quickly to a watery grave was yet to be determined.

But I was forgetting the third option. The harmings might still get us.

———

At dusk I checked the bag that Rodden had saved. It contained his crossbow, a handful of plain points and some coin. My bow was lost, my beautiful bow that had been my silent companion for the past two years. I mourned it for a moment, and then thanked the stars that I hadn't joined it at the bottom of the ocean.

Now that the *Jessamine* was well out of view it was time to find out just how good my harming navigation really was. I closed my eyes, braced myself, and let the tor-line pull tight. The pain that gripped my insides told me we were headed straight to Pol. We'd made excellent progress the previous night, but my heart sank as I realised we were still a long way from the shore. About four days at our present sluggish speed, if I was estimating correctly, and I wasn't entirely sure that I was. It could be longer.

The sun sank out of sight and the wind all but dropped. It was tempting to call up a breeze but at this time of day there might be harmings in the area. I gripped Rodden's loaded crossbow in one hand and gazed at the sky. Griffin, who'd dozed through the afternoon, was now a sentinel atop our mast, scanning the heavens. Not for the first time, I was thankful for her alert and steady presence.

Rodden hadn't moved all day and I was beginning to worry about him. He was already thoroughly dehydrated from his days of illness, and the water we had wasn't going to go far. I didn't dare touch the flasks until moonrise. Then, I poured a little into my hands for Leap and Griffin, took two mouthfuls myself, and helped Rodden into a sitting position.

'Don't puke this up,' I said, and gave him the flask. He managed a little before slumping down again.

'Wishing for a fat husband and a cold castle?' he murmured as I lay down next to him in the bottom of the boat.

'No. Orrik and a horsewhip.'

'Ah. Even better.'

Long into the night I stared at the sky, but saw only the stars above.

————

In the morning I was pleased to find we hadn't been murdered in our sleep. As I washed my face with seawater, Griffin dropped a fat silver fish in the bottom of the boat. I gashed it deeply and squeezed, but there was little blood to speak of and it wasn't the least bit satisfying. Still, it was food, and I scaled it with my knife and divided it into four portions.

Rodden looked askance at his breakfast, assessing whether his stomach was about to cooperate with the pale, uncooked flesh. He nibbled some, grimaced, and lay down again. Leap and Griffin were more than happy to finish his share. I gave them all some water but didn't drink myself, preferring to wait. I knew my limits with thirst, and while I didn't relish the sensation I wasn't about to keel over.

Rodden slept the day away. I did my best to keep him out of the sun, bullying him into the shadow cast by the sail as the sun moved across the sky. In the afternoon I gave him some more water, but ten minutes later he threw it up. It was on the tip of my tongue to yell at him. I was hot and terribly worried about him, and it was a dreadful waste. We were already a quarter of the way through our supply. But he looked miserable enough already so I kept my mouth closed.

In the late afternoon, I tested our distance from Pol. I felt like crying when I found we hadn't travelled nearly as far as I'd hoped. Instead, I cleaned Rodden's crossbow and sharpened all the points we had, Orrik's face floating before me.

Night fell, and my anxieties grew. I clutched some bolts in one hand and the crossbow lay across my lap, ready if we were attacked. Leap kept an anxious vigil, his body curled tightly into me. All night I watched the reflection of the stars in his eyes.

The wind blew gentle and steady. The sea lapped at our boat. Dawn came, and after another uninterrupted night I realised that not even harmings could find us. We were no more than a drop in this great ocean, and though this should have gladdened me it only made me feel more forlorn.

At breakfast time – ridiculous to call it that as we had little breakfast to speak of – I couldn't rouse Rodden. I poured seawater on his face. I kicked him, shouted at him, but nothing drew a response. I clutched the thread between us and found that it was weakening. He was slipping away from me, the cool water of his soul becoming stagnant and cold.

I forced down the fish Griffin caught, though the clammy flesh sickened me. I eased Rodden's head into my lap, feeling for the first time the softness of his black hair, the heaviness of his skull. I smoothed a hand across his brow and found it feverish.

Taking the knife from his belt I regarded my wrist. There was a network of bluish veins beneath white skin as thin as tissue paper. I'd never noticed it before but wrists are vulnerable things. I was reminded of the delicacy of birds' bones and the soft underbellies of fishes. I imagined gutting my wrist like I had our breakfast, blood and nameless viscera spilling from my arm to lie in the bottom of the boat. I shuddered, and decided to approach the problem mathematically, like Orrik's sextant: I would do this by degrees. First, no more than a scratch to see how the blood flowed. I drew the blade across the inner edge of my wrist, hissing in pain as a thin red line appeared. I rubbed the wetness across Rodden's lower lip. He frowned and took a deep breath. I cut again, deeper this time, and the blood began to bead up. I placed my wrist against his mouth, letting the dark red liquid trickle over his lips. He didn't open his eyes but reached up to grasp my forearm, the way I'd seem him hold the carcass of a rabbit or squirrel as he fed. The reflex gladdened my heart. I felt a sharp tug on my insides, the thread between us, and wondered if he knew that the blood in his mouth was mine. My wrist looked even more insubstantial in his large hands, and I despaired at the insufficiency of it, doubting that I would ever be able to keep him alive.

A few minutes later the wound clotted and Rodden slept a proper sleep. I felt light-headed and ate some more fish, though it was a poor substitute for the blood I needed.

By afternoon I was tired of our sluggish progress and certain that if there were harmings around, they would have found us by now. I sat in the bow with the sun warming my back and began to summon a wind. Leap sat tall and proud beside me, his eyes slitted in the strong breeze. The little craft surged forward, and I managed to keep it up for an hour before spots danced in front of my eyes. I thrust my head between my knees, trying not to faint. The boat slowed to a crawl.

A moment later I checked our distance with the tor-line. If I was right we would reach Pol in two days' time, perhaps a little more. We still had one full flask of water and all the fish we could eat thanks to Griffin, but I didn't know how long we were going to last without blood. If it was just me I could probably manage. I'd been strong and well-nourished when we'd been thrown overboard. But Rodden hadn't fed properly in nearly a week, on anything. I wasn't sure how long I could go on giving him my blood. But I would continue, no matter what. I knew he would give the last drop in his veins for me.

There was nothing for me to do but estimate and re-estimate our distance from land, press the usually puffy vein in the bend of my elbow and wonder how much blood I could spare before I too was too weak to move.

———

At first light I swallowed some raw fish and gulped some water. I waited ten minutes for the liquid to thin my blood, and then cut my wrist again.

This time, Rodden woke for a moment. He fumbled at my wrist with one hand as if expecting to feel a furry body and was surprised by its smoothness. Then he frowned and his eyes opened. He looked up at me, eyes unfocused and confused. I put the cut against his lips again. His body went rigid and he tried to sit up, an angry flash of refusal blooming in his mind. But with my free arm I easily held him down, my embrace a restraint. His eyes closed again, and he drank.

Later I was too weak to call a wind. I chewed at a piece of clammy fish and wished for anything at all to break the monotony of the empty horizon. The sense of space was an illusion. I could see miles in every direction, sense the dark fathoms beneath. But we were trapped on this tiny vessel, an eight-by-four wooden structure that was becoming our open-air coffin.

I remembered how often I'd gazed out at the ships from my room at the palace in Xallentaria, wondering where they were headed with their sails so full of wind and purpose. The sea, which had once seemed like freedom, was now a prison.

I began to dream the old dreams, the ones I'd had until, unwittingly, I'd drunk from a flask of blood in

Lharmell. The dreams of the slowly starving.

I was a vengeful angel, black-winged and wielding a sword. I descended on the *Jessamine* with a never-ending banshee scream and killed all I found there. Orrik was always last, and I lapped at his carcass like a cat.

I woke to find Rodden convulsing next to me, his body racked by the blood-hunger. I held him until his shaking subsided, hoping that in his stupor he couldn't feel the pain of the violent cramps.

When I tried to sit upright, spots appeared in my vision again. I would trigger an attack of cramps if I persisted, so I lay still. Lying listlessly in the bottom of the boat, I felt for the tors, but couldn't find them. The cord was there, yanking at me like a restless child, but I couldn't sense its direction. I'd lost us in this great ocean.

Griffin dropped fish on me and screamed, but I batted her away. Leap stuck his whiskery face in mine and I pushed him away too, his fishy breath making my face crease with disgust.

At last when the sun was high I remembered the water, and the three of us drank the rest of the flask while Rodden lay motionless. I gnawed listlessly on some fish, and then cut my wrist again and held it to his mouth. He swallowed once, twice, and then was unresponsive. I licked at the blood that flowed down my arm until the wound clotted and I could hold myself upright no longer.

From then on, time became a liquid concept, flowing back and forth like the rocking of our boat on the sea. I was young, and then I was old. A baby once more, and then an old, stooped woman. The only certainty was the blazing light from the sun or the moon on my upturned face, and the white-hot cramps that gripped my body.

EIGHT

Perhaps it was the eagle screaming blue murder atop our mast, or the frantic pacing of one of their native cats, but something roused the attention of the Verapinians who approached our little craft after it washed up on shore, eighteen miles south of the capital.

In the bottom of the boat they saw a man and a girl clasped to each other, as if in death, faces reddened by days of exposure, lips cracked and bleeding.

We weren't dead, only deep in torpor, and under the watchful eyes of a golden eagle and a drain-cat we were taken to a hospice, little more than a room with rough white walls on the edge of town.

For two days I lay, administered by gentle hands, hearing strange words around me. My burns and cracked lips were softened by salve. My sleep was restless, anxious lest I allow myself to slumber too long. After only a little while I knew I wasn't going to die, but I hadn't yet the strength to rise and get the blood we desperately needed. These were human nurses, not harmings, and couldn't understand why my gaunt, black-haired companion remained unresponsive though he swallowed the water and thin gruel they fed him. The cuts on my wrist began to heal and itch, reminding me how desperately Rodden had needed, and still did need, blood. It was this that shocked me out of sleep at the end of the second day.

The nurses were absent for the moment, and, clad only in a scratchy smock, I found our coin, a flask, and the door and struggled outside. I was blasted by the full force of a scorching sun, and understood what Rodden had meant about the desert and its golden light. At an hour before sunset it was still blistering hot and my sunburn started to pain me. I shielded my eyes and looked about at clusters of mud brick buildings and uneven rocky ground webbed with dusty paths. Donkeys heed and hawed and munched on dried grass, tethered to windows by lumpy ropes.

Raising my nose to the wind I inhaled deeply, smelling the heat from the desert, the fermented aroma of dung. Then a whiff of maggoty meat reached my nostrils, and I turned gratefully in its direction. After walking about thirty shaky paces into the town I had collected a clutch of ragged children in my wake. They chattered to each other like birds, the sound perplexing me as I was unable to understand a word of it.

I knew I had found the right place when my feet touched a dark red slick outside a doorway. Flies were thick under the striped awning. I braced my arm against the squat building and peered inside. The children watched me solemnly, their only movement occasional shoves and staggers as they tried to push each other into the bloodied dirt.

'Hello?' I called, and my voice was creaky with disuse. I coughed and tried again.

After a minute a hefty man in blood-spattered shirt and trousers came to the door. In his hand was a gory meat cleaver. This was, I hoped, the town butcher, and not some flagrant serial murderer.

'Hello, please, may I …' I paused to swallow, my tongue too thick and dry in my mouth. 'May I please have some blood? I have coin.' I held out the flask with a shaking hand. I wasn't going to leave without getting any. The dread that I would return to find Rodden dead was growing stronger with each passing second.

The man frowned, and then rapped out a command at the children and they scattered.

I slumped against the building, realising why I couldn't understand a word anyone was saying: Rodden had neglected to mention that they spoke another language in Verapine.

Trying to make myself understood, I tapped the big vein at my elbow, shook the flask in the man's face and pointed at him. Then I held out two coins, enough to buy a horse in Pergamia. 'Please,' I added, hoping that my tone was universally pleading. I held out the flask again.

He took it, and the coin, and then held out his hand again. I dropped two more coins into it, and when he disappeared inside I slid down the doorframe and rested on the stoop. A minute later I was being hauled up by my underarms. The flask, heavy now, was pressed into my hands. I was given a shove into the red mud and the door slammed behind me.

Not caring where I lay or who could see me, I opened the flask and gulped a third of it, disregarding what the rich pigs' blood would do to my insides after a week of starvation. I felt the liquid hit my stomach and the shock of it made me gasp. I was suddenly gripped by the most awful indigestion, but instead of crying out in pain I clutched my stomach and laughed like a madwoman.

I struggled back to the sick tent and found a matronly looking woman tending an old man on a pallet in the corner.

'Would you mind leaving us for a moment?' I asked her, pointing to the exit. I glanced at Rodden. I had no way of knowing how long a harming could go without blood and any second might be his last.

The woman stared.

'Go!' I said, 'Outside. Now. Please,' I added.

Still she didn't leave, and instead tried to shoo me into bed.

Impatient, I began to shout at her, flinging my arms towards the exit. She flinched, but seemed determined to stay, so I resorted to dancing about, screaming the words to a ditty from home, hoping to convince her I was mad and it was safest to leave me alone. She scuttled out. I glared into the old man's yellowed eyes until he closed them.

Turning to Rodden, I eased him up and shoved several pillows behind his back. His eyes stayed closed, and I couldn't detect even a flicker of his eyelids.

I opened the flask and dipped my finger in the blood, then wiped it across his lower lip. No response.

I waved it under his nose, hoping the aroma would rouse him. Still nothing.

Praying that I wouldn't choke him, I put the flask to his lips and tipped it up, dribbling the viscous liquid into his mouth. When he had a mouthful I clamped a hand over his lips and tipped his head back, hoping he would swallow by reflex.

Nothing happened for a moment. Then I felt him gag, and his eyes flew open. I thought he was about to spit blood all over me but after a confused second he swallowed. I took my hand away and he gasped.

When he'd caught his breath I held the flask to his mouth again and counted the swallows: three. I screwed the cap back on after that, knowing his stomach was weak and not wanting to risk him throwing up again.

He subsided back into sleep. I watched him for a few moments, finally allowing myself to hope that he would be all right. My hand itched to stroke his hair back from his face, to feel the softness of it as I had when we were lost at sea. But he had regained his customary composure, a slight frown creasing the bridge of his nose, and I sensed that this was a liberty I could no longer take. Instead I pressed his hand briefly, the one on which he wore my silver ring, and got back into bed.

Not trusting our nurse, I curled my body around the flask like a child with a coveted toy, and slept.

———

When I awoke it was dark and still and I could hear the high chirping of crickets. The moon shone brightly and there was a chill in the air. The town was silent and still. Through the window I saw a lithe, silvery cat pace atop a wall in the distance.

The old man was fast asleep, snoring lightly. I propped Rodden up, shaking his shoulder to rouse him. I put the flask to his lips and he drank, the blood slipping easily down his throat. After having his fill he lay back, breathing hard from the effort. His eyes opened, and in a slice of moonlight I saw him smile at me. He seemed lucid for the first time in days. Raising his hand he fumbled for my cheek and I felt the warmth from his fingers.

I smiled in return, and was about to feel for the thread between us when he spoke. The words came as tender as rose petals.

'Ilona, my darling.'

His hand fell back to his side and he was asleep.

———

I recovered quickly after that. Not two days after Rodden had spoken, I moved out of the hospice and into a little room behind a shop that one of the nurses found me.

We had lost nearly everything after being hurled from the *Jessamine*. I needed a bow for starters. I needed to shoot something. It was the only thing that could possibly make me feel normal this far from home. But the marketplace didn't have a vendor who sold bows.

I got our other provisions instead: cool robes for the day and heavier items for the desert nights. Soap. Knives. Salve for my sunburn. The woman who sold me the salve also pressed another lotion on me, and pointed to her own eye and then mine. I gathered it was for the black eye Orrick had given me. When I found a mirror hanging at another stall I saw the bruise was now mottled green and purple.

Language was no obstacle to haggling in the marketplace, gestures being all I needed to communicate my needs. I loved the rich colours of the local women's clothing. They wore loose beaded tops paired with trousers that could have fitted two of me until I crossed the fabric in front and tied them snugly to my hips. They had the fullness of skirts but still allowed for sensible horse riding. To keep off the sun I bought a matching gauzy scarf that doubled as a shawl when the night turned chilly.

I bought more than I needed, because if I was idle too long I heard Rodden's voice whispering in the moonlight.

Ilona, my darling.

And my body burned as if from the blood-hunger. I burned through sleepless nights, listening to the yowls of cats on heat and the incessant crickets. Lost on the Osseran Sea, my days had been filled with nothing but worry for Rodden. I had kept him alive with my own blood. And he did not know the name of the one who had saved his life.

Who was she? I cursed Rodden yet again for his secretiveness, that he had never told me the names of his sisters and mother and childhood friends. The name meant nothing to me, and so became everything.

I bought us horses, two pale, stocky creatures with black hooves. They were impervious to the heat, composed even at midday when I retreated, slick with sweat, to the shelter of my rented room.

Soon, a week after I'd left the hospice and well before I was ready for it, he recovered. One of the nurses found me in the market place and, with smiles and pointing, communicated the good news.

No longer able to avoid him, I stowed the belts I had just purchased in my room, and made the short walk to the hospice. I entered to find him sitting upright. His eyes widened at my attire. I wore the loose pants and cropped top of a local woman in rich orange fabric.

'What?' I asked, hearing the defensiveness in my voice.

He said nothing for a moment, and then smiled ruefully. 'You reminded me of someone.'

Someone? Someone? I was Zeraphina Hermione, Second Daughter of the House of Amentia, sister to the future Queen of Pergamia.

I wasn't *like* anyone else.

We sat in silence, listening to Leap purr as he lay heavily across Rodden's legs.

'We'll need to prepare for the next part of our journey,' he said at last.

'It's done,' I replied. 'Horses, clothing. A few knives, but they don't have proper weapons here. All packed and ready to go.'

He nodded, regarding me. The nurse had shaved him, and apart from the thinness of his cheeks and a ruddy, burned complexion, he looked as he always had. I should have been ecstatic but instead my mouth was filled with the taste of sour milk. I found I couldn't hold his gaze for long.

'We should leave for Pol tomorrow, then. The journey will only take two hours or so.'

'All right,' I said, slapping my thighs with a heartiness I didn't feel and rising to my feet. 'I'll see you at dawn.'

'Zeraphina,' he called as I turned to go, and I started. I had forgotten the sound of my name in his mouth. I wanted to take the word back from him. He had lost the right to speak it.

I stopped and waited, still with my back to him.

'Are you all right?' he asked.

I should have been happy he was better. Felt less alone. But it was worse somehow, seeing him awake and knowing he'd lived a life before we'd met that he'd never tell me about. In an unfamiliar land with a dubious future, it made me feel as if I were nothing. Like I could walk into the desert and disappear and no one would ever think of me again.

I drew the scarf around my body, nodded, and left.

———

We departed the town in silence, riding single file on our desert horses. I held Griffin on my wrist and we competed over who could look the most thunderous. Leap had cleaved himself to Rodden for the moment, always the comforter. I could feel Rodden's confusion at my attitude, but it was my turn to clamp down on our connection. My turn to cut him out.

Eventually Rodden drew up next to me.

'What's got into you? Did something happen while I was recovering?'

I had steeled myself to be silent, but words rushed out of me in a bitter flood. 'What, you think you're the only one who's allowed to brood?' I clutched at the first thing that was weighing on me that wasn't Rodden's late-night name confusion. 'I have a lot on my mind, you know. Pretty soon I'm going to be seventeen.' Just speaking the words made my stomach tighten with fear. I had discovered the date while in the markets and my seventeenth birthday was barely a fortnight away. We were far away from my mother right now, but very soon we would be in Amentia. I was going to be seventeen and in Amentia. Oh, by the stars, I was afraid of what might happen when we arrived. I wished I hadn't provoked my mother in the last letter I had sent. And Lilith was bound to have written and told her how I'd snuck away with Rodden in the dead of night.

He frowned for a moment, and I could see him

wondering why the occasion should vex me. 'Oh,' he said at last. 'Of course. Your mother.'

'Yes, my mother. My responsibilities. You're not the only one people are relying on. The only one who has to make sacrifices.' My anxiety, I felt with a flutter of guilt, was for myself right then. But I was worried about my people. If I had been infected with Lharmellin blood as a baby, so could other Amentines have been. I knew my place was out here, fighting, and not married and hidden away in a castle giving some king or prince heirs.

Even if nobody else knew it, I thought sourly.

Rodden gave me a long, steady look, and I could see a spark of annoyance in his eyes. He spurred his horse forward without another word.

I don't know if it was the foul mood I was in or the fact that Rodden had spoken of it so fondly, but I found Pol to be a squalid, dirty dump of a city. It was enormous, too, spreading only laterally where Brivoran architects would have built upwards to make the most of space. Shacks were haphazard, one supporting another and so on like a trail of dominos waiting to be knocked down. Women squatted in front of cooking fires, dressed in rags, while scruffy children played nearby. Older children queued forty-deep for a well, a motley collection of vessels clutched in their hands. The men made ceramic pots at foot-pedal wheels, or sewed beadwork, or butchered carcasses within a cloud of flies.

And everywhere there were drain-cats, lounging atop walls with their scrappy kittens or seated next to filthy gutters, gleaming silver and fastidiously clean. Their silhouette and attitude were familiar to me, but their numbers were astounding. The humans and cats seemed oblivious to one another, and I guessed that familiarity accounted for their companionable disregard.

Rodden looked about him, his manner attentive but grim. He peered down alleyways and into faces as they passed. He seemed to be searching for something. Or someone.

We found rooms in a mud-brick house and he spoke Verapinian to the clerk, the words coming to him as easily as breathing.

Showing me to my room and stowing his things in his own, he turned to me.

'I must go out for a little while, and I must go alone. I'm sorry.' His eyes flicked to my face, wary.

I shrugged, pretending not to care.

'Promise me you'll stay inside where it's safe? And lock the door?' He reached out and squeezed my forearm. 'Don't forget you have a knife in your pack.'

'I'll be fine. Please stop fussing,' I snapped.

His hand dropped back to his side, and his face clouded. Had I hurt his feelings?

Good.

He disappeared onto streets that were familiar to him, leaving me to the loneliness of a traveller who does not speak the language. In less than five minutes I was regretting my coldness, but didn't dare venture onto the streets alone to find him. What a strange city Pol was.

I may have regretted my harsh words, but I was still furious with Rodden. It wasn't fair that he knew all about me, my history, my future, and could read me like one of his precious books, but to me he was an enigma. I had no idea where he was going or where he had come from, except for the few words he'd told me about Verapine.

There was parchment and ink in my room so I tried to write letters to my sister. But the words wouldn't come. I sketched Leap and Griffin, watching them doze, but my efforts were so unsatisfying that I screwed the sheets into balls.

When the sun set, I went to bed. I lay sweating on the sheets with the inadequate window open as far as it would go, listening for Rodden's return. His room was next to mine and close to midnight I heard footsteps. His door opened, and clicked shut. We'd barely spoken a word to each other all day.

With a pang I realised that he could be searching for this Ilona, his own private quest that had nothing to do with the task we'd set out to do. What if that was really it? What if my idea to get bennium was just an excuse for him to return home after all these years and find her?

A thick, ugly feeling spread through my guts. I was incapacitated by the strength of it, unable to do anything but clench my fists and stare at the ceiling as if I could burn right through it with the force of my gaze. It was jealousy, vicious and crippling. But betrayal also; if Rodden had lied to me about the true purpose of this journey, I'd never speak to him again.

As soon as he left his room the next day, I followed. I just had to. I'd rather be with my mother and a dozen eligible princes than here with Rodden being tricked.

I'd dressed in my simplest, darkest clothing and thrown a scarf over my head. Keeping twenty paces behind him, I felt for his thread, keeping it as thin as gossamer and trying my hardest to remain undetected. That way I'd be able to follow him even after he'd disappeared from my sight. If I concentrated, and he remained distracted, I might just get away with it.

Rodden roamed up and down the warren-like city streets. Every now and then he stopped to question someone. Then, as I began to discern landmarks above the roofline of the city – the smart blue and gold flag of the Pergamian embassy, a wagon train hitched in a circle on a sand dune at the edge of the desert – I realised his method. He was dividing the town into a grid and searching each square.

Late in the afternoon I stood in an archway, chewing at some flatbread I had purchased from a street vendor while Rodden questioned yet another old woman just out of my line of sight. Then he was on the move again, nearly running. I panicked when I found he was doubling back, heading straight for the laneway I was standing in. I pressed myself into a doorway, which was barely any cover at all, but in his haste he flew past without noticing me.

I waited thirty seconds, and then pursued, jogging to keep up. Several times I stopped and closed my eyes, letting our thread go taut. I ran this way and that for a time before realising he was no longer on the streets but had entered a building.

I found the right place: a mud-brick house like the one we were staying in. The windows were shuttered.

I skirted my way round the block and found the rear entrance in an alleyway. It was blocked by a rickety fence, and the courtyard was empty. Praying that Rodden or anyone else wasn't about to burst outside, I crept across the paved expanse. There was a window high up and I needed to stand on a crumbling brick ledge in order to peek inside.

Everything was bare but clean, as if the premises had been vacated recently. I was wondering if I had the right house after all when Rodden came into the room. I immediately ducked out of sight, wobbling a bit on my precarious perch. After a tense minute, curiosity got the better of me and I peeked in again.

All traces of triumph had seeped from him and I could detect only disappointment. He leaned against the wall and slid down, defeated. I rose on tiptoe to keep him in my sights, but suddenly the wall gave beneath me and I tumbled off, the shock of the landing making me forget to cloak my presence.

I felt a burst of alarm from Rodden as he heard me fall, and then a surge of anger as he realised who it was.

Winded, I scrambled up and was out the gate in three seconds flat, darting this way and that down darkened laneways, hoping I wasn't about to hit a dead end. My chest was tight but I didn't dare stop.

I felt rather than heard the thunder of his pursuit.

I spotted a drain just large enough for me to crouch in and scrambled inside. There was an inch of brackish water and a drain-cat standing paw-deep in it, not seeming to mind the run-off in the slightest. I, however, did, and gathered my clothing to me to keep it out of the wet. The smell was appalling and I covered my mouth and nose with my scarf. The cat regarded me with astonished eyes, then sat down and purred like a one-cat welcoming committee, her tail undulating sociably in the water. *Welcome to my humble abode.* I guessed that humans did not often grace these parts with their presence.

I concentrated on building my wall up again and thought I had outwitted Rodden, but then heard his familiar, imperious voice somewhere over my head.

'I'm prepared to stand here all night, Zeraphina. Do you think you can stand the stench that long?'

I dropped the wall I had so carefully built and let him feel how annoyed I was. In answer I felt a surge of pure fury.

I looked into the blackness of the drain, wondering if I dared to crawl down it.

I didn't.

So I got out.

With all the composure I could rustle up I emerged back onto the street and brushed myself off. Rodden regarded me silently, his arms folded.

I drew myself up to my full five feet seven inches and said, in my best princess voice, 'Excuse me.'

I moved to pass him but he caught my arm.

'We need to talk.'

———

He took me west, to the edge of the city where laneways and haphazard buildings gave way to desert sands. The sun was setting and everything was drenched in orange light. On a dune several hundred feet away I saw the ring of wagons that I'd noticed earlier, and a motley crew of men and women practising acrobatics in the early evening light. They were lithe and beautiful, all with thick brown curls and ropey bodies. Their coloured clothing flashed as they tumbled and twisted.

We sat on the slope of a dune and stared across the vast, empty expanse.

'You were following me,' he said.

I scooped up a handful of sand and let it slip through my fingers.

'Why?' he asked.

'I needed to know.'

'Know what?'

I shrugged. 'Something. Anything.'

'Why are you so determined to know my business?'

I shook my head, exasperated. 'Don't you see the unfairness of it all? That you should know everything that matters about me, and I should know nothing of you? It's driving me mad.'

His voice was soft, but I could hear the anger in it. 'I thought you'd given up on snooping, but here you are, back to your old tricks.'

'I have no choice when you keep things from me.'

'Maybe you should try minding your own business for a change.' The words were said without malice, but they stung. If he'd yelled like Renata or Lilith did when they were angry, I might have borne it easier. His quiet fury unnerved me.

'This isn't why I came. I thought we were done with secrets.'

He shook his head. 'I don't know what to tell you. But we'll be in Amentia soon and ...' He trailed off.

'And?'

He looked at the acrobats, who were laughing as they swept their dark curls from their faces.

'Maybe you should stay when we get there,' he finished.

Tears stung my eyes. I realised I was more wretched at the thought of being left behind, of being without him, than I was frustrated by his secrets. I remembered the heaviness of his skull in my lap; the taste of his blood on my tongue. His fingers were laced together, and my ring glinted on his right hand. I thought of him one day removing it and giving it back, unable to meet my eyes.

It was tempting to tell him it didn't matter, I wouldn't ask again, please don't leave me behind. But pride is a stubborn thing, and it reared suddenly through my wretchedness. Maybe I didn't need to know – but I should at least know why I didn't need to know.

'Perhaps –' I said, hesitating, 'perhaps if you gave me a reason for keeping things from me, I might understand. I might not need to know.'

'Besides the fact that they're my secrets and have nothing to do with you or our undertaking?'

I nodded.

He sighed, and his eyes searched the horizon. 'There are things I've done that are painful to speak of, and even less pleasant to hear.'

'Things that happened when you became a harming?'

'Yes.'

I felt some of my frustration slip away like the sand through my fingers. I could understand that. Hadn't I kept my confusion and terror to myself for as long as I could? I was still unable to tell my own sister the truth about what I was.

'I don't want to be left in Amentia,' I said.

'I don't want to leave you there.'

With these words the tightness left my chest, and I discreetly blinked away tears. 'I won't ask any more,' I said. 'And I won't follow you. They are your secrets. But ...'

He glanced at me. 'But?'

'But if you should feel like talking, I'm well equipped to be understanding. Being a harming myself.'

He brushed sand from his fingers. 'You are probably right.' He stood, offering his hand to help me up. 'But that doesn't make the speaking any easier. Come on. We've got things to do.'

I took his hand and he pulled me to my feet. 'You're right. It is beautiful,' I said, looking at the city lit by golden light. It was just as he'd described. 'Do you think you'll come home for good one day?'

Rodden looked long and hard at the city. 'This isn't my home any more.' He turned to the desert again and nodded at the wagons. 'Those are the Jarbin.'

The Jarbin. I felt a thrill run through me. These were the people who would give us access to bennium. 'Do you know them?'

'Not personally. Shall we go and talk to them?'

Together we walked down the dune towards the troupe, and I was content to let secrets lie.

For the moment, at least.

NINE

The glassblower's shop became a theatre at night, a bright hot coal in the centre of the city. Rodden and I gathered with the locals to watch the show. The meeting with the Jarbin had gone well, Rodden slipping easily into the dialect. We would be leaving with them in the morning.

The workshop, a twig-and-mud roof on posts, was lit by an enormous furnace at the rear and many coloured-glass lanterns. The audience gathered around sweet-smelling pipes that were placed here and there, tall as a child and made of brilliant brass. Men sucked on nozzles and blew reams of apple- or strawberry-scented smoke, always with one eye on the glassblower.

We chewed on flat bread wrapped around spiced

potatoes, and watched. The sun had set and the air was cooler now, and I had a scratchy woollen shawl gathered about my shoulders.

A boy worked the bellows, exciting the flames into a roar. The furnace was closed but the doors glowed red-hot at the edges where the seals met. The glassblower limbered up, cracking his knuckles and arranging his tools on a rag. He picked up a clay pipe about as long as my arm, checked it for cracks and then peered through it at the crowd like it was a telescope. His face was serious, but I saw a twinkle in his eyes.

He barked a command at his apprentice, who leapt for a rag and eased open the first door. I was yards away but I felt the heat of the fire blast my face. The glassblower eased the clay pipe in and twirled it like he was gathering honey on a spoon. Still twirling, he took the pipe out and turned to the crowd. We watched, mesmerised, as he lowered the glowing red ball of molten glass onto a marble slab and began rolling back and forth, shaping it into an elongated bulb.

He barked another command and the apprentice dashed forward and put a damp pad of paper into the master's hands. They switched places, and the boy knelt and blew into the tube while the man shaped the growing vessel with the wet paper pad. Steam and smoke billowed up around him.

At the glassblower's command, the boy put the glass into the second chamber of the furnace – which seemed even hotter than the first, if it was possible – while the glassblower strewed bits of coloured glass on the marble slab.

The pipe was now back in the master's hands and he rolled the glass in the blue chunks on the table. The pair repeated the process, blowing, shaping and reheating, until they had a brilliant blue vessel two feet long and a foot across suspended on the end of the pipe. With a set of shears the smith severed it from the pipe and the boy placed the glasswork in the third chamber of the furnace.

The glassblower gave a curt nod to the crowd and after a smattering of applause they began to disperse.

Rodden passed his bread to me and stepped forward to speak with the craftsman. I watched as they moved to one side of the shack where an enormous crate stood and Rodden eased off the lid. He brought out a sphere covered in rags, cradling it with two hands. Unwrapping it, he revealed a glass ball the size of his hand-span. After examining it, he held it aloft to show me.

They covered the crate and secured the lid, and stood talking a moment. Then the glassblower clasped Rodden about the shoulders and kissed his cheeks three times. They murmured to each other for a moment. Then, with a tight smile, Rodden said his goodbyes and made his way back to me.

'Let's get out of here,' he muttered, taking his bread back from me and giving it to a clutch of cats that had gathered atop a wall.

'You hardly ate,' I protested.

'Not hungry.' He strode back towards our quarters, leading the way through the maze of streets.

'You knew him,' I said in the darkness, keeping to the edge of the laneways as I walked to avoid the muck that had collected in the middle of the street.

'Yes.' His voice was flat.

I guessed this was one of the secrets that I wasn't allowed to pry into. I bit into my bread, tearing off a large chunk so I wasn't tempted to ask the questions that burned on my tongue.

———

To a girl who had spent her life surrounded by snow and mountains and an ample water supply, setting out into the heart of the world's largest, hottest, driest desert seemed like a rash undertaking. In three directions, undulating white-gold dunes stretched to the horizon. The mid-morning sun beat down, and shimmering heat blurred the line between horizon and sky. I sat uneasily in my saddle, trying not to look back as Pol shrank behind us, giving me a peculiar feeling of vertigo. Rodden got seasick; it seemed I got desertsick. I was gripped with nausea at the thought of the city disappearing altogether.

Behind me, Rodden sat sanguine atop his desert mare. Leap paced in the leggy shadows of the horses, pupils shrunk to a thin line, eating up the sand with an easy gait. We were with the Jarbin, and the entire caravan stretched yards behind and ahead of me. There were a dozen wagons and scores of horses, and so many people that I couldn't imagine getting to know all their names.

The sunburn I'd acquired while lost at sea was starting to peel and fizzed painfully in the desert sun. I kept my white robes wrapped about me, not allowing even an inch of skin to be exposed. I'd been offered a seat in a covered wagon with a handful of Jarbin girls. Rodden, to my annoyance, had told them my royal title as we'd milled about on the dew-damp sand that morning. I'd endured several minutes of exaggerated curtseying and tittering before, teeth gritted, I'd mounted my horse. Now, as I sweated and squinted in the sun, I regretted my decision. I could see the Jarbin girls chattering to one another, shaded and comfortable.

Our caravan reached the crest of a dune and began to descend. I felt Pol disappear as my horse picked its way down the slope. The tors tugged my insides, whispering the distance I'd travelled. I tried to ignore what my eyes and mind-map told me: I was far, far from home.

None of the Jarbin spoke Brivoran. Rodden was deep in conversation with the leader of the tribe, a young but grizzled fellow with a theatrical air. He gesticulated to Rodden as they rode side by side, reins forgotten in his lap as he described something in a wild manner. Rodden nodded, added a word here and there, and then the pair burst into raucous laughter.

I grimaced and turned my gaze elsewhere. Griffin was sitting on my wrist, determined to stay as close as possible while ignoring me at the same time. I was not the only one, it seemed, who grew cranky about being left out. Having spent the last few days being left at the inn while Rodden searched the city, I searched for Rodden, and Leap courted all the queens within a two-mile radius, she was inclined to be annoyed.

I eyed the buzzards overhead, the only shapes in a barren sky. The huge birds rode the thermals rising from the desert sands on lazy black wings. They followed our passage all day and I found their company ominous.

That night when we stopped to make camp, I collected a mound of blankets and tried to make my bed under the stars. I was tired and stiff, and wanted nothing more than to be alone. The Jarbin girls laughed at me. They laughed, it seemed, at everything. Rodden explained that it was too cold to sleep out in the desert, and I would be soaked by the falling dew. I was bundled in with the girls instead and they were as raucous as parrots late into the night; more so, I suspected, for having a mute audience. There were three of them, two who shared one pallet and one who shared the other pallet with me. I had asked their names in the few words of Jarbin that I knew on three occasions but they spoke so rapidly that I couldn't decipher the foreign syllables. It had become embarrassing so I'd stopped asking.

———

The days unfolded much like the first: mute on my part, boisterous on the Jarbins'. By day I rode my horse at the rear of the train; by night I retreated into the wagon to pull a pillow over my head.

My one pleasure was watching the Jarbin at dusk. They were a joy to watch, able to accomplish things that I'd never even contemplated the human body was capable of; often dangerous things, like juggling fire or even swallowing it, and treading, barefoot, on tight wires they strung between the wagons.

But an evening came when I didn't want to venture out even to watch the Jarbin. Instead I sat, arms wrapped about my knees, listening to the crackle of flames outside. I had an oil lamp for company and its soft yellow glow lit the painted interior. Leap sat at my feet, watching the moths dance before the light.

Practice usually ended after dusk, but tonight there was festivity in the air. Instead of settling quietly onto mats to eat the evening meal, the Jarbin rushed about and I could hear musicians tuning their instruments. My sleeping mates had changed into dresses that rattled with silver coins and tinkled with bells, their attire as noisy as themselves. Instead of the scratchy woollen poncho I usually donned of a cold evening, I'd put on a pair of the diaphanous pants that hung like a skirt and a matching shirt that hugged my ribs. It was a heavier version of the attire I'd bought when first coming to Pol, made of burgundy wool and angora. I'd meant to join the others as soon as I'd changed, but now I sat on my pallet, hugging my knees, uncertain.

For today wasn't like the other days in the desert, where I could sit quietly and lose myself in the antics of the colourful Jarbin. Today was my birthday. I was seventeen.

In this pale abyss the date meant little. It could just as easily have been yesterday or next week or not at all for all that it mattered here.

But I knew. And across the miles, Renata knew.

We were travelling further from Amentia every day, but I could feel its pull on my body as surely as I could feel the taut thread of the tors. I felt as if I was being torn asunder by my two fates, each one as hateful as the other.

There was a rapping on the door. 'Are you decent?'

'No.'

Rodden opened the door and stepped in. His black hair was neat and damp with water and he wore a shirt in the Jarbin style, with long cuffs and full sleeves. My heart flipped as I looked at him; desert life agreed with him. He was looking more handsome all the time. Tanned and vibrant in the heat. I realised that every day on this journey could be one less that I would spend with him.

'I said I wasn't decent.' I clutched my knees tighter with indignation.

'You can't lie to a harming.' He frowned. 'What are you doing in here?'

'What does it look like?'

'I've been waiting for you.'

'What for?'

He sat beside me on the bed, reaching out to scratch Leap on the chin. 'Your mother is a long way away.'

I looked at him in surprise.

He smiled. 'Happy birthday.'

I was silent a moment. 'How did you know?'

He raised a hand to the sky like a fortune-teller. 'It was written in the stars.'

I punched his arm.

'I waited until your sulking reached epic proportions.'

I punched him again.

'Ow,' he said, laughing. 'All right, I asked Amis to find out from your sister before we left Pergamia. Are you coming out?'

'No.'

'Wait here, then.' He disappeared outside.

'I *said* I wasn't going anywhere,' I called.

He came back brandishing a long object wrapped in a black cloth.

'What is it?' I asked when he handed it to me. He sat beside me again and pulled Leap into his lap. My cat purred and rubbed silver fur all over Rodden's black shirt, flexing his claws in delight.

'A birthday present,' he said.

'I can see that. You shouldn't have.' I hesitated, the parcel resting on my knees. 'Actually, you should. I've been entirely miserable since we left Pol and you've ignored me to be with all your new friends.'

He raised an eyebrow at me. 'Have you made any attempt at all to learn the language?'

'Yes. I asked those girls their names so many times but I couldn't understand them. Why didn't you teach me any Verapinian or Jarbin? You didn't even tell me they spoke other languages here. I woke up in the sick tent and thought my brain had melted in the sun when I couldn't understand anyone.'

'Sorry. I was distracted. And worried that I'd made a mistake bringing you.'

'Thanks.'

He reached for my hand and clasped it in his. 'No, Zeraphina,' he said, half-laughing. 'You are determined to think the worst tonight. I meant I was worried for your sake.'

I felt a pang when I looked at our joined hands, the silver rings we each wore. I remembered what he'd asked all those months ago on the parapet in Pergamia when I'd given the ring back to him. *Something to remember you by?* Would he remember me once we were parted; would he still wear the ring? Would I, once I was married?

'Are you going to open it?' he asked, nodding at the parcel.

Reluctantly, I let go of his hand. I unravelled the black cloth to reveal a bow. It was the perfect size and weight for me: half the length of my body and made of taut, honey-coloured wood. I'd been without a bow since we'd been thrown from the *Jessamine*. I'd intended to buy one, but hadn't found one of the right quality. I turned it in my hands. 'It's perfect,' I breathed. 'When did you buy it?'

'That first day in Pol.'

I thought back. That was the day we'd quarrelled, the first day he'd disappeared into the warren of laneways in search of something or someone he wouldn't speak of. I thought that he'd forgotten me altogether as soon as he'd left our rooms. I wanted to ask, *What came first? The bow for me? Or had there been someone else foremost in your thoughts?*

'It's made of Amentine ash,' he said, and I nodded, having already recognised the grain. I felt homesick as I stroked the polished wood, which was ridiculous considering how reluctant I was to return.

'I miss the mountains,' I said. 'The desert makes me dizzy. What's it like for you? To be home again after all these years, I mean.'

Rodden rubbed at Leap. 'Peculiar. I never thought I'd see my home again. I banished myself years ago.' He nudged me with his shoulder. 'There's more,' he said, nodding at the black cloth.

I searched the folds and found bowstrings and a quiver of arrows.

'Not Griffin's,' he said as I examined the mustard-coloured feathers the arrows were fletched with. 'Local falcons. Fast ones. Lucky for arrows.'

I hooked a string to the base of the bow, rested the butt on the floor and, holding it secure with my foot, looped the string over the other end with one fluid movement. I hefted the weapon with my left hand and pulled the string with my right. It flexed under my firm grasp. 'It will be good to shoot some arrows again.' I turned to Rodden. 'Thank you.'

He was watching me, and I realised he had been the

whole time I was distracted by my present. I lowered the bow. Unbidden, my eyes flicked to his mouth. I felt the thread between us tighten. Though we sat close he held that part of himself distant, the part that could blend with my own like two rivers running together, if only he would allow it. I hadn't expected to ever want that. I hadn't expected to need that.

I hadn't imagined I would ever fall in love.

He couldn't help but hear the direction of my thoughts. I let him hear, and see their manifestation on my face.

'You're welcome,' he said. His lips when they came touched my cheek, soft but chaste. He stood and tugged on my hand. 'Come on. They'll be wondering where you are.'

I fumbled with the cloth in my lap, eyes lowered so he couldn't see the sudden sheen to my eyes. 'Of course they won't be,' I muttered. But in my confusion I allowed myself to be pulled to my feet and out of the wagon. He stayed close as we paced through the darkness. I peered sidelong at his face but it was impossible to tell what he was thinking. Though it was foolish, I allowed myself to hope that his kiss had been for my cheek and not my mouth due to an observance of chivalry. He'd kissed me once before; now I found myself hoping that he would do so again.

The Jarbin had made a circle of rugs around a flat, hard-packed expanse of ground. Lanterns cast bright yellow light, and as we stepped into the circle a greeting rose above the chatter and music. Two boys jumped up and guided us to a carpet beside the leader. He stood and kissed my hands, and spoke a few words. Then he smiled, his large white teeth glowing in the lamplight.

'He says happy birthday,' Rodden translated.

I turned to Rodden in surprise. 'You told him?'

He grinned. 'I told everyone. An easy thing, as you might imagine, to keep secret from you.'

My hands still in the leader's, I gazed around the circle in amazement at upturned faces and warm smiles. After feeling like a ghost among them for many days, I blushed at the attention.

I was bade to sit, and settled between the leader and Rodden.

'How do I say "thank you" in Jarbin?' I whispered.

'"*Preibek,* Uwin." Uwin is his name.'

I turned to Uwin, and bowed my head respectfully. '*Preibek,* Uwin.'

Uwin's eyes shone with pleasure. He grasped my hand once again and called out to the tribe, which brought on cheers and delighted smiles.

Beside me, Rodden laughed and applauded with the rest of them.

'What? What did he say?'

'He told them you just spoke your first words of Jarbin.'

I reddened all over again. 'For heaven's sake,' I muttered, smiling.

Rodden accepted two cups of wine from a man with a flagon. '*Preibek*,' he said, before turning to me. 'I don't think they've ever heard an Amentine princess utter a word of Jarbin, do you?'

I looked around the animated circle and thought of the girls whose wagon I shared, and wondered if their effusiveness of an evening was their normal behaviour after all, rather than a ploy to annoy the foreign girl.

Drumbeats filled the air. Six men leapt into the circle brandishing crossed swords over their heads. They were clad in boleros and white trousers. After displaying their swords – and their bared teeth – to the crowd with a zeal that bordered on threatening, they placed their crossed swords on the sand and began an intricate dance. They leapt over the blades, their bare feet just missing the sharpened edges, and twined around one another, arms akimbo, fists pressed into hips. After a short but wild performance, they retrieved their swords and flung their arms over their heads with a loud '*Yah!*'

At our rapturous applause their stern faces melted into grins and they hopped about, bowing. Before running off again into the darkness they each gripped both their swords in one hand and held the blades behind them, and with their free hands took turns to grasp one of mine and kiss it. I barely had time to murmur '*Preibek*' to each of them before they darted off.

The sound of a lone pipe twined upwards in the evening air. A hush fell over the circle. A tattoo was rapped out on a tambourine, accompanied by the twangs of a stringed instrument. The tune was cheeky and rapid, and on its heels followed a troupe of dancers, ten women in coloured silk skirts and beaded halters. Arms rippling like water, they stepped into the arena. To the rapid beat of the music they assembled in two rows and began rolling their hips and stomachs. Their bellies were not one curved plane but several independently moving parts. Their spines seemed disjointed. I was as hypnotised by the swaying and popping movements as a snake by a charmer.

When the women finished their dance and the applause died away, Rodden rose and tugged at my hand. He called to the musicians and they laughed and nodded, taking up their instruments once more.

'You remember the brinle?' he asked me, a twinkle in his eyes. The brinle was a courtly dance from Brivora.

'You want me to dance – after that performance?' I tried to take my hand back but he held fast. 'The musicians won't even know the brinle,' I protested.

He pulled me to my feet. 'They know "ol Gesta", which is close enough.'

'I need to practise – I can't remember –' I hissed, conscious of everyone's eyes on us.

He put a finger to my lips, eyes shining with amusement. In spite of myself, I found myself smiling back, and as the first notes began I allowed myself to be tugged into the centre of the circle.

The brinle was a couple's dance but this particular one was unusual as it was danced by only a single pair. I turned out my feet and fanned my loose trousers like I would a skirt. Rodden pressed his arms to his side. He caught my eye and winked, and I bit back a smile as the beginning of the dance demanded an aloof expression.

Then we began. Like most court dances, the brinle consisted of simple steps and turns. But this dance told a story, one almost comic, of a girl purposely oblivious to the attentions of a suitor. I kept my chin up and face turned away from Rodden, my eyes on the stars when I knew he was looking, but sneaking looks when I knew he wasn't. My alternating expressions of detachment and fascination drew laughter from the crowd. The music became rapid. The steps became skips, the dance a chase now, and the laughter became shouts of amusement as I evaded Rodden, still pretending I had no idea he was there. The finale came with a crescendo of beating drums. I evaded, turned – and found myself nose-to-nose with him, breathing heavily.

We were both smiling as the applause erupted. On impulse I stood on tiptoe and pressed my mouth against his. He returned the kiss, but quickly broke it. As he pulled away I saw anger flash in his eyes.

My pleasure at the dance faded. Why did I have to go and do a stupid thing like that?

Rodden grasped my hand tightly – too tightly – and we bowed and curtseyed to the Jarbin. I kept a smile plastered on my face but my stomach was churning. He was angry. I had kissed him and he was angry.

He steered me out of the circle of light, his grip hard and unfriendly, and into the hush of the desert. In the light of the moon I could see the familiar agitated set to his shoulders. His mouth was a grim line. When we'd disappeared behind the crest of a dune he at last came to a halt and dropped my hand.

'Sit.'

'*Please*,' I corrected. 'What? Did I offend you? Did I break some rule of propriety?'

He paced before me, hand to his mouth. The minutes stretched between us.

'I've changed my mind,' he said at last.

'About what?'

'You want to know everything. I will tell you everything.'

I felt a flash of triumph.

He knelt before me in the sand and gripped my forearms. 'I've been lying to you.' His voice remained flat.

I searched his face in the wan starlight; explored the thread between us. I shook my head. 'No. *That* is a lie. You said it yourself: you can't lie to a harming.'

'I can,' he averred. 'I can hide things from you. There is such a thing as a lie by omission. I am not proud of what I have done – that is certainly the truth – but it is my knowledge, and my price to pay. But I will tell you now because of the way you feel about me. I see myself reflected in your eyes and it is not the man I really am. Since we were lost at sea, I've felt you …' He released my arms. 'You shall change your mind soon enough. But I do not want your forgiveness, or your pity, though you might think to extend it. I will tell you all because I do not wish to lead you further down this path we're on. You will not thank me for revealing the truth. In fact, you may hate me from this night on. So be it.'

'You can tell me anything. It won't change what I feel,' I said. 'I don't care about your past. I can see you're a good person. Don't you think I can see that?'

'You can't see it. I haven't let you.'

'I know you, Rodden,' I insisted. 'I know everything about you, just as you know everything about me – everything that matters. I might not know the details, but I'm not blind. When I look at you I can see your goodness.' I reached up to touch his cheek.

He slapped my hand away. 'You know nothing,' he growled. He pulled himself from my grasp and turned away, sitting with his back to me on the slope of the dune.

'Once,' he said, in a voice as cold as Amentine ice, 'I killed everyone I loved.'

I waited in the blackness of the night. Shook my head though he couldn't see me. But even as

I denied it, I felt the truthfulness of his words as he finally, deliberately, relaxed the tight hold he kept on himself. Then I didn't just feel the truth, I was struck by it. Wave after wave of pure emotion like a ship battered in a storm. Grief and fear and a great pounding guilt. I clutched my head, reeling from the sensations.

'You see?' he whispered, his voice faint to my ears as my head throbbed to the beat of his remorse.

——

'My family was poor, like most others in Pol. We eked out a living doing whatever was necessary. My mother wove cloth from the few goats we kept; my sisters helped her as soon as they were tall enough to hold a spindle. My brother, older than me by eight years, hired on with mercenaries to the south, but was killed before the coin he'd been promised could be sent home.

'My father was a clever man, and saw the virtues of an education that he himself had lacked. Though my mother denied the privilege to her daughters, who would never leave to be killed in someone else's war, she feared the fate of my elder brother might befall me, and consented to my education.

'The money my father made crushing sand and metals to make dye for rich Brivorans paid for books and a tutor. I was sent to a man called Levin Servilock, who ran a school for boys on the far side of the city. Six days a week, from the time I was seven years old, I attended what was known as the Clan. The lessons began innocently enough: geography, mathematics, the sciences, languages. I was taught not only the intricacies of my native tongue but other local dialects, such as Jarbin, and the languages of other continents. I became fluent in Brivoran. Then came archery and tracking. Swordplay. Knife skills. We were taught to fight and to hunt. This made little sense at the time. We were to be tradespeople and caravan masters, not warriors, after all.

'I began to crave the sights of the strange lands whose languages I learned. I hungered for escape from Pol and the bland fate that awaited me. Servilock told me that I would leave Pol one day as an important man, not just as a trader. That I was destined for greatness. He flattered me constantly, praising my intellect and insight. It was true that I had a knack for learning that excelled that of my peers, that I was a proficient fighter. Under Servilock's misguided tutelage I grew proud. He made me resent the humbleness of my existence and

I despised my family for the menial way they earned a living. I ordered my mother and sisters around. I sneered at my father. My family endured much of my insolence, but when I was fourteen my father decided that I'd had enough book learning, and that it was time I was apprenticed to a trade. Servilock came to see him, reluctant to lose his star pupil, as I was reluctant to lose my place in his academy. But my father was adamant: my education was over.

'I was apprenticed to the glassblower and was mad as a snake for many months. Servilock disappeared from my life. For the first time I worked with my hands and not my mind. I reviled the tasks I was given by my new instructor; the dirt and ashes and burns that accompanied my daily existence.

'I had always been a thin boy, taller than most but as skinny as a drain-cat. Under the pressures of my new occupation I grew strong and tanned. I also learned humility under the glassblower, and to take pride in something, rather than simply be proud. I learned the wonders of glass. I also discovered that girls weren't necessarily as annoying as life with my sisters had led me to believe.

'When I was sixteen I met Ilona. She came to buy a glass trinket for her mother one afternoon when I was alone in the workshop, labouring over the bellows. It was sweaty work and I was accustomed to doing it shirtless. She blushed when she saw me, but I bade her stay and jested with her. She laughed, and I found myself suddenly bewitched. She found excuses to come to the glassblower's again and again, and lingered over the pieces, her hands on the vases but her eyes on me. Soon I found I was going to her. I discovered why she had the money for glass: she was the daughter of what passes for a rich man in our city. This bothered me not in the least, for I was still a proud boy and on the inside I felt as good as any king. So I courted her in the secrecy she insisted upon until she would be old enough to marry.

'It was about this time that Servilock came back into my life. He was snide about my work and stirred up all the old resentment in me. I was too important for this menial work, he told me; my destiny was more illustrious than I could imagine. I was tempted to defy my family and return to my education, but told him that I was happy with the way things were. That I was going to be married and stay in Pol. We argued bitterly, and parted in anger. I thought that would be the end of it, but his words were like poison. They niggled at me, day and night. I started to question why I had to keep my courtship of Ilona secret from her family. Was I not good enough for her? When my family discovered whom I meant to marry they howled in protest. Such a girl would not be happy as a crafter's wife, they scoffed. She would drive me mad with her extravagance and dissatisfaction. They could not have chosen a more expedient manner with which to drive me back to Servilock. But they weren't to know. They were, with the wisdom that comes with hindsight, probably right.

'I quarrelled then with Ilona, demanding to know why we must keep our love secret, and at the height of my fury and confusion, when Servilock had seen to it that I had no one to turn to but him, he dosed me with Lharmellin blood. He was a harming, though I never heard the word until after I'd joined their ranks. The Clan was not a school, but an enclave; a cover for infecting students Servilock had groomed and who would then become infectors themselves and infiltrate every corner of the world. Hence the languages and geography that were taught, the hunting and fighting skills. While learning mathematics and the sciences wasn't directly helpful to a harming, I suspect that Servilock, as a scholar, couldn't help but impart a well-rounded education to his pupils.

'It is a blessing that you were infected as an infant, if such a thing can ever be called a blessing. The change is painful and protracted for the fully grown, and the ingestion of blood is required immediately to ease some of it. But for days I lay on a pallet in a secret part of the school, Servilock in almost constant attendance. He whispered to me throughout my delirium of my greatness, my destiny, the betrayal of my loved ones. He told me they were demons who would forever haunt my days and nights unless I liberated the evil from their bodies. I refused to believe him at first – my mother, a demon? My dearest Ilona? – but wracked with pain, tormented by hunger, I began to accept it as the truth. He should have given me blood to ease my passage. But he wanted me hungry. He wanted me angry. And inside me a great rage gathered, as a storm gathers over the seas. Servilock asked me if I wanted greatness, and I said that I did. He told me that my family and Ilona would smother my destiny, and I howled in agreement. I lost all sense of time, of day and night. In the brief moments he wasn't with me I paced the prison that was my room – for he locked me in, and my captivity, too, I blamed on them.

'Finally, when I was more wild, starving animal than human, Servilock let me out. And they were there: my mother, father, sisters and Ilona. I think they were in chains. Possibly it was rope. They were already bloodied and mutilated by cuts on their arms and faces. I smelled the blood. Servilock put a knife in my hand, and the storm was unleashed.'

———

In the silence that followed I realised I was shaking. I was soaked with sweat that was turning icy. My fingernails cut into my flesh. My teeth rattled like stones in a drum.

Rodden sat stock still, his breath the only sound audible over the noise of my own shivering. Minutes dragged by. Then, without turning, he stood and was gone.

It wasn't until much later that I realised he'd been waiting for me to speak.

TEN

Sleep was beyond me that night. The camp was quiet when I returned. Leap and Griffin sat by my wagon, uneasy sentinels. I retrieved my wrap and paced the sand. My hands clenched and unclenched at my sides. I needed to think. I needed to shoot something.

My new bow and arrows had been placed at the foot of the pallet. I took them from among my sleeping companions, buckled on my gauntlet and called to Griffin with my mind. She fluttered to my wrist.

The lid of an empty water barrel made an excellent target once I'd dragged it and the barrel a short distance into the desert. I propped the lid up in the sand. My eyes had adjusted to the darkness hours earlier and my makeshift target was easily visible at forty paces. Leap curled up on the sand beside me, eyes half-closed, and Griffin perched on the empty barrel next to me.

I notched an arrow, drew, and fired. The arrow bit into the wood with a muted *thunk*.

I waited, wondering if I'd woken anyone in the camp, but there was only silence. I drew again, and fired.

Thunk.

The bow became an extension of my arm and I felt the tension in my body begin to ease. Rodden had chosen well.

With Leap and Griffin beside me and the coldness of the night, I could almost imagine I was back in Amentia. Unhurried, I shot arrow after arrow, emptying my quiver into the barrel lid, then collecting them and beginning all over again.

Too soon the sky lightened in the east. I continued to shoot as the Jarbin began to stir. My eyes were focused on the target before me, but I kept a small part of my mind tuned to Rodden, that I might know the minute he woke.

There. In my mind's eye I saw him: knife in his hand, he made his way to the cages. Selected a bird. With a short, sharp twist the chicken's neck was broken and then severed, the body upended over a flask.

Thunk.

I felt him approach my wagon with the morning's repast. He rubbed a hand over the morning stubble on his face. He wore the same clothes he'd had on the previous evening, the shirt rumpled now and his hair dishevelled.

I sighted him down an arrow, drew back on the bowstring and shot it at his feet. He jumped as the arrow sprouted in the sand near his right boot. I hailed him with another arrow, notched it, and turned back to my board.

Thunk.

He stopped beside me and handed me the arrow.

I took it. 'Thank you.' My voice was crisp. 'Tell me,' I said, examining the tip. Blunt already. 'What happened to the *Jessamine*?'

Rodden looked at me in surprise.

'You asked at port, didn't you?' I prompted.

He cleared his throat. 'I did, now you mention it. She never made it to Pol.'

I nodded. 'I thought as much.'

I notched and fired.

Thunk.

I turned the bow in my hands, choosing my words carefully. He wanted no love from me. No pity. But

I had another gift for him. 'What you told me. I've been up all night thinking about it.'

He waited for me to go on.

'Would you have killed Servilock, had you found him in Pol?'

He never hesitated. 'Yes.'

'If you'd told me I would have helped you. I'll happily kill him myself. I can think of nothing I'd like more.' I wanted to kill Servilock so badly I could taste it. I burned for revenge on the man who'd caused Rodden so much pain. I would keep burning until everything else inside me was reduced to ashes. There would be no love left. I wasn't allowed to give it, so I would let it burn.

In my mind I saw the queen I would one day become: a husk; a living effigy to duty, honour, obedience. Loveless, but free of pain, loss. Free of fear.

Thunk.

'Thank you for reminding me why we're here,' I said.

Rodden's hand reached to bridge the distance between us, and then dropped to his side. He looked tired and unhappy.

I indicated the flask in his hand. 'May I?'

He passed it to me and leaned on the barrel next to Griffin, his movements stiff and tired. My bird's beak was sunk into her chest, her eyes closed. She muttered in her sleep.

I gulped the blood, and it erased the effects of my sleepless night. There. Everything was smoothed over. It was almost as if he had never told me the truth about his past. Almost as if I'd never let him see my love for him. Almost.

'Here,' I said, passing the remainder back. 'You look like you need it.'

He cocked an eyebrow at me. 'No doubt.' He took the flask and his fingers brushed mine.

Pain sprang up afresh, like kerosene on a bonfire. There was much in me yet to burn. I stalked to the target and yanked out the arrows.

The Jarbin were awake and stirring. It would not take long to break camp. I filled my quiver with the arrows.

'How does it shoot?' Rodden asked, indicating the bow.

'Well enough. But I'll let you know for sure once I've tested it on a harming.'

I saw the wrangler hitching horses to the wagons. I wondered what the Jarbin thought about our performance the previous evening, the fact that we'd not returned. Had they seen the thunderous look on Rodden's face as he'd pulled me from the circle, or two lovers disappearing into the desert? Either way, I didn't want to ride alone today. The Jarbin might talk even more if they thought we'd had a fight. My pride had taken enough of a beating, and if even one of the Jarbin girls laughed up her sleeve at me I would be tempted to test my bow on her.

'Ride with me?' I asked.

He nodded and rose from the barrel. 'I'll saddle our mounts.' Hesitating, he said, 'That wasn't the way I wanted things to turn out on your birthday. I'm sorry.'

'Actually, it was perfect.' I pushed past him. I'd been given a weapon and the best reason in the world to use it. It had been foolish of me to hope for more.

───

When I had washed with a wet rag and changed into my travelling clothes I felt like a new person. I boosted myself into the saddle when Rodden handed me the reins. Having a firm purpose refreshed me. Kill Servilock and defeat the Lharmellins. Nothing mattered beyond that. Nothing after that, a voice whispered, would hold any pleasure for me.

We were the last riders to mount, and let our

horses set their own pace as they followed the train out of camp.

'What happened after?'

'After what?' Rodden asked. 'Oh. I was very ill. Glutted. Servilock left me with ... the bodies.' He took a deep breath, and then went on briskly. 'I was eaten up by remorse. Servilock hadn't expected that. I didn't turn out like other harmings, just as you didn't. On the eve of our departure to Lharmell for the Turning, I ran away. I went to the port and bought passage on the first ship I saw. It was then that I discovered my seasickness and I nearly died making the crossing.'

'You seem to be making a habit of it.'

'Quite. We docked at Jefsgord and I was turfed from the ship. I had nowhere to go, no money. But I didn't need it. I had all the blood I needed from the city's rats. When I found harmings I killed them. It was so easy. They never thought to fear one of their own.' He took a deep breath. 'But I was careless about it. Soon I was arrested for murder by the king's guard and brought before Captain Helmsrid. He saw immediately that I was a harming myself and was fascinated to know why I had been killing my own. His own guards could never seem to get close enough to the scourge that riddled his city. Not long after that my arrest papers went missing and I found myself in paid employment for the King of Pergamia. Chief harming hunter. I refused to join the guard – life in the barracks as a harming would have been intolerable – but Helmsrid didn't mind in the least when he saw the zeal with which I led squads of his troops on extermination forays.'

I was amazed by how easily he was talking, after months and months of silence. I bit the inside of my cheek, loath to interrupt him.

'I began to try to atone for the things I had done,' he went on. 'I'm still trying. I will probably be trying till I die.'

'It wasn't –'

'Don't,' he said. 'I told you, I don't want that from you.'

Your fault, I was going to say. I glared out into the desert. Ashes. Let it all be ashes.

'Why must Pergamians insist on so much secrecy about the Lharmellins?' I finally choked out.

He shrugged. 'Because that is the way it has always been. Pergamia has been riddled with harmings since time immemorial and the rulers have always kept the citizens in the dark. This means even the soldiers don't know exactly what they're hunting. I argued with Helmsrid that the only way to remove the

scourge once and for all was to educate the people.'
He gave a hollow laugh. 'I still believed in education,
for all the good it had done me. Helmsrid refused to
even consider it. Simply speaking the words *harming*
or *Lharmellin* is an act of treason against the king of
Pergamia, punishable by death.'

I remembered how reluctant Carmelina had been
to speak the name of her enemy that time in the
palace gardens; how adamant she'd been that I left
well alone. I'd always believed it had been Rodden
to insist upon secrecy, but it seemed the order had
originated higher, from the king himself.

He sighed. 'I've always deemed this profoundly
stupid. Secrecy can only lead to more deaths. Pergamia
is on the front line, the major entry point for Turned
harmings once they return from Lharmell. Through
it they access the rest of the world, overland or by
the ports. As long as King Askar refuses to reveal
the truth to his people, the rest of the world remains
in peril.' Rodden thumped the saddle with his fist.
'He's a fool! I can say that now we are thousands of
miles from the capital: King Askar is a fool, like all
the foolish kings before him.'

'If you think so, why do you stay at the palace?'

Rodden raised a sardonic brow at me. 'The
juiciest books on the Lharmellins, as you well know,

are housed at the palace. In fact, the only books. All others have been destroyed. That penny dreadful you found at the markets last winter – what was it called?'

'*Creetchers Moste Fowl.*'

'That's it. The only one I've seen of its kind. The rest must have been burned. As a scholar – no, as a human being –'

'Of sorts.'

'As someone with half a brain between my ears, then,' he amended, 'I find book burning to be one of the most atrocious crimes a king can commit against his citizens. Open discourse can only strengthen society, but Askar is terrified of widespread panic and civil war if the citizens find out that they've been lied to for centuries. So instead of progress, we have parties. At the very least we should share our knowledge with the other kings and queens of Brivora.'

'You rotten hypocrite! Last winter all I wanted was for you to tell me the truth about the Lharmellins, and you wouldn't. And I'm going to be a ruler of Brivora one day. You knew that and still you kept things to yourself.'

He smiled and rubbed his neck. 'That's because I'm rather attached to my head. Second, you're a harming, and therefore not to be trusted. Third, you're a princess. The only princess I've ever known is Carmelina, and she lives and breathes gossip. But I told you everything eventually, didn't I?'

I snorted. 'I never know with you. You hoard secrets like a squirrel hoards nuts.'

'Habit.'

'Why do you stay in Xallentaria if you can't stand the way King Askar handles things?'

'Because he won't let the blasted books out of the palace! Do you know, when Helmsrid finally sent me to the capital to meet the king, after he first ascertained he wasn't going to be hung, drawn, and quartered for his troubles, I found the tomes kept at the palace on Lharmell hadn't been opened in nearly seventy-five years? They'd been relegated to a locked, damp room in the library and were covered with dust and mouldering with age. Many had to be thrown out. The waste reduced me to tears – these books were one-of-a-kind. Irreplaceable, thanks to the king. It took months of wheedling just to get him to let me take them to my turret. I established myself up there pretty quickly, I can tell you. As far away from everyone else as possible, and I only came down for the most important of state occasions.'

'Like the visit of harming princesses?'

'Quite. And only then for the prettiest ones.'

I glanced away. Yesterday his words would have pleased me. Now they only caused me pain. When my humiliation had dissipated, I asked, 'You said once that you heard me resisting the Lharmellins all the way in Amentia. Have you heard any others?'

'No.'

'A pity. We could use the help.'

He agreed.

Ahead, the dunes stretched to the horizon. 'How much further?' I asked, trying to keep the frustration from my voice.

Rodden was silent, and I knew he was picturing his mind-map. 'If we're lucky, we'll reach the flood-plains tonight.'

'Are we ever lucky?' I grumbled.

He was silent a moment. 'There's something I want you to keep in mind once we arrive at the Jarbin village.'

His tone was careful and I glanced at him in suspicion. 'Oh, yes?'

'There might be harmings.'

'Good. I'll break in my new bow.'

'No, you won't.'

'Why not? I'm dying to shoot something.'

'I'd rather avoid it, if it's all the same to you. There's no guarantee that we'll kill them all, and the last thing we need is to announce our presence while we're stuck in the middle of the desert with no yelbar. I'd like to get back to Pergamia in one piece.'

'But what if we're attacked?'

'Then we defend ourselves. Just don't go starting any fights.'

I sighed. 'Fine.'

'That's not all. Your cloaking is shabby.'

I turned on him, eyes flashing. 'That's not true!'

'Yes it is. Remember the harming in Ercan?'

'He could have picked up on either of us.'

'Then why did he end up in your room? And in Pol, I knew there was a harming following me that day. If I'd bothered to check I would have realised it was you.'

'Why didn't you?'

'Because I thought you were one of Servilock's minions and that I was on the right track. You were lucky I didn't stab you in some dark alleyway.'

'I kept us safe –' My voice hitched. 'I kept us safe those days and nights when we were lost at sea and you were unconscious.'

'Probably a sheer fluke,' he replied. 'And last night …'

I glared at him. 'What about last night?'

He hesitated. 'In the wagon. You were very ... audible.'

Embarrassment flared red in my cheeks. 'I *meant* to be,' I hissed.

'Oh.' It was Rodden's turn to look away. 'Well, despite your other talents, such as wind-drawing, you have trouble concealing your thoughts. So be careful at the Jarbin village, all right?'

'I'm always careful,' I insisted, though it was a lie. I hadn't made a conscious effort to guard my thoughts since we left Pol. But I could do it now. I was certain. As long as I concentrated.

'If you say so.'

We rode in silence after that. Sometime in the early afternoon I saw dark shapes circling in the sky, and remarked, 'The buzzards are following us again.'

———

The first sign that we were approaching the end of our journey was a faint strip of green on the horizon. A ripple of excitement went through the Jarbin. Horses pricked their ears up and strained against their harnesses.

Rodden leaned forward in the saddle. 'We're almost there.'

I shifted restlessly. There were still many miles of sand stretching between us and that hint of vegetation. 'What is that up ahead, anyway? A lake?'

'Used to be. Now it's an oasis.'

'What happened?'

'Time. Hundreds of years ago this whole area for miles around was a vast floodplain, and the oasis was Lake Keole. It was fed by a river that began as run-off from the mountains to the north-west, and swelled by monsoon rains. The monsoon still comes, most years, but the mountains are ice-locked all the year round now. There's not enough melt to feed the river, so it dried up. It flows when the rains come, and then the oasis floods, but not nearly to the extent it used to.'

'Why did the mountains freeze?'

'They just did. Weather patterns change. Temperatures drop.'

'The Lharmellins attempted to freeze Amentia so no one could mine the yelinate,' I pointed out. 'Couldn't they have done the same thing with the mountains? If the oasis dried up completely, could anyone live here to harvest the bennium?'

'No, they couldn't. This is the only waterhole for miles in any direction, and the only place where bennium is found. It's an interesting theory, and possible, I suppose.' He looked worried all of a sudden. 'In fact, you could be right. I don't know why it didn't occur to me.'

Soon our horses trod sparse, low-lying grass instead of sand. Undulating dunes gave way to flat gravel. Smoke from cooking fires rose against a setting sun. Beyond thick reeds I spotted a thin line of silver that must have been the oasis, and a collection of squat huts on the far side. The temperature dropped, muggy but pleasant. I unwound my white outer layers and relished the fresh air against my skin. Instantly I was surrounded by a cloud of whining midges.

'What the – look at these things!' I flapped my scarf at the insects.

Rodden called out to one of the women and she rode back with a jar in her hand.

'What's that?' I asked, as he began rubbing the salve onto his bare arms.

'Mosquito repellent. It's made from natron, the mineral the Jarbin collect and sell in Pol. Here.' He tossed it to me. 'Keep it with you after dark. The mosquitoes carry a nasty fever.'

I rubbed the grainy white cream on my arms and ankles and the midges dissipated. 'Rotten bloodsuckers,' I muttered, and Rodden snorted with amusement.

A ululation filled the evening air, a greeting from the villagers. The Jarbin in our wagon train threw back their heads and sang out in reply. A few riders broke free of the train and cantered to meet the rest of the tribe, who were now emerging from their huts.

Unable to bear being in the saddle a moment longer I dismounted and slid to the ground. Rodden did the same and we led our tired, dusty horses into the Jarbin village. Dozens of men, women and children came forward, deeply tanned with unruly curls. They greeted the travellers with shouts and hugs, and began pulling supplies from the wagons. Several small children, holding fistfuls of their mothers' skirts, stared up at us with large liquid eyes. I smiled at them and they ducked out of sight.

A woman with the longest hair I'd ever seen, past her waist, ran to Uwin, who was just dismounting his horse. She threw her arms around his neck and kissed him. He murmured to her for a moment, and they were an island of stillness among the mayhem. Watching them, I felt a flash of envy.

Uwin led the young woman over to where Rodden and I stood, hovering at the edge of this mass of jabbering people. He made the introductions. I couldn't catch her name but murmured hello, wishing I knew the right word in Jarbin.

The woman turned her eyes on me, and I saw that they were green, not brown like the eyes of the other Jarbin we had travelled with. 'Your Highness, I'm very pleased to make your acquaintance,' she said, dropping into a curtsey so graceful we could have been in the Pergamian court. It was incongruous in this dusty landscape, her barefoot and in trousers. I must have been standing there with my mouth hanging open as Rodden nudged me.

'This is where you say "how do you do". I do apologise, Oilif,' he said, turning to the woman. 'We've been travelling for weeks and it seems the princess has forgotten her manners.'

I scowled at him. 'Rot. I'm tired, that's all, and I haven't understood any voice but yours in forever.' I turned to the woman. 'Sorry, I didn't catch your name.'

'Oilif,' said the woman, smiling and glancing from Rodden to me with evident amusement.

She spoke perfect Brivoran, but in an accent I couldn't place. 'Where are you from?'

'Lippa. On the western coast.'

'I know it – south-west of Amentia, is that right?'

'Yes. It's been so long since I've seen anyone from home. I want to ask you a thousand questions, but you have had a long journey. Can I offer you a bath?'

I was emphatic. 'You certainly can.'

She led me away from Rodden and Uwin to a hut enclosing a well and a flagged floor. In the dim light, Oilif helped me strip off my filthy travelling clothes and then poured ladle after ladle of very cold water over me while I scrubbed myself with rough white soap. When I was clean she wrapped thick white sheets around me.

'Better?'

'Yes, thank you.'

'Come outside and I will comb your hair,' she offered.

We sat on a stone wall facing the sunset, and Oilif pulled the snarls from my hair.

'How did you get here?' I asked.

I heard her snort of amusement. 'How did you? If you don't mind me asking, Your Highness.'

'I asked first. And don't call me that.'

'Very well. I ran away.'

'Oh?' My interest was piqued. I liked the sound of those words. *Run away. A runaway.*

'You're a runaway too, of sorts. Aren't you?'

I turned my head to look at her in surprise. 'Yes, I suppose I am. Of sorts.' I sighed. 'But I have to go back.'

'You don't want to?'

'Not really. But I must.'

'Why?'

Because either my mother or a horde of blood-sucking monsters will hunt me down and kill me if I don't. 'Oh …' I said, giving a blustery sigh. 'It's complicated.'

'It usually is,' she mused. 'Do you love this man?'

'Who, Rodden? We're not – I'm not …' I sighed again.

'Ah. It's complicated too?'

'Yes.'

'Maybe you have not run far enough yet.'

'There's nowhere to run. They'll find us.'

'Your mother and father will never find you in a place like this.' Her voice was dry. 'Trust me, I am living proof.'

'My father's dead, and it's not my mother I fear will find me. Not who I fear the most, at any rate.'

Oilif's hands stilled in my hair. I could feel the question on her lips, but instead she said, 'There are many reasons to run away. Some of them very good reasons. If you have the right reason, when you run you may find happiness. Or you may just run forever, lost.'

I thought of Rodden, running from Servilock for all the right reasons but still unable to find happiness, his demons following him wherever he went.

'But if you run for the wrong reasons,' she continued, 'you will only find misery. There will be no going back, no hope for tomorrow. But either way, right reason or wrong, there will be loneliness, perhaps regret. But if it is truly what you want, or need, you'll have as good a chance as any.'

I frowned. Running away from my mother and my duty to Amentia had never crossed my mind. But once the Lharmellins were defeated ...

The question was, would he run with me? Why would he, if he didn't love me?

'How did you know I want to run away?'

'You have the look of one who is chased.'

I sighed. 'It's all conjecture. I can't run away, not properly. He doesn't love me back.'

'Oh, yes.'

I could hear the amused disbelief in her voice, and it grated. What did she know?

The temperature was dropping and I wrapped the damp sheets tighter around me. I gazed out over the oasis, at the silhouettes of birds as they flew low across the water, black against a darkening sky.

I pushed Oilif's words out of my mind. Rodden

and I would have no peace while the tors still sheltered the Lharmellins. I wanted revenge for what the Lharmellins had done to me, to Rodden, to countless other people before us. I wanted to kill every last one of them. I would do it, too. Or I would die trying.

But then? a small voice asked. If you do kill them all, what then?

If they were all dead, and I was free ...

Would I go home to mother, to marriage? Would I willingly surrender myself?

Or would I run?

I didn't know. I couldn't see beyond the tors and those that resided within. I didn't want to see.

My eyes were closing of their own accord. Oilif put me to bed, where I slept like the dead.

ELEVEN

I woke to find the village quiet and empty. A cup of water and a bread roll had been placed next to my pallet, and a pile of neatly folded clothes. They weren't my clothes, but rather the rough-woven shirts and trousers that I'd seen some of the village women wearing. I drank the water and dressed, and went looking for everyone, chewing the roll. A few hundred yards from the village I spotted a group of people labouring over the flats. The heat rising from the desert blurred the horizon in the distance. As I made my way to the group, the low-growing grass underfoot gave way to white-crusted dried mud. I shielded my eyes. In the glare reflected off the ground, I almost didn't see Rodden.

'Hello, sleeping beauty.' Rodden wiped the sweat

from his brow with the back of his hand, smearing white crystals over his forehead. 'Come to see what the peasants are up to?'

'I was tired,' I said, my voice tart. 'What *are* you up to?'

'Harvesting natron. Are you here to work?' he asked, nodding at my clothes.

I nodded. 'Why not? What do I do?'

He passed me the flat metal object he held in his hand. 'Bend and scrape, Your Highness.'

I took it, biting back an irritated retort.

Rodden went to find another scraper and I watched the other workers for a moment. There didn't seem to be much to it: scrape the white crust from the ground and deposit it in one of the clay trays that were scattered about. The villagers seemed to be avoiding the areas streaked with yellow and grey, so I did too.

After a few minutes of scraping, the natron began to sting the tiny cuts and scratches on my hands worse than salt in a wound.

'What's so good about this stuff, anyway?' I grumbled when Rodden returned. We worked side by side, prising the white crust from the floodplain, avoiding the veins of grey and yellow.

'I'll never understand the ruling classes. You're surrounded by beautiful things every day and you don't think to question where they came from or how they were made.'

I clenched the scraper in my hand. 'Do stop going on about it, Rodden. Every time I start feeling just like any other person, you have to go reminding me I'm not.'

'I don't forget so easily,' he muttered.

'What?'

'Nothing. Do you really want to know about natron?'

'Yes.' It was something to take my mind off the baking hot sun.

'The blue of the Pergamian standard,' Rodden began, bent double with the scraper in his hand, 'is the blue my father used to make. Verapinian blue.'

I glanced at him, wondering if this was bringing up painful memories, but his face was impassive.

'It's a mixture of copper, lime, sand and natron, crushed together and heated in a furnace.'

I leaned on the tip of my scraper. 'This stuff, plus metal and sand, makes blue?' I shook my head. 'I'm astonished, but ...'

'But what?'

'Doesn't it seem an awful lot of bother, transporting natron all that way just to make some blue cloth?'

'Can you see kings and queens – and princesses – dressing themselves in the drab colours of peasants?'

I thought back to my own clothes over the years: scarlets and yellows and purples, the delicate blues and pinks of Lilith's gowns. I hadn't spared one thought for where the cloth had come from. It was just ... there.

'And it's not just for dye. Natron is used for all sorts of things.'

'Like what?'

'Insect repellent, as you know. Soap, lamp oil, teeth cleanser, wound cleanser. It's used to tan leather, preserve meat. My mother used it to bleach fabric. The glassblowers use it to make coloured glass and the potters in their ceramics. It's also used in the rites for the dead.'

'Really? How?'

'It desiccates bodies and preserves them.'

'Why would anyone want to do that?'

'In Brivora you might bury your dead, or cremate them, but in some cultures that's horribly disrespectful, as bad as leaving the bodies to wild animals.'

'What do they do instead?'

'Wrap them in cloth and entomb them.'

I shuddered. 'Sounds lonely.' I wiped my stinging

hands on my trousers. 'Much more of this and you'll be able to entomb me, no rites necessary. Would you look at that?' I held out my reddened hand to Rodden.

'Careful!' He grabbed me before I could plant my foot in the middle of a vein of grey and yellow natron. 'Those impurities in the natron. That's bennium.'

'Is it dangerous?'

'No, but if you stand in it you'll get it mixed in with the sand.'

I looked at the dirty crust on the ground. This was what we'd almost killed ourselves for: a patch of grey and yellow crystals. They seemed so insignificant.

'But this is what we've come all this way for. Why aren't we harvesting it right now?'

'Because that would be rude to our hosts. We do a day's labour. Then we collect the bennium.'

'Tomorrow?'

'Tonight. Before the sun sets and the dew falls. It's best to harvest it at the end of the day.'

I couldn't help grinning at him. 'The glass. The bennium. There's just the yelinate to collect at the mines and we'll be ready.' I stood, arching my back. 'It's a good feeling, Rodden. It's like we're finally getting somewhere.'

He gave me a sardonic smile. 'Well, you're not

getting anywhere fast. Back to work. Did you think this was a holiday, Your –' He caught himself. 'Zeraphina?'

I arched my eyebrow at him. 'Thank you. And no, I was never under the impression that this was a holiday. The sleeping rough, living in constant fear, going unwashed for days, almost dying on several occasions. I figured it out.' Sweat trickled down my forehead and into my eyes. I wiped my brow on my shoulder, not daring to touch my face with my hands.

'We can have a holiday tomorrow, if you like. Do whatever you want. A sort of celebration for getting this far.'

'Really? You wouldn't rather we level a mountain or paint the sky pink?'

He smiled. 'We could perhaps sweep the desert of sand in the afternoon if we got bored.'

'What I want,' I said, staring at the dirt under my fingernails, 'is to spend all day swimming in the oasis.'

'Your wish is my command.' He bowed, as if we were in court and I was in one of my finest dresses. 'Now get back to work, princess.'

———

I stayed by the oasis all day, lying on the banks, getting back in the water as I dried off and grew hot again. The water was deliciously cool with soft, squishy mud at the bottom, waist-deep near the edges and seemingly bottomless in the middle. Oilif had given me a linen bathing wrap. Weeks at sea and in Verapine had taken their toll on my skin: I'd tanned right through my clothes on the trek through the desert and was now a warm brown all over. What would Mother say? I lay on the grassy bank, squinting up at the sky and smiling to myself.

The bennium was safely in our saddle bags: five small sacks of it, a dark crystalline substance. It would be enough to makes hundreds of arrow points once we had the yelinate.

It was odd, this sense of accomplishment. I wasn't used to it. Still smiling, I gazed at the dragonflies that hovered over the glassy surface of the oasis. Grasshoppers creaked and rustled in the reeds. On the far shore stood white cranes, their long black legs descending into the water, thin as twigs. Their heads bobbed this way and that on elegant necks as they scanned the water for titbits.

I could almost pretend I didn't have a care in the world.

There was a mighty roar, and something large

and dark flashed overhead before plunging into the water. The cranes leapt into the sky, honking. I snatched up my bow and had an arrow notched before the last bird had cleared the water.

Rodden's head and torso broke the surface. He shook the water from his hair and grinned at me.

I sagged with relief. 'I could have shot you,' I called, putting my weapon down.

'Well, I would have died happy in the knowledge that I'd impressed some battle-readiness on you.'

I grabbed the bow again. 'I can still shoot you – you're a sitting duck right now,' I threatened.

He laughed and dived under the water. I watched him swim laps. The cranes watched him too, wary of this noisy, splashy intruder.

Eventually Rodden emerged, dripping, and sat beside me on the grass. He pushed the water off his arms and legs as we had no towels. He wore trunks, but I hadn't been this close to him when he'd been wearing so little and I didn't quite know where to look. 'When must we leave?' I asked, sneaking glances at him. He had very long, brown limbs, lightly muscled. I longed to trace with my fingers the silvery scar that ran down his left thigh.

Rodden cleared his throat with a strangled cough.

Horrified, I realised I wasn't concealing my thoughts, and my eyes snapped back to the oasis.

'Tomorrow. The next day at the latest. I've hired us a guide who will escort us to Rilla, south of Pol, where we can get passage to Varlint and then on to Amentia.'

I sighed. 'Another sea-crossing.'

'Yes.' Rodden lay down and covered his eyes in the crook of his elbow.

'Try not to kill yourself vomiting this time.'

'Yes, Your Highness.'

I elbowed him in the ribs.

'Thank you, Your Highness.'

'Oh, shut up.' But I couldn't keep the smile from my voice.

I sat back on my elbows. The only thing that spoils this afternoon, I thought, staring at the sky, are those damned buzzards.

There were five of them, forever circling, as if waiting for something to drop dead. They'd been with us on and off all the way from Pol …

I sat up, peering at the sky. 'Rodden,' I whispered.

'Hmm?'

'Do you notice anything strange about those birds?'

'What birds?'

'The birds right above us.'

Rodden let his arm fall back from his face and squinted up at the sky. Then he sat up. 'Piss and blood,' he swore. 'Do you think they're brants?'

'They've followed us from Pol, I'm sure of it.'

'Why didn't you say anything?'

'I did. I said, "Oh look, the buzzards are back". That's what I thought they were. But look at their wingspan. They're huge. Buzzards aren't normally that big.'

'How's your cloaking?'

'Fine,' I said, and mentally thickened the walls around my mind. 'Do you think they have riders?'

'Undoubtedly. Let's stop staring at them.'

We looked at each other instead. Rodden's jaw clenched. Harmings, here. My skin crawled as I imagined them looking down on us.

'What now?'

'We go back to the village. Slowly. Don't look up.'

Fighting the urge to run or at least notch an arrow in my bow, we walked back to the huts.

'Why haven't they attacked yet?' I hissed. 'What are they waiting for?'

'Put them out of your mind.'

'But what do we do now?' We had no yelbar. Only my bow and a crossbow Rodden had bought himself in Pol to defend ourselves with. We stared round at the Jarbin village: the flimsy reed and mud structures; the children playing tag among the bushes; the old women crouched in doorways, sewing. What had we brought to this peaceful place?

Rodden looked grim. 'We find Uwin.'

———

We sat in our soggy bathing clothes on a reed mat. Oilif offered us tea and cordial, but Rodden shook his head, tight-lipped.

Uwin regarded us with solemn eyes as Rodden explained what we'd seen. For once there was no glimmer of amusement on his face. I began to shiver in my damp clothes, though not from cold.

Rodden reached the end of his short speech, and said one word over and over. '*Lika.*'

'What's *lika*?' I asked.

'"I'm sorry",' murmured Oilif, draping a blanket round my shoulders.

I turned to Uwin, pressing a hand to my breast. '*Lika.*' I felt wretched that we'd put the villagers in danger.

Uwin shook his head and began to talk, addressing both Rodden and I though I couldn't understand a word he was saying. The conversation went back and forth between the pair and I clenched my thumbs in my fists to prevent myself from crying out in frustration.

Finally, Rodden turned to me. 'He says once we're alone in the desert with our guide, the harmings will attack. So he won't give us a guide.'

'Could we get to Rilla by ourselves?'

'We'll be killed. Five harmings on brants against two with no yelbar, we don't stand a chance.' Rodden glanced at Uwin, and then at me. 'He wants to help us fight them.'

'No. These people are dancers, not fighters. And besides, it's our fight, not theirs. We can't ask them to put themselves in danger.'

Rodden repeated what I'd said. Uwin jutted his chin and motioned for us to follow him outside. He called out to a clutch of young men standing in the shade of an awning, and watched them, hands on hips, as they scattered, grabbing things from inside the huts. With a flick of his hand he bade us follow him to the eastern side of the oasis. Overhead I felt the birds tracking us. I called to Leap and Griffin with my mind, needing them close. Griffin alighted on my arm, wings hunched.

'Griffin didn't even know,' I said to Rodden. 'She could always sense harmings in Lharmell.'

Rodden shook his head. 'I'm a fool. I don't know why I thought we could outwit them. We're harmings, just like they are. They know exactly what we're capable of and our weaknesses too.'

I looked back and saw that the village men were following us, coils of rope and wickedly curved hooks in their hands. Their expressions were grim, and I remembered the ferocity of the sword dance in the desert.

We entered a copse of trees, the canopy so thick it blocked out the sky. The harmings wouldn't be able to see what we were up to.

Uwin turned and called back to the men, and they jogged past us. On Uwin's command they surrounded a dirty blob, eight feet tall, made entirely of mud.

'What is that?' I asked Rodden.

'A termite mound. Stand back.'

The men swung the metal hooks over their head, faster and faster. Each hook resembled an anchor, but barbed on four sides instead of two and twice a hand-span in size. Uwin barked a command and the men swung faster, so fast that the hooks became a blur. On his word they let fly; the barbs whistled through the air, wrapping around the mound and embedding with a dull thud. The men grasped the ropes and pulled. The mound imploded with a crack, sending up plumes of dust and termites.

I hastened back as thousands of tiny pale bodies erupted out of the shattered earth.

A whirring sound filled the air and I turned quickly, anticipating an attack from vengeful insects. Oilif stood with a half-dozen women, all whirling bolas above their heads. They were long ropes that split at the end into three cords tied with weights. I'd seen them for sale but never in action. Fascinated, I watched as Oilif cried out a command and the women flung the bolas. Six men, including Rodden and Uwin, found themselves hobbled as the ropes encircled their legs. Rodden grasped my shoulder for balance. He glanced around at the Jarbin, all straight-backed with ferocious expressions.

'All right, then,' he said.

———

'There.' I pointed to the eastern edge of the flood-plain. 'That's where we surrender.' I stood with Rodden, Uwin and Oilif on the edge of the village, hidden under the eave of a hut. 'The trees surround that spit on three sides. They don't give complete cover, but it should be enough.'

Rodden turned to Uwin. 'We might not kill them all. If a harming escapes back to Lharmell with the news the Jarbin have allied themselves with us, there will be nothing I can do to help you. Zeraphina and I must get back to Pergamia as quickly as possible.'

Uwin bade us follow him to a mud-brick building. He waved the two guards aside and ushered us in. The afternoon light barely touched the room, but my rapidly adjusting eyes saw a tell-tale orange glow. Lining the walls of the room were swords, spears and daggers, all glowing faintly orange. Yelbar weapons.

'Stars above,' Rodden breathed, reaching for a sword and then thinking better of it.

'They're very old, but they're in perfect condition,' Oilif said. 'There are tales, you see, of creatures that attacked and killed our ancestors, and only a special type of weapon would work against them. This stock-pile has been maintained in case we ever need them again. We listen to our old stories, you see.'

I turned to her. 'You know how the truth about the Lharmellins has been suppressed on Brivora,' I guessed.

'I thought they were superstition and nonsense. But they're not. The bennium draws them here from time to time. They froze the mountains to the north, but they cannot stop the monsoon.'

I'd been right about the mountains. The Lharmellins had locked up all the water in the ice caps.

I noticed she made no distinction between harmings and Lharmellins: she didn't realise that the ones who froze the mountains and the ones who had come from the north to attack the Jarbin were two different creatures. They knew enough to keep the weapons, but not more. I didn't want to disabuse her and the rest of the village of the notion, fearing she'd discover that Rodden and I were harmings too.

She gazed at the weapons. 'So we are not helpless after all. We have found ways of protecting ourselves.'

'I can see that,' Rodden said. 'Pity there are no yelbar-tipped arrows in your armoury.'

Oilif translated for Uwin, and the man snorted. He hefted a sword from the rack. Rodden and I stepped back instinctively. Uwin gazed at the weapon, the sharp metal lit from within. A harming wouldn't hesitate to attack a sailor who carried a cutlass, but they would think twice about coming near the bearer of such a sword. I didn't need anyone to translate Uwin's words.

Who needs arrows when you have this?

With our weapons concealed in our packs, Rodden and I sauntered west of the village, unhurried. I had my bow and Rodden his crossbow. We each had a yelbar dagger, gifts from Uwin, sheathed at our belts. Rodden had taken them gingerly from the man, thanking him but suggesting quietly that I fetch our gloves. We hadn't told the Jarbin of our harming blood, nor had they asked why the brant-riders were so interested in us. We let them assume that it was because we sought yelbar for the king of Pergamia. Which was half-true.

Overhead, the brants tracked our progress. We were drawing them away from the village to give the Jarbin time to secrete themselves among the thin scrub and trees that bordered the eastern corner of the floodplain. The men had their barbed hooks and ropes and the women their bolas.

We reached the oasis and stopped. I tried not to think of the Jarbin hidden in ambush. Rodden's foot beat the ground in an irregular tattoo.

'I don't like this at all,' he muttered. 'We're putting these people in danger for no one's benefit but our own.'

'They are fully informed and helping us willingly,'

I countered. 'You just have trouble relying on anyone but yourself.'

'I wonder if they know what they're getting themselves into. It's my responsibility to get us home safely. Not theirs.'

'Don't I get a say in this? I'm the one the harmings are after for killing the Lharmellin leader.'

'You know I would have that another way also, if I could.'

'You can't have all the glory.'

'I don't want glory, I want you to –'

'Oh, shut up.'

The sun had begun its descent and the shadows were lengthening. There were three more hours until sunset. I hoped it would be enough time to lure the harmings from the sky and kill them. 'Do you think the Jarbin are in position yet?'

'A little longer.'

The silence stretched, punctuated by the drowsy chirps of crickets among the reeds.

I took a deep breath. 'Oilif ran away from home.'

'Oh, yes,' Rodden said. His eyes darted over the surface of the oasis. He was too distracted to listen. Perhaps this wasn't the best time to discuss the idea that had been forming in my mind since I'd spoken to the leader's wife.

I glanced towards the village. Not a creature stirred.

'All right,' Rodden said, hefting his pack higher on his shoulder. 'Let's go and surrender.'

Like moths to a flame, the harmings wheeled their mounts to follow our progress back through the village and out onto the plain. We dumped our bags on the dried mud.

'Ready?' Rodden asked.

I nodded. We looked up at our enemy. Pushing all thoughts of the Jarbin out of my mind, I let down my walls. With not a little malice I brought forth my memories of killing the Lharmellin leader, its brackish blood flowing in rivers down my arms. With the full force of my resentment, I flung these pictures at the harmings.

I did it. It was me.

From their great height, I heard the harmings scream in anger. The brants dipped and wheeled violently as they sensed their masters' turmoil.

My memories had a bigger effect than I'd expected. They actually seemed to be in pain.

'Can you sense that?' I whispered to Rodden.

'Yes,' he said, frowning. 'Your memories seem to be hurting them. Can you do it again?'

I did, and they yelled in fury. One brant broke

from the others, drew in its wings and hurtled to the ground. It landed at speed and staggered, twenty yards from where we stood. The harming rider dismounted, his body tight with anger. He approached, halting at ten paces distant. The desert sun had not been kind to him. His face and hands were a mass of angry red blisters. Breathing heavily, he snarled, 'You! You are the traitorous one.'

'Glory to Lharmell,' I hissed.

'We wish to parley,' Rodden said. He nodded at the sky. 'With all of you.'

The harming's lip curled. 'You do not order us, you traitorous wretch.'

'Zeraphina, show them again what you did to their beloved leader.'

With all my strength I hurled my memories of the Turning at the five harmings. The screams of the dying Lharmellin. The orange light in its eyes as the yelbar coursed through its body; the screams of the crowd as they beheld their dying leader. I showed them the arrows sprouting from the other Lharmellins and their bodies crumpling and smoking. And then I showed them our escape.

There were screams of anger overhead.

'We will come willingly,' said Rodden, 'as we realise we will never make it out of this desert alive. The Jarbin refuse to help us or hide us. But we will discuss the terms of our capture with you first. We've killed many of your kind and my friend here would be more than pleased to share her memories with you.' Rodden gave his most charming smile. 'Please. Indulge us.'

The harming shot us a look of pure loathing. Silently, the brants above began their descent. One after the other, they landed with a thud on the cracked ground, encircling us. The riders slithered from their mounts.

The first harming glared at us. 'Tell us your terms, and be quick about it.'

Rodden wet his lips. I heard a whirring sound from the bushes. Two harmings cocked their ears to the sound. The first stared at us, puzzled at our silence. Then he too heard the low humming that filled the air and realised his mistake. 'It's a trap!' he screamed.

They leapt for their mounts as the Jarbin let fly. Two brants were ensnared with ropes and pulled to the ground. They screamed and lashed out with their beaks and talons. Three harmings found their legs hobbled by bolas but one was already worming herself free. She and another leapt for Rodden.

The first harming came at me.

'You will die a thousand deaths,' he screamed. He was weaponless, but I saw the mad glint in his eye and didn't doubt that he was strong enough to tear me limb from limb with his bare hands.

I whipped the yelbar dagger from its sheath and dropped into a crouch. 'One death from you is all I require.' My heart pounded in my chest. I wished for the certainty of a bow but the harming was too close. I'd practised knife-fighting with Rodden but this was the real thing. As the harming lunged, instinct kicked in and I dodged his attack. I slashed at his arm but he was quick to avoid me.

The screams of harmings and brants filled the air. The Jarbin were now on the floodplain and I heard the whirr of bolas again. Out of the corner of my eye I saw Rodden cut the throat of a harming and let her fall to the ground. The body began to smoke and burn before her dying gurgles had faded.

I struck out with the knife, but the harming evaded my blow and kicked me in the stomach. I fell to my knees, winded, and the harming was on me, pushing me flat and trying to wrest the dagger from my grasp. His cracked and burned face was inches from my own.

'The Great One will visit such agonies upon your body,' the harming growled, spittle flying from its lips.

I elbowed him in the nose, hard. There was a

crack and blood spurted over both of us. He howled in pain and I took the chance to buck his body off mine. Knife firmly in my grasp, I sank both my knees onto the harming's shoulders, pinning his arms. I pressed the tip of the blade against his throat and watched the skin sizzle. He glared up at me through the blood on his face.

'Who is the Great One?' I demanded, pressing the point harder.

'Torrents of poison rain will strip the flesh from your bones,' he said, somewhat hoarse from the pressure on his windpipe. 'Your accomplice will have his body torn asunder by the power of the tors and we will drink his corpse dry.'

'*Who is it?*'

The harming began to laugh.

I flipped the knife in my grasp and smashed the hilt into his broken nose. He howled. 'You will show me who it is and where they are.'

The harming still laughed, his mirth punctuated with grimaces and hisses of pain.

He was not going to reveal anything, no matter how hard I beat him. I remembered the way the harming in Ercan had plundered my mind, searching for information. I could do the same, I realised. Or I could at least try.

I shot thoughts like arrows into his mind. They were deflected easily. I called to mind shooting the harmings in the pass at Lharmell as Rodden summoned the brant from its nest, and I flung that memory at the harming.

He stopped laughing. Rage parted the walls of his mind and images tumbled through. I was ready for them. Pictures of Lharmell. The forest and the tors. Then places I hadn't seen before. A vast, underground cavern. Hundreds of harmings, their faces upturned in admiration for a figure I couldn't make out. I had to know who it was, who had taken over and was making the harmings smarter since last winter.

The harming heaved his body under me and the images stopped.

'Show me who it is,' I demanded, and punched him with my fist, splitting the knuckles of my glove on his teeth. My hand stung.

I bombarded him with memories of killing his kind, but he was ready this time and his mind stayed tight as a vice.

Anger flared. I would do this for Rodden. Rage made me strong. I punched him again.

He laughed, spat blood, and laughed some more.

I stood and pushed the sweat and blood and hair back from my face. 'Tell me!' I screamed. 'If you don't I will kill you.'

The harming giggled at my feet despite the oozing blood and his burned flesh.

I tightened my grip on the yelbar knife. 'This is for Rodden,' I said. My arm rose, and plunged.

Hands caught my wrist. I struggled against them. I was blinded by blood and sweat but could still tell enemy from friend.

'No! Rodden, let me go.'

'Give me the dagger.'

'I want to kill this one. Let me at least kill this one.'

He wrested the knife from my grasp and threw it far from my reach. Grabbing a fistful of the harming's cloak, Rodden dragged him a few yards from me and dispatched him with his own bloodied dagger. Then he threw the knife aside.

Silence fell, broken only by the scratching of talons on mud and the brants' weakened cries.

Rodden knelt beside me. 'Give me your hands.' He stripped off my gloves and cradled my bleeding hands in his lap.

'I wanted to kill one for you,' I said.

He smoothed the hair back from my face and

wiped away some of the blood. His own face was splattered with gore. Looking into my eyes, he smiled. 'Thank you. What is it they say? "It's the thought that counts"?'

My shoulders shook with mirth and tears.

The Jarbin receded, leaving us alone on the blood-soaked plain with the blackened bodies of our enemies.

TWELVE

Eventually, Leap and Oilif approached. Leap's eyes were large with worry. Rodden was bandaging my knuckles while I sniffled my way back to composure.

'Look at you,' Oilif tutted, surveying us.

We were both covered in blood. Well, I was spattered. Rodden was soaked.

Leap sniffed at my sticky hands and had a tentative lick. 'Yuck,' I said, holding them out of his reach. 'One of us doing that is quite enough,' I whispered to him.

Rodden got to his feet. 'I must talk to Uwin.'

'It can wait, surely,' said Oilif. 'We'll get cleaned up and see to these birds –'

Rodden cut her off. 'Zeraphina and I must leave, and by nightfall there must be no trace of what happened here. There will be more harmings on brant-back sent to relieve the ones we killed, and if they realise the Jarbin had anything to do with their disappearance, and ours, it will be the worse for you. Yelbar weapons or no.'

Oilif paled, and nodded.

'Will you go with Zeraphina and help her get our things ready? We'll need warm travelling clothes, if you can spare them.'

Ignoring both Rodden and Oilif's offered hands, I struggled to my feet. Rodden held his knife and I realised what he meant to do. I looked at the brants, which were struggling against their bonds. They were magnificent creatures and had never done us any harm of their own volition.

'Must you kill them?' I asked. They reminded me of Griffin.

Rodden pressed his lips into a grim line. 'Not all of them.'

Oilif began to lead me away, but I stopped. 'Wait. I must tell you something, Rodden.'

When Oilif had receded out of earshot I said, 'I saw something in that harming's mind. A Turning, I think. But it was underground, and it wasn't a Lharmellin that was leading it. In fact, there weren't any Lharmellins that I could see.'

Rodden considered this. 'A harming.' He frowned. 'The taking of destitutes, and sailors from ships. These are new things. Innovations. Lharmellins aren't much good at innovation.'

'It's the Lharmellins that have control of the weather, though. The real control, not like my wind-calling. If Amentia has thawed, but the harmings are still active, do you think it could mean the harmings have taken over?'

Rodden looked alarmed. 'But that's unheard of. Why would they do that?'

'Maybe they're impatient. Maybe they're sick of waiting for the Lharmellins to turn things in their favour.'

He nodded. 'It makes sense. You know,' he said ruefully, 'this could be our doing. Killing the Lharmellin leader – it might have been the catalyst for the harmings to take charge.'

'You mean we might have done more harm than good,' I said grimly.

'Possibly.'

'The enclaves that are being set up. They could be springing up all over Brivora. What if it's those we need to put a stop to, and not go back to Lharmell at all?'

He shook his head. 'You saw whoever it was in

Lharmell. The harming who is leading is directing things from there. They'll still need the Turning ceremony to create more of their number. They won't have done away with the Lharmellins entirely. The caves you saw, I've heard about them. They're underneath the tors. My guess is the Turnings have been moved there.'

'Is this going to make things harder for us?'

He squeezed my arm. 'You know, it might actually mean the opposite.'

———

By the time I'd bathed and changed, the shadows were lengthening on the ground and the beginnings of a large pit were being dug in the soft ground beneath a copse of trees. Beside it were piled the harming corpses and three dead brants. On the floodplain, children were scattering dirt over the evidence of our skirmish.

Alone, I carried an armful of clean clothing towards Rodden, who was washing at the edge of the oasis. His shirt was damp and streaked with red, but his face and neck were clean.

'Here.' I passed him a towel, and in turn he gave me a flask of blood. I knew what blood in the evenings meant: we weren't sleeping that night.

I sniffed the contents and recognised the musky odour. Brant blood. It was richer than the small-animal blood we'd existed on for weeks. I drank half and felt like I could run to the moon.

'All of it,' Rodden said as I tried to pass it back. 'I've got my own, and more for later.'

I drank the rest and wondered when I could expect to sleep again. 'Did you kill all five of the harmings?' I asked, turning away while he dressed.

'Yes.'

'How did it feel?'

'I don't remember.'

'Rot. You just don't want to tell me.'

He was silent. I heard the whisper of cloth against skin and the sound of his belt being buckled.

'I swore I would kill one. Ever since you told me about Servilock and your family I've wanted to.'

'You've killed harmings before. Doubtless you will again.'

'I want to do it with my hands, using a knife. A bow isn't the same. You said so yourself.'

'Zeraphina –'

'And don't tell me girls shouldn't say such things, or it's not my place because I'm a princess. I'm a harming, the same as you, and it's my right if I want to.' My voice grew shrill. I was drained from the fight, but pepped from all the blood, a strange combination that was making my heart race, fast and light.

'You can turn around now.'

I turned. He stood, hands on hips. 'What do you want me to say? "I'm sorry for not letting you kill the harming"?'

'Yes.'

'Too bad. I won't. If I'd been busy fighting and you'd killed that harming, then so be it. But what sort of person would I be if I'd stood by while you killed the harming when it was already at your mercy, knowing how I have been tormented by memories of doing just that?'

It irked that he felt he had the right to *let* me do things or not.

'I can see you're annoyed,' he went on. 'It's not because you're a girl, or a princess. I swear. I would do the same for anyone who wasn't used to killing.'

'Are you mad? I *am* used to killing. I do it all the time.'

'Not with a knife.' Rodden set his teeth. 'I am touchy about knives, all right?'

'Oh.' His family. Ilona. How he'd murdered them. 'I'm sorry. Of course you are.'

His eyes dropped to the ground. I closed the distance between us and wrapped my arms around his neck. I pressed my cheek against the dampness there. He smelled of sunlight and rough soap.

After a moment, he clasped me back. Where our chests touched I felt a low vibration spread through me, right to my fingertips and down to my toes. I never wanted to let him go.

Finally, I had to, but he seemed reluctant to pull away also. My hands trailed down his sleeves and over his fingertips, and then the contact was broken.

Rodden's eyes met mine, and his face looked warm beneath his tan. 'Now,' he said, voice husky, 'let's go and say thank you to the Jarbin for saving our sorry skins.'

———

At the edge of the pit, which was now heaped with corpses and rapidly filling with dirt, we said our goodbyes. When it came time for me to farewell Oilif, I flung my arms around her neck.

'I wish I'd had time to ask you what your right reasons were for running away,' I whispered.

'It's my story. Very different from yours.'

'You could write to me. At the palace at Xallentaria. Or Amentia. I'd get your letters eventually. And I'd write back.'

'I will.' She released me.

'I don't have many friends, you see.'

Oilif smiled. 'I promise I'll write. Perhaps you could come and visit me one day.'

'I would like that very much.' I thought of us returning, free from both Lharmell and our duties to Pergamia and Amentia. Just as we were. Runaways who had found a new home. Sadness crested inside me as I realised that the obstacles between now and that future were too numerous to count.

Uwin gathered me up in a big bear hug. I murmured '*preibek*' a few times and he beamed.

And then it was just Rodden, Leap, Griffin and I again, a few hundred yards from the village, facing two tethered and furious brants. They shrieked when they saw us, and Leap flattened himself to the ground. Magnificent they were, but cranky also. We sent calming thought-patterns to them and they quieted somewhat, but they still had a vicious glint in their eyes.

'Easy,' I murmured as I approached one. I sent the feeling with my mind as well. It was used to mental orders, and when I asked it to it crouched low to the ground and allowed me to mount. Leap jumped up before me, curling against my belly, and Griffin flew to my gauntleted wrist.

Rodden mounted and gathered his cloak about him. 'It's going to be cold up there at night,' he warned. 'Are you ready?'

I nodded.

'All right then. To Amentia.'

'Lucky, lucky me,' I muttered, as the brants beat their wings and we lurched into the sky. We flew south-east, with the setting sun behind us and the pain of the tors between our shoulderblades.

———

Amentia wasn't quite our next stop. We rested the brants for several hours just outside Rilla before we attempted the ocean crossing. In the midnight darkness we stood on the outskirts of the city and we shared a flask of blood. My hands were stiff from my knuckle wounds and holding onto the brant in the cold upper air.

'We'll rest in Varlint for a day,' Rodden murmured in the darkness. 'These birds won't make it all the way to Amentia without a proper rest.'

'Varlint has plenty of unpopulated forest,' I said, remembering from my trip there with Lilith and Renata to meet my sister's first betrothed. 'We've got supplies so we won't need to approach a town.'

We clambered back aboard our mounts. Between Rilla and Varlint the Osseran was narrow, but I still felt sick with apprehension. The sea was no longer my friend. It was a deadly, unforgiving force. We wouldn't be so lucky this time if we were plunged into its briny depths.

When dawn came, I saw the blue-black waters far beneath us and broke out in a cold sweat. My stomach lurched. There was no land as far as the eye could see. My brant was tiring. The muscle ache of its wings was becoming my own. I twisted in the saddle and saw Rodden a score of yards behind me and slightly to my right, rigid on his mount. Our eyes met briefly. I saw the white of his knuckles where he clasped the reins. We'd held the thread between us like a life-line all the long night so as not to lose each other in the darkness. As the sky lightened I felt his mind gradually retreat.

Leap wriggled against me and I urged him to be still. It was a long, long way down.

An hour after dawn, I spotted the coast. We flew several miles inland to what we hoped was uninhabited forest, and began a slow, circling descent. As soon as my bird's talons thudded against the leaf litter, I slithered to the ground. My legs were numb with tension. I heard Rodden touch down a few seconds later, and wordlessly we led our exhausted brants to a nearby stream and let them drink their fill. I washed my face and hands and then sat back on my heels, watching Leap. He stood gingerly on a wet rock and lapped up water with a pink tongue.

Rodden strung his crossbow with stiff fingers. 'Meat for the birds,' he muttered.

I strung my bow as well. Griffin and Leap disappeared among the greenery on a hunt of their own.

On the edge of an emerald clearing, Rodden and I picked off three rabbits and a duck. We fed them in gory pieces to our famished brants. I'd had enough of blood and guts to last me at least a week so ate some of the bread Oilif had packed for us instead.

'Travelling by brant,' I said, mouth full, sitting on my cloak, 'might be cold and exhausting and terrifying, but it's the only way to see the world. No vomiting. No mad sailors.'

'Just the attention of any harmings that might see us fly over.'

'I'll take the harmings over the mad sailors any day. We can handle harmings.'

Rodden lay down on the mossy ground, his eyes

already closing. 'We'll travel by darkness tonight and should reach the palace at Amentia at dawn.'

I was filled with excitement and terror at the prospect. I was glad to see my home again, but fearful at the same time. 'If you leave me there,' I warned Rodden, 'I will hunt you down and feed you to my brant.' My threat was met with silence as he was already asleep.

———

From the sky I could see the drastic change in my homeland. The rivers resembled thick lengths of rope. They were swelled with mountain melt and meandered across the countryside. The roads were still in an awful state, but even at this early hour they hummed with traffic.

It was heading into autumn and by now the landscape should have been dulled by frosts. But the forests and pastures were verdant. Amentia had thawed.

I was excited to see the change. Had Rodden and I done this? I hadn't quite believed my mother when she'd written of the temperate weather, but now I was seeing it with my own eyes. Was this the first indication that things were turning in our favour?

The castle was perched on high ground east of Prestoral, our capital, which was roughly the size of Jefsgord. We skirted the city, flying high above the neat houses, banked, and made for the castle. Among the ash and aspen I saw the Amentine banner flying above the battlements, a golden griffin on a rich red background. My heart swelled with pride. I was home.

Manoeuvring to land in the tiny courtyard was tricky. I went first while Rodden circled above. The castle walls rushed up to meet me and the brant's talons clicked loudly on stone. Griffin was jolted awake. Leap looked this way and that, as if unable to believe where he was, and then scampered straight to the kitchens.

I jumped to the ground.

From a stairwell, a serving girl carrying a pail was staring at me, struck dumb. ''Oo are you?' she asked.

At the sound of her voice, my brant swivelled and pinned the girl with its glittering black eyes. It opened its enormous black beak and hissed. She screamed, dropped the pail, and dashed inside the castle, her cries trailing after her up the stairs. Milk pooled white over the flagstones.

I sighed, and searched the sky for Rodden.

'What the heavens.'

I turned. Renata strode through the main arch, encased in russet silk. Her red hair flamed and her eyes blazed. She took in the brant, my dishevelled figure, and she folded her arms. 'Oh, *Zeraphina*,' she said, managing to fill that one phrase with an avalanche of derision and disappointment.

The sky darkened above us. Rodden's brant, wings stretched to their full five-metre span, talons extended, was poised to land.

Renata screamed, her lungs seemingly twice the capacity of the kitchen girl's. Griffin, my brant, and I all winced. The bird landed, Rodden slid off, and Renata's screams died in her throat.

'*You*,' she accused. 'So it is true.' She glared at both of us. 'I did pray that letter was your idea of a joke. Just what has been going on?'

Rodden, face impassive, clicked his heels smartly and bowed. 'Your Majesty.'

Renata's desire to lose her temper warred with her need for composure. Propriety won out. She drew herself up to her full height. 'Thank you for bringing my daughter back to me, Lothskorn, whatever state she might be in. See my steward for anything you may require for your return journey.'

Her meaning was clear: Rodden was to get out of her sight as soon as possible.

She turned to me. '*Up*stairs.' She marched inside.

I kept my grasp on the brant's reins and looked at Rodden, white-hot anger burning inside me. 'How dare she dismiss you in such a way? You're the king's man and you deserve respect, especially here in Amentia. She has a lot to be thankful to you for. Lilith's marriage, for a start. And you were the one to follow me to Lharmell when I was taken there.'

'It is the reception I expected.' Rodden began to unsaddle his brant. 'Now, where do you suppose we'll put our birds?'

'We'll leave them right here,' I said. 'Right where she can see them. Besides, they'll terrify the horses if we try to stable them.'

Sensation prickled down my spine. I whirled around. A man with half-lidded eyes was leaning against a stone archway, watching us. He looked first at Rodden, then at me, cocking one eyebrow as he assessed our appearance. He was dressed in black, and his smartly pinned-up cloak was lined with dark red velvet. A sword was slung at his left hip – he was a noble then. I recognised his broad face as he smiled; an amused, faintly disgusted expression. Prince Folsum.

'Hello, sweeting,' he said.

My hands fell from the saddle buckle that I'd

been worrying at. There was dread in the pit of my stomach. I didn't like that he was here, not one bit.

'I should run you through with my sword, Lothskorn. What the deuce have you been doing to my bride?'

Folsum's face was impassive, but I caught the menace in his tone.

Anger flared in my breast. 'You have no right to claim me so.'

The lidded eyes flashed. 'But my dear, I do. I have the consent of both the Queen of Amentia and the King of Pergamia.'

'You are forgetting my own right, my lord. The right to refuse you.'

Folsum laughed. He cast a look at Rodden and the amusement died on his face. 'Aren't you forgetting something, Lothskorn?'

Rodden's jaw clenched with anger. He straightened and made to bow.

I clutched his arm. 'Don't you dare bow to him.'

Rodden pulled away and gave Folsum a cursory bow. 'Your Highness,' he growled.

'That's better. We can't have you forgetting your place. Now, run along.' Folsum made a shooing motion with his fingers.

Rodden stared long and hard at Folsum. The prince fingered the gloves in his pocket as if he'd like nothing more than to slap Rodden for insolence.

Rodden turned on his heel, and I just caught his muttered, 'I'll be with the servants.'

'Far too much pride in that one,' Folsum said. 'He's been given free rein in Pergamia. It would never happen in Ansengaad. We know our place in Ansengaad. Or we're made to find it, damned quickly.' He looked hard at me.

'Rodden Lothskorn has done more for all of Brivora in six months than you could ever hope to achieve in a lifetime.'

Folsum ignored me, his eyes on our brants. 'Incredible creatures. I've read about them in esoteric travel journals. I thought them to be fictitious, or at the very least extinct.' He stepped towards them across the flags. The brants watched him, black eyes flashing. We might have only recently stolen them from the harmings and pushed them to their limits of exhaustion, but both birds could detect my loathing of this man, and they'd decided they didn't like him either.

I slipped their tethers free while Folsum's eyes were elsewhere.

'Beautiful,' he murmured, his eyes running over

the brants' wickedly curved beaks. 'Imagine the possibilities for war.' He reached for one and its hackles rose in warning. Folsum was either too stupid or too arrogant to heed it, and the moment his hand brushed the bird's feathers it lashed out, snapping at Folsum's shoulder with its beak. The leather of his jacket was sliced open. Folsum flung himself back, gasping, as the two birds advanced on him. They towered over him, wings raised, necks elongated. A low, steady hiss emanated from their open beaks.

'Call them off!' he yelled. He was backed against the courtyard walls. I directed the brants to herd him back out through the archway, urging them not to hurt him but to hiss as much as they liked. Finally, he turned and ran. The brants closed their beaks and returned to me.

I raked my fingers through my hair and tried not to cry out in frustration. I should never have listened to Rodden. It had been a huge mistake to come home.

THIRTEEN

There was a steaming bath in my room when I finally climbed the stairs into the keep. When Renata turned from stoking the fire her face was an angry red.

'Undress her,' she snapped at the maid. It was another girl I didn't recognise. There had been changes to the castle while I'd been gone. New tapestries and furniture. New servants. The place hummed with life, and with money. Renata herself was dressed head to toe in new attire, and she'd grown plump.

I bade the girl to stop. 'Thank you, but you may go.'

Renata looked on, arms folded, as I stripped off the rough Jarbin attire.

'Must you watch?' I asked.

'Indeed I must,' she insisted. She glanced at my stomach as I pulled off my shirt. 'You don't show. Not yet, at any rate.'

I frowned in confusion, and then flushed as I understood her meaning. '*Mother*. I'm not with child. Rodden never touched me.'

She sniffed. 'We'll see. You're nothing but skin and bones so we shall know soon enough.' She began rolling her sleeves up. 'Gallivanting all over the world without a chaperone, and with a man such as he. What was Lilith thinking letting you go?'

'Lilith didn't *let* me do anything. It was my decision.'

She pointed at the tub with an imperious finger. 'Scrub.'

I stepped into the tub and the hot water enveloped me. 'Being a harming does not make Rodden depraved or wicked. After all, I'm –'

A basin of hot water was tipped over my head, making me gasp. I sat in sullen silence while she worked my hair into a lather.

After several more basins of water had been tipped over me without warning, and Renata was working oil through my hopelessly tangled hair, I asked, 'What's *he* doing here?'

'He, if you are referring to Prince Folsum, is here because I invited him. He's an extremely suitable match for you. Not only will he be king of Ansengaad one day, but he's willing to overlook your recent indiscretions. As well as ... other things.'

I stiffened. 'Other things? What other things.'

Renata was silent.

'He thinks I'm a bastard, doesn't he?'

Renata tugged her fingers viciously through my hair. 'Watch your tongue.'

'Ow! Mother, how could you let him think such a thing, about both of us?'

'What else can I let him think? There are no portraits of you father anywhere but everyone knows he was fair as can be. And your eyes. How else am I to explain you?'

'The world has gone mad. Why not the truth? Why is everyone so afraid of the truth? There are monsters in the north!' I began to holler at the top of my lungs. 'There are monsters in –'

Another basin of water was dumped over my head and I came up spluttering. 'Stop *doing* that.'

'Keep your voice down. Do you wish to lose your head? A harming daughter,' Renata moaned, 'and her sister wedded to the future king of Pergamia. We shall all be burned at the stake.' She grabbed a scrubbing brush and began attacking my skin. 'You must marry, Zeraphina, and it must be soon. I haven't forgotten your birthday. You're seventeen now. It's time you did your duty, just like Lilith has.'

'Happy birthday to me,' I muttered, pushed this way and that as Renata scrubbed at me.

'Ansengaad is far to the south, and I think that's for the best. Far away from Lhar–' She caught herself. 'That place. And from Pergamia. It's too dangerous for you to ever go northwards again. I've told Folsum you must stay in the south and he has assured me he will see that my wishes are carried out.'

'How could you do such a thing? Am I to be a prisoner in Ansengaad, my husband my jailer? Am I never to see my sister again?' But it wasn't the thought of my sister that made my throat ache with despair. If I was never to go north, I would never see Rodden again. Not even across the high table at Xallentaria.

'She may come to you,' Renata said. 'And you may visit me here after you have provided your husband with an heir. Until then you must stay away for your own good.'

I watched through blurred eyes as she began scrubbing the dirt from under my fingernails. A prisoner who must bear her foul husband sons. Between the two of us, what sort of monstrous children would we have?

Renata saw my anguish. 'And of course, there's the other reason why it's best you stay away from the north.'

'Nothing happened, mother,' I insisted, my voice thick. 'He never touched me.'

'Maybe not. But you wanted him to.'

'You don't know that.'

'I saw how you were mooning over him when you returned from Lhar– that place. Doubtless he saw it too. If you're speaking the truth, and he hasn't touched you, Lothskorn may have some honour after all.'

Tears spilled over my cheeks. 'He's the best person I've ever known.'

Renata sighed. 'Do stop blubbering. We all have crushes when we're young, and we grow out of them. Now, out of the tub.'

She wrapped me in towels, sat me in a chair and began clipping my ragged nails and rubbing lotion into my roughened hands and feet. I let her, too limp from exhaustion and heartache to do anything else.

'I may have married a landless fourth son,' she said, 'but he was still a prince and I had the means for us both. You have nothing entailed on you and that man is a commoner. A foreign one to boot.'

'He's not a commoner, he's the Honourable Rodden Lothskorn, King Askar's right-hand man.'

'A commoner with a fancy title is still a commoner. Who are his parents?'

'His parents are dead.' I narrowed my eyes in suspicion. 'Mother, where have you put him? Not with the servants, I trust.'

'Of course with the servants. You surely don't expect me to put him in one of the state rooms?'

I was aghast. 'Mother! He is treated with respect in Pergamia. He sits at the high table with the king. The nobles of Brivora are introduced to him along-side the king and queen's own children!'

'Not in my palace.' But I saw her face redden as she realised her mistake.

'Move him.'

'To the room next to yours, I suppose.'

I gritted my teeth. 'I don't care which room. Get him out of the servants' quarters. Now. You will show him the respect he deserves or King Askar will know why.'

Renata wiped lotion from her fingers with a towel and glared at me. 'In my presence not five minutes and you behave as if you were the queen of all

Brivora.' She slapped the cloth down and strode to the door. 'The sooner you're married the better.'

———

Dinner was another argument. Renata insisted I wear a corset with my gown though I detested them. 'What is wrong with my Pergamian dresses? You said yourself I am skin and bones. What do I need with a corset?'

'They favour the corseted style in Ansengaad,' Renata said, holding the horrid thing out. 'Stop snorting like a bull and put it on.'

I tore the corset from her grasp and fitted it around my torso. If my stay in Amentia was going to be at all bearable I was going to have to choose my battles. Corset yes, wedding no.

When eventually we stepped into the dining hall only Prince Folsum rose to greet us. Rodden wasn't there.

I turned to Renata. 'Where is he?'

Renata smiled at the prince and hissed out of the corner of her mouth, 'Sit. Down.'

I crossed my arms. 'King Askar will not be pleased if you dishonour him.'

With barely concealed rage, Renata ordered a footman to fetch Rodden and set another place.

Folsum seated both the queen and then me with a great flourish, elbowing another footman out of the way to do so.

'Thank you,' I said stiffly.

'The pleasure is mine, my dear bride.' His smile was so obsequious I felt ill.

'Don't count your chickens, my lord.'

He laughed. 'Such quaint, rustic expressions you have picked up, Zeraphina. Have you been keeping rough company?'

I ignored him. The door opened, but instead of Rodden, the first footman stood there, hesitating.

'Well?' Renata said. 'What is it?'

'Your Majesty,' he said, speaking as if he could not quite believe the words coming out of his mouth, 'Lothskorn sends his compliments, but he has already eaten.'

I clenched my hands in my lap. Not a day in the palace and he was abandoning me.

'Oh, has he?' Relief and annoyance warred on her face.

'And a good thing, too,' said Folsum. 'Is it customary in this palace to dine with the unscrupulous?'

'The unscrupulous?' I said. 'A fine thing it is, my lord, to remind the queen of her adultery at the dinner table. You shall spoil her appetite.'

Renata glared at me, and I returned her angry gaze measure for measure. I did not enjoy pretending I was a bastard.

We sat through four courses without speaking. I'd lost my appetite and didn't even make the pretence of picking at my food after the second course.

Folsum noticed. 'Are you unwell, princess? I hope you are not experiencing any nausea.'

If I were Griffin, my hackles would have risen. I was not a bastard and I was *not* pregnant. If Folsum thought so little of me, why was he even here?

He put down his knife and fork and rested his fists on the table. His chin jutted with authority. 'Before we are married,' he said, 'I insist the princess undergo an examination by a surgeon of my choosing.'

My face burned.

'If she is not found to be intact I will petition the Crown Chamber at Xallentaria and Lothskorn will be executed.'

Outrage flared in my breast. 'King Askar would do no such thing!' I looked to Renata for confirmation. 'Mother, what is this Crown Chamber?'

'It is the court for those who are above the common law, because they are nobles or the king's favourites. The king has little influence in the chamber. My lord,' she said, turning to the prince. 'I can vouch for her myself, or we can wait several months and see –'

Folsum cut her off without even looking at her. 'I have written letters of consent to this marriage from both King Askar, as your father-in-law by marriage, and Queen Renata. They state my right to the assurance that any offspring of our union be our own. Anyone found to have sullied these writs and threatened the sanctity of the Ansengaad blood-line will be deemed guilty of treason, and executed.'

It made me sick to think I would be inspected in such a humiliating way. Folsum would probably insist on being in the room. 'Any examination would be useless,' I said. 'I've been riding horses, and surely you know what that can do to maidens.'

'Interesting that you leap straight to defence rather than refutation, princess. I don't see what difference horseriding will have made. You will have been riding side-saddle, of course.'

'You think I travelled halfway round the world riding side-saddle?' I scoffed.

'It doesn't matter what I think. It's for the chamber to decide.'

'The chamber doesn't decide how I've been riding horses.'

'The chamber understands the ways of nobles, and

noble maidens ride side-saddle only. Therefore how can anyone, even the king himself, have seen you riding any other way? It is a logical impossibility.'

'That is the stupidest thing I ever heard.' My mind raced. I knew how things could get carried away at Xallentaria. Askar would never execute Rodden of his own accord, but under pressure from the court … The court had power. All Folsum needed to do was stage some public performance, playing the part of the wronged suitor, and he would have their entire support. Under pressure from both the court and the Crown Chamber, Askar would have no choice.

Folsum, seeing the look of horror on my face, picked up his knife and fork and began eating again with relish.

———

First thing the next morning I sent a maid to Rodden's rooms with a summons to meet me in the library. No longer the dusty, shut-up place it had been when I'd left Amentia, it was now clean, ordered and quiet. The shutters had been opened and sunshine slanted through the tall windows. I sat in a high-backed chair, my heels bouncing with impatience on the footstool. I had lain awake half the night agonising over what was to be done. If we returned to Xallentaria, Folsum would follow and Rodden would be arrested. If we ran, the Lharmellins would find us eventually.

I heard footsteps in the corridor and raised my face to the door in expectation. Together, Rodden and I would figure out a way to return to Xallentaria to prepare for our assault on Lharmell without him losing his head.

But it wasn't Rodden who opened the door. It was the maid I'd sent to fetch him. There was confusion on her face.

'Where's Rodden?'

'He wasn't there, Your Highness,' she said. 'He's gone.'

My heart thudded in my chest. 'Gone?'

'There was a note.' The girl held out a slip of paper.

I snatched it from her. 'Where are his things? Are the brants still here?'

'I beg your pardon, miss?'

'The giant birds – are they in the courtyard?'

'I'll go and see. But his things are gone, miss. All of them.' She bobbed out and closed the door behind her.

I unfolded the letter. It was a short missive, written carelessly and without an addressee.

I'll be gone in the morning. I will leave the brants at the palace and instead take a horse as I do not wish to attract unwanted attention at the mines. Be safe until my return. I urge you to stay indoors. Though you will, of course, follow your own advice.

The note was signed with a perfunctory 'R'. I had to read it through several times before I realised that he had not abandoned me in Amentia. He had gone to the mines, but he would return. I crumpled the note in my hands, staring out the window at the mountains to the south. If Rodden rode swiftly he could be there and back in three days; four at the most. He was right about the brants attracting attention, and he might even be right about going alone: a man and a girl, both black-haired and visibly armed, turning up at the Teripsiin mines would raise suspicions among any harmings there. By now they would know we had killed the harmings sent to ambush us in the desert and be more enraged than ever. Alone, Rodden would be safer. He could disguise himself as a worker, or perhaps a merchant. It really was the best thing to have done.

And yet, I felt utterly desolated. He had promised never to leave me in Amentia, and I could not shake the unpleasant feeling that I'd been abandoned.

———

Though the castle had undergone many changes in my absence, the grounds were much the same as they had always been: overgrown, dark, and quiet. I found their familiarity soothing in the days that followed. I stayed out of doors as much as possible and ate in my rooms, pleading headaches whenever I was summoned to table. Renata and Folsum didn't object. They believed I was heartsick for my lover who had abandoned me at the first sign of danger. I did not tell them of the letter; that Rodden planned to return. Folsum would not petition the Crown Chamber if he thought he had won.

Standing in the clearing with Leap and Griffin, my bow made of Amentine ash and the target forty paces down my sights, I could almost imagine that the last year had been a dream; that Lilith was upstairs composing love letters to Lester, her dead betrothed, and I was still trying to come to terms with my strange cravings.

Then I felt the silver ring tingle on my thumb, and smiled. Rodden's consciousness brushed the edges of my mind, as light as a feather. Just as swiftly as the touch came, it was gone. It happened every few hours.

It was a wordless exchange, but it was enough. I looked to the south and saw clouds, heavy with rain, gathering over the mountains. It would storm soon at the mines. I thought briefly of trying to hold off the rain so Rodden wouldn't be soaked, but it might not be wise. The harmings might suspect something was up. But the prospect excited me. What was I capable of – could I hold off a storm? Could I cause one?

Another sensation touched my mind, one of irritation, and a little fear. It was familiar, but it wasn't Rodden. Then the thread blazed in fury, and I recognised it: one of our brants. But it was no longer in the courtyard where I had tethered it. I searched the vicinity, letting the thread go slack, allowing it to tug me in the right direction. There – to the south-east, in the forest. I broke into a run, sending Griffin ahead to scout in case it was harmings. She disappeared among the trees and only seconds later threw a picture back at me: Folsum with a horsewhip in one hand and the brant's reins in the other. I heard shouting, the prince's voice raised in anger.

A second later I broke into the clearing and saw the scene for myself. The bird was confused and furious, not understanding the orders Folsum was yelling at it. He'd got a saddle and bridle on the beast, but he'd fastened them awkwardly and far too tight. The stirrups were too high for Folsum to reach while the bird stood, and he was trying to force it to the ground. He struck the bird over the head with the butt of his whip.

I dropped my bow. 'Stop it!' I cried, running forward. 'It's not a horse. It doesn't understand.'

'Brainless bird. A mount is a mount. I have broken enough horses in my time to know how to handle it. Stand back, girl.' He lashed at the brant's legs and it screamed in pain.

The bird's fear blossomed in my chest. Folsum raised his arm again and I leapt at him, trying to wrestle the whip from his grasp. Surprise flashed in his eyes as he felt my strength but then he rallied. He shoved me to the ground and planted a foot in the middle of my chest. I struggled like a pinned insect.

'Get off me,' I wheezed.

He pressed harder, anger burning like blue flame in his eyes. 'Your pride, your *fight*. It's quite unreasonable for a bastard slut to carry on so. Are you not ashamed of yourself? Were you raised to think yourself better than you are, or is your pride of your own making? Why do you not consider yourself lower than the worms that squirm beneath you?' He pressed harder. 'Because that's what you are.'

I scrabbled to free myself from under him but he landed a vicious blow across my face.

A piercing scream shattered the air and Griffin flew at Folsum, talons first. He yelled in surprise and staggered back, an arm coming up to shield his face.

My hand flew to my hip but I'd left my knife in its belt sheath and had not thought to don the belt that morning. Folsum had dropped his whip and I lunged for it. He spotted it at the same time and we crashed into each another. With a grunt of surprise he shoved me off with his shoulder. A second later the whip cracked across my upraised arms. I screamed. He lashed me again, and I could barely hear my cries of pain over the cacophony of his shouts, the screams of Griffin and the brant, and Leap's terrified hissing. Folsum caught the back of my dress and ripped it open, shoving me to the ground. His foot bore down on the back of my neck. The whip whistled through the air, striking the expanse of my back. I screamed in pain, unable to throw him off. In seconds my whole body felt like it was on fire.

I reached out with my mind to the brant, calling to it through the blazing pain in my back. *Beak and claw*, I urged. *Help me, please.*

The sky darkened over us. Folsum stayed his hand as a long, thin shriek pierced the air.

'What the –'

I looked up. The brant reared on the tips of its talons, wings spreading. It dwarfed the prince, and he cowered beneath the bird's black gaze. I was reminded of the mighty golden griffin on our standard. Then the bird struck, lightning fast, beak slicing through the leather of the prince's garb. It struck again, then leapt several feet in the air and raked down his chest with its talons. He screamed. Blood spurted. The bird went for the prince's face and his screams increased. He fell to the ground and disappeared beneath the brant's huge body.

I heard the thunder of running feet. The queen's guard burst into the clearing. The brant looked up, hissing, wings hunched. The men fell back at the sight of the enormous bird, bloodied in beak and talon, and drew their swords.

I flung myself in front of them, clasping my dress about me with one hand, the other outstretched. 'Don't harm this bird.' Already the brant was heeding my silent urgings and was backing away.

The soldiers looked uncertain, but lowered their swords.

Folsum moaned. He was bloodied and torn and

his left eye was missing. I winced, feeling sick. Blood flowed from the cuts that crisscrossed his chest. One gash on his neck was bleeding profusely.

Amid the shouts from the soldiers to fetch a healer and restrain my brant, I knelt down close to Folsum, gasping slightly from pain. Blood ran down my back and dripped onto the dead leaves.

Folsum's good eye flickered open.

'Your left eye is in the belly of my brant,' I said. 'Touch me again and I will feed it the other.'

I raised myself to my feet and limped back to the castle.

———

I lay on my belly, stripped to the waist while Eugenia, mother's maid, dabbed at the ribbons of cuts that covered my back and arms. Every breath was painful. Sweat trickled over my brow and into my eyes. I heard someone enter but had my face turned towards the wall and could not see who it was.

'She has refused laudanum, My Queen. Sleepin' elixir, too.'

I heard Renata sigh. 'Leave us.' She took up the cloth and the pot of salve and began dabbing at my wounds. I felt her hands shaking. 'You hurt only yourself by refusing treatment,' she said.

She lied. I knew it hurt her to see me enduring this. 'I cannot.' I kept my fingers fastened around the ring on my thumb, desperate for any contact from Rodden. If I disappeared into an opium fog we would never find one another. I needed desperately to know if he was any closer to the palace. If he was safe. If he really was returning to me.

Renata laid strips of bandage over my cuts. Then she bandaged my arms, placed a thin blanket over my body, a light kiss on my brow, and departed with the lamp.

At the door she turned and said, 'It may please you to know that the prince might die. In any case, he suffers. I have mislaid all our laudanum. It is a pity.'

She was gone, and I was left in darkness.

I waited through the sleepless hours. The world behind my eyes turned from black to burning red. My scored flesh swelled and blazed as hot as fire. I sent out thought-fingers to search for Rodden but they came back empty.

Sometime after midnight, a sleepy thought-finger caressed my mind. Rodden, somewhere between sleep and wakefulness, reaching out to me. He'd already begun to fade away when he felt my rawness, my thought-patterns that told him, beyond doubt, that all was not well. That things were, in fact, horrid.

I felt him jerk into consciousness. I let my hurt speak for itself down the thread between us. It spoke volumes. He disappeared.

He emerged again in my mind a short time later, and I felt him vibrant with blood. He'd hunted and fed. I thought I could hear his voice but the words were hopelessly distorted. Then, like a fish rising to the surface of a river, his voice came into focus. He was saying my name. My eyes snapped open.

Twin blue points of light hovered near my face. Rodden's eyes. He was once again the blue-eyed phantom, the form he'd first appeared to me in.

'Hello,' I croaked.

The eyes widened, dazzling me. He spoke rapidly, his words bursting like bubbles before I could catch them.

Cool fingers ran through my hair, traced the curves of my ear, my mouth, my fingers. And then he was gone.

———

When I opened my eyes in the morning, he was there. In the flesh. He sat on a three-legged stool by my bedside, face in his hands. I lifted my head and the sheet came up with it, stuck fast to my cheek.

'You're here,' I croaked.

He raised his head and looked at me, bleary-eyed. His face was spattered with blood. Leaves and dirt clung to his shirt.

With a shaking hand, I pulled the sheet from my face. 'What happened to you?'

'Me?' he said, incredulous. 'Not three days I am gone and you get flogged in the woods. What on earth happened?' He stared at the bandages that encased the top half of my body.

'The prince and I disagreed about proper brant-wrangling procedure.' The pain in my back, which had been dormant embers, sprung up again and burned merrily.

He cursed.

'Is he dead?' I asked.

'Not yet,' he replied, voice tight. 'Did he … do anything else?'

'No,' I said. 'The brant attacked him mid-flog.'

He nodded and rubbed his hands over his face.

'How long have you been here? You look exhausted.'

He sighed and reached down absently to rub my hand. 'A few hours. I rode all night. With one or two stops.' He scratched at the crust of blood on his trousers.

'Did you get enough yelinate?'

'I did. It's there with the bennium,' he said, indicating his bags in the corner. 'I can't think of a safe place to store it so I just prefer to not let it out of my sight.'

'Good idea.' I gripped his hand hard. 'Oh, Rodden. We've done it.'

'Yes. But look at what's happened to you.'

'We've gathered all the materials we need. We're still alive. That's what really matters. And besides, this had nothing to do with the Lharmellins.'

I heard the door open. 'Who is it?' I called, unable to turn my head.

'Eugenia, miss. Come to change your dressings.'

'What salve are you using?' Rodden asked her.

'Clover 'n' goldenseal, sir.'

'I have something better,' he said. 'Leave the bandages with me.' Eugenia hesitated and he snapped, 'Come on, woman. Hand them over!'

I heard Eugenia harrumph and slam out. 'She'll tell Mother you spoke to her so,' I mumbled into the sheet.

'I couldn't care less. Besides, if your mother comes in she's a lot less likely to have hysterics when she sees me smearing blood all over you.'

'Blood?'

'Harming blood. From a Turned harming. I thought I would just use my own on you but I ran into a coven of the things and thought, this is even better. It should help you heal quicker.'

'Good. I want to be gone from here.'

He washed his hands in a basin and began peeling the bandages from my back. I saw the look of horror on his face when he saw the welts and was alarmed.

'Is it that bad? I mean, I shan't *die*, shall I?'

Rodden shook his head. 'Heavens, no.'

'Don't look so stricken, then. Get on with it.'

'It's just …' He didn't speak again until all the bandages had come off. 'I thought I understood violence. What is your mother thinking, trying to bind you for life to a man who would do this to you?'

The cold air was at once a pain and a relief on my ravaged skin. 'She thinks it's for my own good. But what I don't understand is, why would he want me if he thinks I'm a bastard slut?'

'Is that what he called you?'

'Yes.'

Rodden was silent.

'What?' I asked.

'There are men who … enjoy having their low opinion of women confirmed.'

'Why?'

He didn't answer. I thought about Folsum's glee as he had pinned me beneath his boot and was glad all over again that I had sustained only a whipping.

'Oh. Be quick, please,' I said.

He snapped out of his reverie and unscrewed a flask. 'This might sting. Or it might not. Or maybe it will do nothing, I'm not sure.'

'You haven't tried this before?'

'No, only read about it. Here goes. Scream if it hurts.'

'I will.'

He dampened a cloth with blood and dabbed at my shoulder. It stung, but in a clean, cold way, like it was doing some good.

'Is it all right? Do you want me to stop?'

'No, it's – it's good, actually.'

He worked steadily over the cuts, the blood first stinging and then soothing the pain, putting out the fire. Once he'd finished with my back he started on my arms. Lash marks crisscrossed the backs of them. By the time he'd finished he was angry again, swearing to kill Folsum in his bed. 'Unless you'd rather,' he offered.

'So now I'm allowed to kill someone in cold blood?'

'I'll hand you the knife.'

The door opened. Rodden looked up, and then bowed.

'Hello, Mother,' I said wearily.

'Daughter – have you been bleeding again?'

'No, Your Majesty,' Rodden replied. 'It's ... a special treatment.'

'When can I move?' I asked Rodden.

'Soon. Only a few days.' He looked back to Renata. 'Have a cot brought. I will sleep in here until we depart.'

I grinned at hearing him order Renata around as if this were his palace and not hers.

'You will do no such thing, Lothskorn.'

'You will bring a cot or I shall sleep on the floor. The prince's men are in the castle and I don't trust them not to murder Zeraphina in her sleep. Dispose of the evidence, you might say.'

'I have my own guards,' Renata countered.

'Yes, but they might be alarmed at all the blood drinking that will go on in here. Besides, one of them might be a harming and your daughter is rather unpopular with them at this time. I shall stay.'

Renata began to protest, but he cut her off. 'Madam, I shall stay.'

FOURTEEN

I fell asleep, and woke much later in the day. Rodden was slouched in a chair by the window, reading, boots propped up on the stone window ledge. Leap was sprawled over his lap, head lolling against Rodden's thigh. Sunshine washed over them. Dust motes floated in the air. Seeing me watching, Leap blinked his pale green eyes and flexed his claws.

'Ow,' Rodden muttered, detaching Leap's claws from his leg with one finger without looking up from the page.

They were the perfect tableau, and I watched them for several quiet minutes before asking, 'What are you reading?'

He looked around. 'You're awake.' He gazed at me a moment, his eyes running over my face, my back. I could see the concern in his eyes. I thought I saw traces of guilt, too, and wondered if he thought my injuries were his fault.

'It's about Lharmellins,' he said. 'Found it in your library.'

'Surely not.'

'The old name for Lharmellins is the Cold Ones. Your mother must not know that.' He read aloud. '"The cold spreads from areas of lower mean temperature outwards, rather than from north, where the Cold Ones reside, to south." Amentia is naturally cooler than the countries surrounding it, you see, because of the elevation. That has made it easy for the Lharmellins to influence it in the past.'

In the past. I clung to those words. If we were successful at the coming Turning in Lharmell, killing more Lharmellins and harmings, we might be able to disrupt them even further. Innocent people wouldn't be taken from cities and ships, and killed or forced to become harmings.

'I remember those words. Cold Ones, Cold Times. They were in a book on your desk that day I went snooping in your room. I didn't know they had anything to do with the Lharmellins.' I looked at the stack of books by his chair. 'Are they all about the Cold Ones?'

'Mostly. Some are about alchemy. I'm appropriating them in the name of King Askar. Sounds grander than stealing, doesn't it?'

'Alchemy? Shall we be transmuting urine into gold?'

'Ah,' he said. 'All shall be revealed. How do you feel?'

I moved my shoulders. The dried blood had stiffened the bandages, but the pain had lessened. 'A little better.'

He got up, and Leap was deposited on the chair, rumpled and blinking. Rodden peeled off the bandages. 'I'll change the dressing now while the blood's still fresh.'

'How does it look?'

'Your back? Like raw meat. But I see signs of healing. Rapid healing.'

'How soon can we leave?'

'In a few days, I expect.'

'Let's leave tomorrow.' I was anxious to go before Folsum recovered. I never wanted to see his loathsome face again. Or what I had done to it.

'Not a chance.'

When he'd finished with the bandages I said, 'Read to me?'

'What would you like me to read?'

'Anything. Whatever you like.'

He went back to his chair and picked up his book. Scanning the pages, he said, 'It's very dull. Just theories, and not very good ones.'

'That's fine.'

He read, and it was dull. But I enjoyed the cadence of his voice, and his profile as he frowned at the pages. Several pages later he laid the book in his lap and stared out the window. I wondered if he was thinking about the passages he'd just read, but he turned back and said, 'To be wounded or die at the hands of one who is meant to love you. Is there a more miserable thing in the world?'

I did not need to read his mind to know he was thinking of Ilona. 'The Lharmellins,' I suggested.

He shook his head. 'No. Not even close.' He looked back to the page, trying to find his place. Then he put the book aside and stood up. 'I have chosen three guards. They are outside your door should you need them. I must take some air.' And then he left.

———

The next morning I was able to sit up without screaming. Rodden brought blood from the kitchens and I drank until my stomach was fit to burst. 'Bring me that hand mirror on the dresser,' I said to him when I'd finished my breakfast. 'And bring that standing mirror closer to the bed.'

'Why?' His eyes were haunted. I knew he'd lain awake most of the night as I'd heard him tossing and turning on the cot in the corner and sighing at regular intervals. Something was bothering him.

'I want to see.'

'Wait a day or two more. Once the bandages come off.'

I held out my hand. 'Please. Or I'll get it myself.'

He fetched the mirrors, but scowled the whole time. The standing mirror he placed at the bedside.

I eased my shoulder out of my nightshirt. 'Can you peel the bandages away?'

With reluctant fingers, he pulled at the bandages. Holding out his hand he said, 'Give me the hand mirror.'

I gave it to him, and he angled it so that I could see the reflection in the big mirror. Thick, dark red lines crisscrossed my skin. They were no longer swollen and I could see how deep the cuts were.

'I will scar, won't I?'

'Yes.'

Our eyes met in the mirror. 'Good.'

He put down the mirror and sat beside me on the bed. 'What?'

'The scars are evidence. If Folsum tries anything I'll take him to the Crown Chamber and get *his* head cut off.'

'What are you talking about?'

'The prince. The night before you left for the mines he threatened to petition the Crown Chamber at Pergamia to have you beheaded if I wasn't found to be pure.'

'Oh, that. You needn't worry about that. I can't be convicted by a Pergamian court for a capital offence.'

I thumped the comforter. 'I knew King Askar would never let it happen.'

'Oh, the Crown Chamber does not answer to the king. That's the whole point. But one of my conditions when I began working at the palace was that I not be considered a Pergamian subject and that the severest punishment that could be meted out to me was banishment. I needed to be sure that nothing untoward would happen in the event that I am accused of revealing state secrets.'

'Like the ones you have told me about the Lharmellins?' It hadn't occurred to me at the time that he could be breaking the law by telling me everything he knew.

'Yes. But it also comes in handy when uppity suitors want to cut my head off.'

'Does that happen very often?'

He smiled. 'Every now and then.'

I grasped his hand. 'That is a great relief. I was worried that when we returned to Pergamia you would be arrested.'

He raised an eyebrow. 'Why? I haven't done anything, have I?'

'Oh. No, you haven't.' I turned a question over in my mind. 'Rodden, why haven't you?'

'Why haven't I what?'

'We've been travelling alone together all this time, and you did kiss me at the masquerade ball. Those things you did when you were younger – none of it was any of your fault, but ...' I hesitated. 'Your expression when you saw the cuts on my back. I mean, they're bad, but not horrifyingly so. It's because of Ilona, isn't it?'

'You're not making any sense. What's because of Ilona?' He sounded exasperated.

I repressed a groan. Sometimes he could be very stupid. 'You're scared that if we become lovers you might hurt me. Might even kill me.'

Rodden yanked his hand from mine as if it had been burned. He stood, backing away.

'I'm right, aren't I? Please, Rodden, sit down.'

He turned away to the window, a hand to his mouth.

'Rodden?'

Without a word, without even looking at me again, he strode from the room.

——

Suddenly I was made of thorns and needles. Rodden still slept on a cot in my room but he barely looked at me. I realised then how easy we had been with one another. Now it seemed he could not put enough distance between us. Every exchange was awkward. He did not trust his hands, and kept them clasped at his back or balled into fists. On several occasions I caught him looking at me, but his eyes were troubled and unhappy. I chafed under the silence and the bandages.

Two afternoons after what I'd begun to think of as our fight, I got out of bed and went to the mirror. I was alone. I stripped off first my nightgown and then the bandages. I stood naked before the mirror. Looking face-on, I could barely tell that I'd been whipped. A ribbon or two of red snaked around my neck, and the marks were visible on my arms only when I held them a certain way.

I turned around. Looking back over my shoulder I saw the extent of the damage. My upper back was covered in angry red striations. They were thin now, thanks to the time that had passed and the blood Rodden had applied. But my skin was no longer smooth. It was ridged, like the frets of a lute.

No one will make me marry Folsum now, I thought with triumph. I am walking proof of his violence.

I wiped my face and upper body over with a wet cloth. The day seemed warm and I donned a Pergamian dress. The short sleeves showed the marks on my arms, as did the neckline at the back. I felt a pang as I realised that my scars would be visible to all in dresses like these. I remembered the beautiful peacock gown Rodden had given me for the masquerade ball. It had been strapless and cut low at the back. There would be no more dresses like that for me.

But today I wanted my cuts to be seen.

On somewhat shaky feet I went in search of Renata. One of the guards offered his arm but I refused. To my surprise and annoyance, they escorted me as I made my slow way down the passages. 'Is this absolutely necessary?' I asked the one who'd offered his arm. 'I am in my own home.'

He looked at me in surprise. 'Begging your pardon, princess, but recent events seem to suggest that yes, it is.'

I found Renata in her sitting room, thumbing through ornamental garden designs. She glanced up as I limped in, and then back at her papers. 'Is topiary hopelessly outdated, darling? You must know the current trends. You have been gallivanting all over this great continent of ours.'

I eased myself down in the chair opposite.

'Or perhaps a hedge maze …' she mused. After another minute's perusal she looked up. 'I must say, it's good to see you up and about again. I wish I could say the same for the prince.' There was an edge to her voice, and her eyes had grown flinty.

'He is still abed?'

'Yes, Daughter. He lost a great deal of blood. And an eye, if you remember.'

I did remember. I remembered the gory red hollow of his eye socket all too well. 'I rather think it serves him right, don't you?'

Renata put down the designs and folded her hands in her lap. 'Be that as it may, you have crippled the future king of Ansengaad. If you think this will go unnoticed you are very much mistaken.'

'How do you mean?'

She spread her hands. 'Who can say? Folsum's sister is on her way here as we speak. She will advise her father how to proceed.'

Ansengaad was hundreds of miles away. Penritha wouldn't reach the castle for days. Rodden and I still had time. 'We will go, and the princess will not see us, though I would dearly love to show Penritha what her brother has done to me.'

Renata's eyes grew colder. 'You shall go where?'

'Back to Pergamia, of course. Rodden and I have a lot of work to do.' I'd wondered if, after our argument, Rodden would attempt to leave without me. But he'd seemed reluctant to leave me alone despite his obvious discomfort with my feelings for him.

Was I so distasteful to him? Did he still love Ilona, despite her being dead for so many years?

She threw up her hands. 'Forget him, Zeraphina. Enough of these childish games. You must marry.'

I raised my voice. 'This isn't a game. This is about being free. Our people being free. I can do far more for our nation in Pergamia than I could ever do walking up an aisle. You have not seen what the Lharmellins can do. Rodden and I, we're not like the others. We have some modicum of free will, but the others are slaves. They steal children. They kill people for their blood.'

Renata glanced at the guards. 'Keep your voice down,' she hissed. 'It is not your responsibility, Zeraphina. It is for people like Rodden to handle this problem, not you.'

'I shouldn't have expected you to understand. It's your fault I am like this, after all.'

She raised her arm to strike me, but my bruises and cuts must have made her think twice. She stood over me, her face mottled with rage. 'I pray you never have to nurse a sick child while your husband lies in a fresh grave.'

'I will say this for the last time: I will marry whom I please, if and when I say so.'

'You are quite wrong, Daughter. You will marry at my pleasure, not your own.'

'Mother, if you try to force me again I will tell the entire court at Xallentaria what I am and how I came to be this way. Then you can be sure no one will want me.'

'No one shall believe you. At court those creatures are nothing more than a tale to scare little children.'

'Ah, but I have proof.' I looked to my guards.

'Leave us,' I commanded. 'And close the door behind you.' I waited until they'd shuffled out before taking my place in the centre of the room.

'What are you doing?'

The window was open on the dusk. I closed my eyes and felt the dew falling. With invisible fingers, I began to draw moisture inside, covering the ceiling with a thick fog. The room melted away, the palace vanished, until I was standing alone in a great expanse. My feet no longer felt the floor beneath them. I saw wind flowing around me, shining like rivers of sunlit water. Currents whipped at my dress. I felt every drop of moisture for miles around. The rain wanted to be ocean; the ice in the mountain caps wanted freedom. I'd never known that water held such longing. The clouds above my head rumbled like a growling wolf, impatient to release their burden. I held the rain there a moment longer. I turned to Renata, heard her gasp and knew my eyes glowed blue.

I spoke a single word. 'Rain.'

The clouds sighed. Water spattered on the flagstones. The rain brought me back into the room, and I laughed at the spectacle. It was raining inside, great sheets of water flowing down the walls and pooling on the floor. Renata, soaked through, huddled beneath her parchments, ink running in black rivers down her arms.

The clouds were exhausted and the rain stopped. The room shone with moisture. I tugged my clinging dress from my body and squeezed the water from my sleeves. 'I've never done that for fun before,' I said, grinning. 'It was beautiful. I wish you could see what I see, Mother.'

I turned and saw Rodden standing in the doorway, looking in amazement around the sodden room. At me in my dripping dress. He looked at me properly for the first time in days, and I saw admiration in his eyes.

'We're leaving?' he guessed, a smile tugging at his mouth.

I nodded. He held out his hand, and I ran to him.

FIFTEEN

If there had been any light at all, everything would
have gone black.

'Zeraphina!'

Pain exploded in my back and my head thumped
painfully against the ground. I struggled for breath.
Wings beat the air, the breeze a mockery to my
empty lungs.

Footsteps over a hard surface. Skittering stones.
'Are you hurt? Can you move?'

I felt wetness beneath me. I shifted side to side,
trying to coax the breath back in my body. Finally,
air rushed in. 'I've split – my cuts,' I gasped.

Rodden felt beneath my shoulders. 'It feels like it.
I can't see a thing. The clouds are too thick.'

The memories of just a few moments ago

returned. 'I fell,' I said, indignant at my own body. I remembered being in the saddle of the brant, and then suddenly here, on the ground, with no memory of the seconds in between. 'I fainted and fell. How high were we?'

Rodden's fingers probed my scalp, feeling for cuts. 'A dozen feet or so. We'd only just taken off. Can you move everything?'

I wriggled my fingers and toes. 'Yes. Nothing broken.'

'Wait here.'

Only too pleased to oblige, I lay still. There was the sound of feet stumbling over uneven ground. More swearing. A brant hissed in the darkness. A faint mew from Leap and coaxing noises from Rodden.

He came back. 'Leap and Griffin are in saddle-bags,' he whispered. 'They're not happy but they'll be safe. Now, try not to scream ...' His hands went under me and he lifted. Pain exploded in my back and I choked off a yelp. He settled me on a brant's saddle and got up behind me, one hand around my waist and gripping the saddle horn.

This was one way, I thought as a settled myself against his body, to get him to stop treating me like I was a porcupine. Though ever since he'd seen me cause a storm in my mother's sitting room he'd come out of his moodiness. I wondered why that was so.

'The birds are tethered together. Are you ready?'

I managed a faint moan to the affirmative, and we lurched into the air.

———

I slept for a day and a half when we returned to the palace in Xallentaria, trussed up tight in fresh white bandages, courtesy of Rodden, and administered nothing more powerful than a herbal draft to take the edge off the pain. I received no visitors, and wondered what could be keeping my sister.

I did receive a lovely note from Queen Ulah, telling me she hoped I recovered quickly from the malady that had struck me down on the last portion of our journey. I puzzled over this, until I realised Rodden must have made my excuses to the king and queen, knowing I didn't wish to speak of the flogging unless I must. The scandal that would ensue wasn't something I wanted to cope with right then.

I was relieved to receive the letter. Our clandestine departure, it seemed, hadn't angered the king and queen. Rodden must have made suitable excuses for us before we left, or Amis might have smoothed things over. I felt a little guilty that I hadn't even considered such a thing.

Several days later I felt strong enough to get out of bed, and the first thing I did was seek Lilith out. I paced the palace halls on stiff legs, gritting my teeth and holding myself rigid beneath the shawl I'd draped over my shoulders. I felt like an old woman.

I found Lilith in her suite of rooms. Her hands were folded in her lap and her eyes were directed out the window. I went to embrace her but something in her countenance made me pause. I stood before her a long time, waiting to be acknowledged. Finally, she flicked her gaze to me and her eyes raked my figure. She turned back to the window with a twist of her mouth.

'Hello, Sister,' I said. I felt the first twinges of guilt for having sneaked from the palace in the middle of the night directly after she'd told me not to.

'Do you have any idea,' she bit out, 'the humiliation and worry that I have been subjected to?'

'Why, Lilith, what has happened?' Humiliation? Surely, that couldn't have anything to do with me. I had disobeyed her, but I hadn't humiliated her. What else could it be? My eyes flicked to her belly, which was flat. Remembering Renata's letters, I felt a flash of anger. The pressure she put her daughters under was criminal.

Lilith turned her cold eyes on me. '*You* is what has happened to me.'

My heart sank under Lilith's glare. 'You sounded just like Mother then.'

'Don't speak to me of Mother,' Lilith spat. 'I have had letter after letter from her these last months. It is I who has suffered her rants, her fury, while you have been away gallivanting about the countryside with that man. But has that not always been the way: you shirk duty and responsibility and it is me who bears the brunt of it? In Amentia all Mother needed to do was open her mouth and you would flee to the grounds. You were always leaving me with her. And then when Lester died, where were you?' Her eyes were bright with angry tears. 'Well? Where were you?'

She didn't know what I was, I told myself, as white hot fury built in my breast. The fire was stoked with guilt, for what she said was right. I had always left her with Mother. But I hadn't realised she cared until now.

'You were still shooting that silly bow and arrows,' she cried.

'I know that's the way it looks, but I couldn't help it.'

'No, for you are irresponsible. Shameful. Instead

of doing your duty you consort with that man. I suspect you are no longer fit to be married. The whole court suspects it.'

'I do not give a fig what the court suspects. Rodden has been the perfect gentleman.'

'He is no gentleman. He is crude and coarse.'

My patience snapped like a bow string. 'How dare you speak of him so! You have no idea how much gratitude you owe him. The whole kingdom should be grateful to him.'

Lilith's lip curled in disgust. 'You are not only infatuated, you are deluded. Tell me this: why do you return to Pergamia instead of staying in Amentia where you belong? It is not for my comfort, so do not say it is.'

I was silent.

'Go on, tell me. You stay for love of that man. Don't you?'

I turned and hobbled out.

———

'"The alchemical endeavours",' I read aloud, '"are transmutation, the creation of the panacea, and the search for the universal solvent."' I had one of Rodden's alchemy texts open on my lap, a huge, dusty tome filled with fancy lettering and esoteric diagrams. We were in his turret room and I had been propped up on a low couch in a corner while he, wearing goggles and a rubber apron, conducted strange experiments that crackled, flared and smoked. It was rather like being at a magic show. The skylight was propped open for ventilation but the room still reeked of rotten eggs. The funny thing was I hadn't seen an egg all day.

My back throbbed with pain and heat and I sweated continuously. I hadn't seen Lilith in several days. I had avoided the high table of an evening, not only because of my sister, but because I also suspected she'd been telling the truth about the court: they would stare and gossip about me the minute I made an appearance. Until I could hold myself up straight I would hide in Rodden's turret of an evening. Besides, we were busy.

I turned my attention back to the book in my lap. I knew what transmutation was: the conversion of one object into another. Rumours sprang up now and then that an alchemist had turned urine or lead into gold, but the claims always proved false.

'What are the panacea and the universal solvent?' I asked.

'The panacea is the elixir of life,' Rodden said.

He scraped a blackened substance out of a beaker, his nose wrinkling at the smell. 'It cures all diseases and allows immortality. A solvent is a substance that can dissolve other substances while remaining unchanged itself. The universal solvent dissolves everything, hypothetically speaking.'

'Hypothetically? By the way, is that supposed to happen?' I asked, nodding at the burnt beaker.

'No. It's not,' he muttered. 'The universal solvent has never been discovered. And if it was isolated, the trick would be containing it.'

'Because it would dissolve its container.'

'Exactly.'

'What about the panacea, has that been found?'

'No.' He paused a moment, thinking. 'I wonder if they've experimented with Lharmellin blood ...' He shook his head. 'No, the side effects rather outweigh the benefits.'

'So alchemists can't make gold, they can't cure disease and they are unable to dissolve ... everything. Do they do anything useful at all?'

'Once in a while. A very little while.' A beaker of viscous yellow liquid was about to boil over and he made a grab for it with a pair of tongs. He held the glass vessel up at eye level and shook it. 'When they're not keeling over from lead poisoning or going mad from the distillation of mercury they manage to accomplish one or two things that are useful in the practical sense, such as manufacturing vitriol. As I'm trying to do now.'

'I saw that word, "vitriol". Hang on.' I flicked through the yellowing pages, past diagrams of stars and representations of the cosmos. 'Here it is, vi–'

There was a flash of light accompanied by a loud bang. Rodden dived for cover as glass shattered over the bench and a plume of sickly yellow smoke wafted up to the ceiling. It was the eleventh beaker to explode that morning.

'Oh, dear. You're not very good at this, are you?'

'It's not me,' he huffed. 'It's the alchemists. My raw materials are inadequate. Pure sulfur and saltpetre they promised, and look –' he stabbed a finger at a clutch of leather bags – 'seven different coloured compounds from seven different alchemists. They're all supposed to be the same. Look at this saltpetre. It's pink. Pink! The stars know what's been mixed in. Full of impurities. Imbeciles, the lot of them.' He swept broken glass from the bench and set out a fresh clutch of beakers.

I turned back to my book without saying a word. '"Vitriol is the most important alchemical substance. Highly reactive, it is used in the purification of gold, as it dissolves many salts, metals and other compounds without reacting with the more precious metals. It is named for the motto *Visita Interiora Terrae Rectificando Invenies Occultum Lapidem*." What does that mean?'

'"Visit the interior of the earth; through purification you will find the hidden stone,"' he intoned, not looking up from the powder he was spooning into a vessel.

'Gold?'

'Yes.'

'If vitriol could be used to purify gold, then can it be used to purify other metals?'

'Yes.'

'Like yelbar?'

'Yes.'

'Ah.'

'But not only that,' he continued, shaking the beaker, 'when we react pure yelbar with hot, concentrated vitriol, we get gaseous yelbar: thick, strong and lethal. The tiniest amount is enough to kill you. Or me. Or any harming or Lharmellin.'

'Oh, my,' I breathed. I turned to the crate that had been shipped from the desert, all the way from Verapine. 'That's what the glass balls are for.' The first thing Rodden had done upon our arrival was check them, and they were all intact. I met Rodden's eyes across the room. 'We're going to poison the air, aren't we?'

'That is the plan. It would have worked well in the open air, but underground? Even better.' He strode to the crate and lifted out a glass ball. Holding it aloft, he looked me in the eye – and then hurled the sphere to the floor.

I gasped, expecting the glass to shatter. The ball bounced and rolled harmlessly to a standstill.

'Are they magic?'

Rodden laughed. 'There's no magic. There are only laws.' He dug around in the crate and pulled out a box. 'Inside this,' he said in reverent tones, 'is the master glass. Break it, and they all shatter.' With care, he placed it back in the crate.

'How does it work?'

'All the glass balls were drawn from the master glass when they were made. It's a special technique that only the master glassblower of Verapine knows. He would have taught me the secret one day, had I stayed.'

I must have looked doubtful, as he went on.

'Think of them as one glass, not dozens of glasses. Their properties are all linked. There is a theory among alchemists – some of the better ones at least – that matter can become entangled like this, but it's almost always too small for us to see. These glasses are entangled on a larger –'

Two beakers exploded, one after the other. We both ducked for cover. I heard Rodden muttering from beneath his bench.

'Do you have to do this yourself?' I asked.

'Want to.' He reappeared and pushed his goggles on top of his head. His face was sooty except for two clean circles around his eyes.

'We don't have to do everything ourselves. We can ask for help,' I said, then muttered, 'Clearly you need it.'

'I don't want any help. I know basic chemistry. This should be easy.'

'And manufacturing gaseous yelbar, is that basic chemistry?'

He glared at me.

'Well, is it? At any rate, it sounds a rather dangerous thing for a harming to do. One exploding beaker and you'll drop down dead. Could a human do it?'

'Hypothetically.'

'Rodden, I could do it *hypothetically*. What I mean is, would it be dangerous for them?'

'No more dangerous than handling hot vitriol.'

I closed my book. 'Well, then. Find an alchemist.'

'And what I am supposed to do in the meantime?' He looked around at the mess he'd created, irritated and forlorn at the same time.

'That's easy. Anything you like.'

——

My cuts were still too fresh for me to ride so I didn't accompany Rodden into the city in search of an alchemist who wasn't completely potty. I couldn't train either, so I found an arbour in the grounds and spent the days in the shade of rosebushes. Carmelina sat with me sometimes and brought me all the gossip from the great hall. I listened politely, but in truth it didn't interest me at all. I read frivolous books when the words could hold my attention, but mostly I sat in quiet contemplation. My eyes would follow a peacock as it picked its way across the grass or the path of a dragonfly as it careened over the flower beds. Often I wasn't seeing the palace grounds at all, but the oasis where the Jarbin lived, and I would be filled with longing to be there. How peaceful it had been.

Rodden sat with me sometimes but he would fidget so restlessly that it was a relief when he went back to his turret room.

One perfect sunny morning I sat with Carmelina

on the grass playing with a clutch of fluffy white kittens that had been presented to her mother from one of the city nobles. Leap looked on, bemused by their antics. They were so tiny they were dwarfed by dandelion blossoms. One clung to the front of my dress and stared up at me with wide, shocked eyes. Two simultaneously attacked Leap, gnawing at his paws with their tiny teeth. Good-naturedly, he let them clamber all over him.

Then Carmelina spoke words that made my blood run cold.

'Princess Penritha will be arriving at the palace shortly, did you know? A messenger from the main party reached the palace last night.'

I hadn't even told Carmelina about the flogging. She'd noticed my stiffness and I had muttered something about sunburn acquired in the desert. At first she'd asked a lot of awkward questions, about why Rodden and I had snuck away in the middle of the night, and whether we'd eloped, and what on earth I'd been doing all this time. I made the whole journey sound very dull and she eventually stopped asking.

'How long until they arrive?' I asked, trying to keep my voice level.

'Oh, a day or two at the most. The messenger left

them just outside Delafor,' Carmelina said, naming a town that was a mere hundred miles from Xallentaria. Penritha must be in a great hurry to cover the distance between Ansengaad and Prestoral and then on to Xallentaria so quickly. And I could well imagine what had spurred such haste.

I disentangled the kitten from my dress and handed it back. 'I must go in,' I told Carmelina, scooping Leap into my arms. 'There's something I forgot to …' I trailed off, not bothering to finish the thought as I hurried across the grass.

Leap butted his head against my chin, but I was beyond comfort.

———

Rodden was unmoved by my news when I finally ran him to ground at the stables.

'Let her come. She can't do a thing to hurt you now. You mustn't worry.'

'It's not me I'm worried for.'

'Oh? And what do I have to fear from a scrap of a princess?'

I kicked straw around the stall and watched Rodden groom his horse. 'Princesses can make an awful stink when they want to.'

Rodden cast me a dark look. 'I've noticed. But so can I.'

But you're not a royal, I wanted to scream. The court will favour Penritha and whatever sob story she constructs for her brother.

'How long until we're ready?' I asked.

'Oh, days probably.'

'More than enough time to cut your head off.'

Rodden gave a short laugh. 'I would like to see them try.'

'Well, I wouldn't!' I cried, and tore from the stables.

SIXTEEN

The next afternoon, under a heavy grey sky, I watched Princess Penritha and her retinue gallop the final distance to the palace. The princess sat atop a large black horse surrounded by a contingent of soldiers in full armour and armed with halberds. Her long brown curls hung loose down her back and she wore a riding habit of crimson and ebony. The Ansengaad standard, a black serpent against a red background the same shade as the princess's dress, flapped in the wind.

Never did a royal party look more like it was about to go into battle.

Standing on my balcony a hundred feet above, I was too far distant to see the expression on Penritha's features. But her brother's face flashed before my eyes, flushed red and ferocious as he wielded the whip. I shuddered. I had never met the princess but if she was anything like her sibling it was an introduction I would rather forgo.

Rodden had departed that morning for the alchemist's, swearing to do all he could to hurry things along. He'd mentioned that there was something strange about the yelinate he'd collected in Amentia – that it was discoloured somehow, perhaps impure.

'What if it doesn't work?' I'd said, suddenly sick with worry.

'It will work,' he'd assured me. 'But trying to purify it has delayed things.'

He'd warned that he could be absent all day and possibly the evening, and seeing the fearsome retinue approach, I was glad. Princess Penritha was out for blood.

At the appointed hour I entered the great hall for the first time since returning to Xallentaria. As reluctant as I was to be in her presence, I would face this woman. She wouldn't be given the opportunity to spread lies without someone holding her accountable.

I took my seat at the high table next to Carmelina and received a greeting from the king and queen. Amis gave me a warm smile, and I allowed myself to relax slightly. Amis was on Rodden's side. He would protect Rodden no matter what.

The trestles below were filled with courtiers glistening with jewels and clad in fine velvets and silks. How strange it was to look upon them again after being among the ordinary folk of Pergamia and the Jarbin of Verapine. How much collected wealth, I wondered, was in this room tonight? And it was for this that my mother schemed and forced her daughters into marriages. I recalled the rich clothes Renata now wore, the plans she had for improving the castle. My union and Lilith's were for the good of the people, she insisted, but how much was for her own satisfaction?

Lilith took her place next to Amis and she kept her pinched white face turned away from me. I was still angry with her – and she, evidently, with me – but I felt a stab of regret. Maybe I'd been wrong of late to keep the truth from her. She was not only my sister, she would be queen of Pergamia one day and would have to know the truth about Lharmell. I did not relish her reaction when I revealed myself to her.

Princess Penritha entered. She had her brother's wide mouth and hard eyes. Her shoulders were broad in her scarlet dress and she held herself with pride. Some might think her handsome, just as they did Folsum. But I read cruelty in her features.

Several ladies of Ansengaad proceeded into the hall behind the princess and settled themselves at various tables. They all gave me cool looks before turning to their neighbours and speaking in low voices. The rumour mill had begun. By the end of the second course many of the courtiers were casting looks in my direction. At the other end of the high table, Penritha remained as silent as stone.

'What is happening?' Carmelina asked, noticing the tension in the air. 'Why is everyone looking at you so?'

I pressed Carmelina's hand, aware that she was the closest thing I had to a friend in the whole room. 'You must know that no matter what is said tonight, Rodden has done nothing wrong. You do believe me, don't you, Carmelina?'

Her eyes grew as round as saucers. 'What happened in Amentia?'

I saw Penritha rise and my stomach lurched.

'Swear it,' I begged. 'Swear that you believe me or I don't know how I shall bear it.'

Carmelina nodded, holding fast to my hand.

Penritha addressed the king. 'Your Highness, while I appreciate the hospitality, I have come to Xallentaria on the most urgent business. I cannot be silent on the matter any longer.' Her voice was pitched to carry; the hall fell silent.

King Askar smiled at the princess. 'My dear, we do not discuss business when there are far more pleasant pursuits before us. Eat, drink. We can talk of sober things on the morrow – for I see from your expression that the matter has some gravity. Besides, this is the first time I have seen my daughter-in-law's sister at table these past weeks. I have a mind to scold her, and that is all the solemnity we can bear tonight.' The king winked at me.

Penritha did not sit. 'I have not the time, Your Highness. I must return to my brother early upon the morrow. He is convalescing in Amentia.'

'Oh dear,' Queen Ulah said. 'Has he been unwell?'

'More than unwell, My Queen. Prince Folsum was attacked and mutilated in a place from which he expected nothing but shelter and protection. He will never be the same again.'

Out of the corner of my eye I saw Penritha's guard edge into the hall, blocking every exit. They were unarmed, as protocol required when they were in a foreign king's court, but I felt their menace just the same. Their gaze was focused squarely on me.

I realised my mistake. Penritha hadn't come for Rodden. She'd come for me.

'An alliance was proposed between my nation of Ansengaad and Amentia,' Penritha went on. 'My brother, who will one day be king of our great nation, to be wedded to a princess of Amentia. All parties approved the match.'

I never approved it.

'As you will remember, King Askar,' she said, nodding reverently to him, 'given Pergamia's ties to Amentia you yourself were consulted and were generous enough to bestow your blessing. Papers were drawn up. There was much celebration in my kingdom. The people could not wait to greet their future queen.'

Penritha looked down as if overcome by sorrow. 'I have seen my brother. Since the attack he cannot stand to be out of doors. He takes fright at shadows and wakes screaming every night. His body bears terrible scars and his eye –' Penritha covered her face with her hand a moment. 'His left eye was torn from its socket.'

There were gasps from those at the high table and the courtiers. Queen Ulah began to fan herself.

Lilith turned to me, a question twisting her brow. Her eyes flicked to my shoulders; she had noticed my stiffness after all. Her frown deepened.

Penritha raised her head. 'You have all seen the great and terrible birds that are stabled near the northern turret. You have heard their fearsome cries. I myself approached them this very afternoon. They are wild and vicious creatures, brought back from northern parts. It was these birds that assaulted my brother. But make no mistake –' she glared round the hall – 'wild as they are, they answer to one person. Princess Zeraphina, Second Daughter of Amentia. The princess my brother was promised in marriage.'

All eyes turned to me.

'The princess, learning that she was to be affianced to Folsum, sought to do away with him. While walking in the grounds of the Amentine palace he was set upon by one of these birds in a deliberate attack.'

'That's a lie,' I shouted. 'Your brother is a bully and a brute. He attacked my bird.'

Penritha and I faced each other down the table. 'Heated words, princess. They are stoked out of love for another, are they not?'

The court held their breath. Even the king was engrossed.

'Well? Speak, Zeraphina. Or shall we ask the one who knows you best?' Penritha turned to my sister.

Please, Lilith, I silently begged. *You must know this is all lies.*

Lilith's eyes roved over the courtiers, the king and queen. Penritha. Her expression was filled with resentment and anger. I had brought scandal and upset into the court she was to one day rule, and she did not like it one bit. Finally her eyes rested on me. She seemed to come to a decision. 'It is true that she loves another.'

The room erupted with scandalised whispers. Penritha looked triumphant.

'That proves nothing,' I yelled over the din. Eventually the hall quieted. 'I was set upon by Prince Folsum in the grounds. He attacked both my bird and myself. We acted in self defence.'

'A giant eagle and a wild princess against one man?' Penritha asked. 'The defending was undoubtedly his. Do you not know how to fight, Zeraphina? Did you not best the greatest archers in the kingdom only a few months ago?'

I did not want to do it but she left me no choice. I stripped off the wrap that covered my shoulders. I yanked down the shoulders of my dress. 'This is what your precious brother did to me.' I turned, and let those at the high table and all at the trestles below gaze on Prince Folsum's handiwork. The cuts had healed over the past weeks but they were still a bright, angry red. Anyone could see that I'd been flogged.

I turned back to the high table. 'Lilith. Sister,' I implored, clutching the dress to my breast so that it did not slither to my ankles. 'Stand as my witness and tell the court that this woman has it wrong. That I could never do such a thing as she describes.'

Lilith studied the whip marks that crisscrossed my arms; the shiny red ribbons that snaked over my neck and around my shoulders. She was still angry with me, I could tell. Her eyes slid away from me. 'Cover yourself, Sister, it is unseemly.'

She didn't denounce me. She didn't call me a liar. Not out loud. But she'd as good as done so. If I didn't have the support of my own sister, no one was going to believe me. I sat in my chair, pulling my wrap around me.

Penritha said, 'Her guilt is written all over her face.'

I shrank into the cloth about my shoulders, ashamed now. Wanting to hide from all the stares, the whispering. Did Lilith really believe that out of love for Rodden I had attacked the prince? There had been mortification in her eyes, as if my display had embarrassed her. Surely my safety was more important than what the court thought of me, and, by association, of her, wasn't it?

A new voice joined the fray. 'Now, wait a minute.' It was Amis. He looked furious with Lilith. 'Those are whip marks on her back. How do you explain that if Folsum was acting in self-defence?'

'They are from an unrelated injury. Or her lover gave them to her as false evidence – or for other purposes,' Penritha said darkly.

'Listen here, I know Rodden –'

I winced.

Penritha arched her brow. 'Oh, so it is common knowledge that they are lovers? I wonder that no one thought to inform the good people of Ansengaad.'

Amis began to stammer a reply but he was drowned out.

'I noticed he is absent, this Rodden Lothskorn,' she said, her voice thick with scorn. 'It is no small matter, meddling with the property of Ansengaad. There could be grave consequences.' She let these words settle over the crowd a moment. 'But,' she went on, her voice brisk, 'my brother and I want a speedy resolution to this whole affair. I am here to ensure that what was promised to the people of Ansengaad is delivered. A bride for their prince.'

I felt sick. Folsum still wanted to marry me. I remembered what Rodden had said, about men who enjoyed having their low opinion of women confirmed. If I was wed to Folsum I was as good as dead.

'The princess has assured my brother that she remains pure of body if not of heart, and despite his present condition and all indications being contrary, he is willing to take her at her word – if she will honour the agreement that exists between Ansengaad and Amentia. If his generosity is refused, however, the prince and I will see to it that all parties involved in this sordid, underhanded affair are brought to justice.'

I looked into Penritha's grey eyes. Rodden. She would kill Rodden if I didn't agree to marry her brother. He might believe that he couldn't be convicted of a capital offence in Pergamia, but I knew that Penritha would find a way – legal or otherwise.

I heard the thud of heavy footsteps. Penritha's guard approached the high table.

'My dear, you forget where you are,' King Askar said, an edge to his voice. His own guard, fully armed and armoured, watched Penritha intently.

The princess held up her hand, and the men halted.

I didn't mistake their purpose. How fitting, I thought numbly, that I be escorted from the room as if for execution.

I couldn't stand the staring eyes any longer. 'The prince is very generous,' I whispered. I rose, clutching my disarranged clothing around me. As I left the dais the soldiers closed in and I was shepherded from the hall. Not a single voice spoke in protest.

I felt the silence of one in particular most keenly.

———

It was only once I was back in my room that I began to panic.

Penritha's guard was stationed outside my door. I ran to my balcony, already knowing that it was hopeless. There was a hundred-foot drop to the ground below. Even if I had that many sheets to tie together I would be too terrified to attempt the climb down. I looked up and saw only the sheer face of the palace walls rising to the battlements above.

I went back in. The room was dark and I huddled behind a sofa, needing the security that concealment brought. I hugged my knees to my chest and shivered on the cold marble floor.

I had to kill Folsum. If I didn't kill him he would kill me, or worse. I must do it soon, and do it properly. I would never get a second chance once he was on his guard. If I killed him in Amentia while he was still bedridden I could take a horse and disappear into the forest. There was the risk that I'd run into harmings but, honestly, being taken to Lharmell would almost be a blessing. Anything to get me away from Penritha and her guard.

Could I do it; murder him in cold blood? Creep into his room at night and slit his throat? I thought of the harming in Verapine that Rodden had not wanted me to kill; his words, all those weeks ago.

No matter how remorseful you are or even if you have no choice in the matter, you'll always be that person, the one holding the knife, with blood on their hands.

I wondered what would be worse: being a cold-blooded murderer or wedded to Folsum. I felt the sting of my scars against the cold marble wall and knew what I'd choose when the time came. No matter what it made me.

Something thumped on my balcony. I sat up. There was silence, and then a slithering sound and a louder thump.

I froze. Harmings? I reached out tentatively with my mind –

Rodden. I leapt to my feet. I was on the balcony in a second and threw myself into his arms with such force that he staggered. I pressed my face into his shirt and squeezed him with all my might.

'Zeraphina, I have been gone less than a day.' His voice was exasperated but his hands buried themselves in my hair, and for a moment he held me as tight as I held him. He smelled of wood smoke and strange chemicals and the sharp tang of the desert.

'I need to rescue you more often, it seems,' he drawled.

I pulled away and looked up at him. 'They're going to make me marry him.'

'Nonsense. I've a fate far worse in mind for you.' With a flourish he indicated the knotted rope he'd used to climb down to my balcony. 'You might want to change, though. Warm clothes and boots.'

For the first time I noticed he wore his black harming cloak. My eyes widened. He saw the question in them and said, 'We're going to Lharmell tonight.'

———

Minutes later I stood on the balcony wearing boots and trousers and my own black cloak. I clutched Leap in my arms. 'How am I going to get him up there?' I asked, looking at the sheer climb ahead of me. I was only barely certain that I could do it myself, let alone while carrying my big silver cat.

'I don't know if you can bring him,' Rodden said.

'Of course I can bring him! He's very capable, aren't you, Leap?' Leap was looking about with big worried eyes. He knew something was wrong. 'I need him.'

'We're going to be in the very heart of Lharmell for days. He might get spotted. They'll kill him.'

I hugged Leap to my chest. 'But he's very careful …' I trailed off. Leap wanted to come, I could feel it. He wriggled in my arms, pushing himself up under my chin and holding tight to my cloak with his claws. I bit my lip. Rodden was right. Leap couldn't fly to safety like Griffin could. He would be safer at the palace. It wasn't right to bring him just because I would be heartsick without him.

'Griffin can come, though,' I said firmly. On the balcony rail, Griffin glared as if daring anyone to suggest otherwise. Glared even more than usual, that is.

'Griffin will be very useful,' Rodden agreed. 'In fact, she's a vital part of the plan.' He took Leap from me, carefully detaching his paws. I planted a kiss on my cat's fuzzy head and told him to be good. He looked very forlorn, sitting there watching us leave. I made him promise to keep out of Penritha's sight, to hide until our return. And then I was climbing the rope, hand over hand, my feet braced against the castle wall, up into the darkness. After twenty feet my hands were burning in my gloves. I was only halfway and the thought of the drop beneath me – not just twenty feet, but a hundred and twenty, because if I fell I was unlikely to stop at the balcony – made a pang go through the soles of my feet. Somewhere above me, Griffin made a clicking noise in her throat. I saw myself in her mind's eye, a deficient, wingless creature who was forever struggling over flat surfaces. I reached the battlements and tugged myself over, gasping. I held fast to the rope as Rodden climbed up after me, knowing it was tied securely but still seeing that drop into darkness. As soon as he appeared I grasped his arms and pulled him over the top. He was breathing heavily too and shot Griffin an annoyed look.

'I would like to see how silly you'd look if you had to walk everywhere,' he said.

Griffin ruffled her feathers and glared in the other direction.

The sky was full of stars and an enormous moon. It was not quite full. When it was, there would be a Turning. Our brants were tethered a few yards off. In the darkness their beaks shone black. As I took stock of our situation I found it uncomfortably familiar – fleeing one danger in Pergamia only to land in even more peril across the straits in Lharmell. But this time I had Rodden and we were prepared. My feet wouldn't burn in the forest, because I had boots. I wouldn't stumble unarmed into a coven of Lharmellins. I would shoot them full of arrows and hear their dying screams.

The brants had bulging saddlebags strapped to their girths – the glass balls, filled with yelbar gas. Enough to kill all the Lharmellins in Lharmell? Possibly. But probably not. But if we destroyed their leader – their true leader this time – we might stand a chance at knocking out the rest one at a time. As well as the gas we had quivers filled with yelbar-tipped arrows and a yelbar knife each. I itched for some target practice.

'We've only got a small window of time to depart,' Rodden whispered. 'I've told the captain of the guard to stand down his archers. It puts the palace at risk for an attack so we only have minutes. After that, they'll fire at anything in the sky. Are you ready?'

My stomach lurched but I nodded. We mounted our birds. I saw that Griffin was settled on the saddle horn and with the beating of sooty black wings, we were off.

Looking down, I saw the outline of archers against the battlements, their bows lowered but ever vigilant, watching the skies. Rodden hailed a figure as we banked the birds and shot past the eastern parapet. I heard a shout of triumph and recognised Hoggit's voice. Then we were climbing, up into the night sky. The ground fell away to forest beneath us, then briefly cliff and rock and pounding spray. And then open ocean. In just minutes the temperature dropped from freshness to crackling cold. My ears stung in the frosty air.

For the first time in months the pain in my back began to shrink. The tors could feel me coming.

I kept my eyes fixed on the horizon. I could see the silver-tipped swell of the ocean. Then in almost no time at all, the silver gave way to a black hole of nothingness.

Lharmell.

It frightened me all over again just how close it was to Pergamia. I searched the blackness as we passed over but nothing in the burnt forest reflected any light. It seemed to suck in the moonlight.

I wondered how many Lharmellins and harmings were abroad, and tightened the hold on my mind.

I lifted my eyes and saw the tors, craggy on the dark horizon, outlined against the stars. Something twisted painfully in my breast. There was part of me that longed for the tors. The pain disappeared altogether and was replaced by a rush of euphoria.

Home.

The word beat out a rhythm on my bones. I was home. The Lharmellins were my family. My blood.

And I was going to kill them all.

SEVENTEEN

We didn't put the birds down where we'd hidden the last time, at the dolmen just outside the tors. Instead, after skimming the forest we began to rise again, flying over the mountain and into the very heart of Lharmell.

I searched the skies with my eyes and mind. All seemed quiet. We reached the peaks and hurtled down the other side, our birds wing to wing. I flew with Rodden round the curve of the bowl-shaped valley, an ancient spent volcano crater filled with trees and rocky outcrops. With a whisper of feathers and the thud of talons on soil, we put the birds down. I slid from my mount. There was a copse of trees and not far off the yawning mouth of a cave. I felt a flash of recognition. That was the place I'd seen in the harming's mind at the Jarbin village. The new Turning place.

Rodden cut through the cords that held the saddlebags. I took one from him, hearing the faint tinkling of glass. The bag was almost as big as I was, and very round. It weighed next to nothing though and I followed Rodden into the trees. Branches scratched at me in the darkness and the litter was very thick and crunchy underfoot. We hid the bags under some bushes and scattered them with leaf litter. It was a poor camouflage, but the earthy colour of the bags would help disguise them. As long as no one was actively searching the area they would be safe. We did the same with the second set of bags and then mounted our brants.

At any second I expected the blood-curdling scream of a harming to pierce the darkness, but all was eerily quiet.

This time we alighted in the forest outside the tors. I stared round at the trees, marvelling that little had changed since we were last here. The trunks were still blackened. Not a leaf or blade of grass grew. I'd walked alone through this forest in the tatters of my ball gown, alone and afraid. Somewhere not far from here was the cave where I'd first convinced Rodden that we had to start fighting the Lharmellins; that we couldn't afford to wait any longer. I still marvelled at that: that this man who could be so stubborn, so frustrating, had listened to me. But then, I could be just as stubborn. And more to the point, I had been right.

I stroked the brant's neck for a moment. This had been the one to turn on Folsum after he'd given it a beating, and likely saved my life. 'Thank you,' I whispered. It shuffled left and right for a moment, and then nudged at my shoulder with its beak. The force nearly knocked me down but I could recognise an affectionate gesture.

Rodden swigged from a water skin. He passed it to me. 'Three nights till the full moon. That gives us time to get everything in place. If we're able to seal that cave … nothing is getting out alive.'

'Including us,' I said. 'We have to be careful.'

Rodden was lost in thought.

I nudged him with my foot. 'Rodden, did you hear me? We have to be careful. We could get trapped at the Turning.' I remembered the press of bodies, the uncontrollable urge to strain towards the Lharmellin blood. I thought I would be able to keep my wits about me this time, but Rodden and I could so easily be separated.

'What? Oh. Of course. You'll be fine, don't worry. I wouldn't let anything happen to you.'

'To us,' I corrected.

'Listen, I've been thinking ...'

I shoved the cork back in the water skin. '*What* have you been thinking?'

'There's no need for us both to go to the Turning. Only one of us needs to seal the exit and break the master glass. I should have thought of it back at the palace, but I've gotten so used to us doing things together. And I didn't want to leave you to Penritha and her sabre-rattling.'

'That's because we're better when we work together. What if you're trying to seal the exit and you get seen?' What if he got trapped inside and broke the master glass anyway, thinking he was doing the right thing? I wouldn't put it past Rodden to do such a thing.

'Well, I'd fight them off,' he said with a shrug.

'There could be too many. Anything could happen. And you're forgetting the most important thing.'

'What?'

'I'm not going to let you.'

He gave me a wry smile. 'I should have realised as much.'

'Yes, you should.'

'All right. But I'm taking the master glass. And

I'm not breaking it or sealing anything unless I know you're well away from the Turning.'

I nodded. 'Fine by me. What do we do in the meantime?'

'We could see what we can learn from the other harmings,' he suggested. 'Who's in charge. How many harmings they're expecting. It could help us in the future if this plan fails somehow.'

'Is it safe to talk to them, do you think?'

'It would mean splitting up. We're more recognisable together. I would prefer you not going in at all, but –'

'But I'm stubborn,' I finished for him. 'We can learn more if we both enter the tors. I'll seal my mind like a vice. Hide behind my hair. They shan't recognise me.'

———

Pre-dawn blackness lightened to blue-grey gloom. Black slashes became the twisted, burned trunks of trees. Heavy grey clouds threatened rain, or possibly even snow. It was cold enough for it. Frost glimmered on the forest floor.

I shivered. I'd relinquished my cloak and hidden it in some bushes. Alone, I'd run snarls into my hair.

I would have liked to rub dirt under my nails and into my face, but it would have burned me. The Lharmellins made the trees and ground around Lharmell toxic by calling down acid rain.

I'd positioned myself on what seemed to be a well-worn track half a mile from the tors, hoping I looked like a forlorn, confused part-harming who'd gotten this far but was too scared or stupid to go any further. I had a yelbar knife concealed beneath my clothes and had to resist the urge to pass my hand over it for comfort.

Rodden was approaching the tors from another direction. We might not see each other until it was time to seal the cave.

I heard a crunching noise. Footsteps. There wasn't just one harming. It sounded like a whole group of them.

They appeared through the trees. The two in front stood straight, their cloaks billowing around them. Trailing after them was a clutch of figures with shoulders hunched, wearing a collection of rags. The Turned leading the un-Turned.

Half a dozen pale blue eyes fastened onto me. I forced my mind blank but didn't bother to conceal my look of terror as they approached. I stayed where I was, teeth chattering, my eyes darting among the figures.

'Praise for blood,' said one of the figures at the front. He lifted a sardonic brow.

The other, a female, snorted. 'Close your flipping mouth, girl.'

I closed it.

The woman, in her late twenties perhaps and short and stout, narrowed her eyes, and I felt something dark and sticky brush my mind. She sighed. 'Another half-wit, and half-starved too by the look of her. Look at her skin – all the way from Pol, I'll bet.'

'And cut up good, too,' remarked the man, noticing the stripes on my neck. 'Runaway slave. Someone catch you feeding?'

'Aye, look at the way she perks up at that. Hungry, are you? Well, so am I, so get in behind,' she snapped.

I scurried to the rear of the group. The woman started off at a brisk walk and the un-Turned trailed after, clutching our goose-pimpled arms.

The man noticed me trailing and slowed his pace. 'Cold, are you?'

I nodded and looked at the ground.

'Never mind, girl, we'll have you at the tors soon enough and get you a belly full o' blood.' He made to clutch me about the shoulders but I evaded him. 'Scared, were you,' he asked, 'coming all this way by yourself? Aye, I imagine you were. And been scared many a time before, I can see.' He nodded at my shoulders. 'Them cuts go all over, I bet.' He tutted. 'Humans. Rotten creatures.'

I was surprised by his words. Could he really think of humans how we thought of harmings? But then, it had been a human who'd done this to me. I'd put Folsum on a par with most harmings I'd met.

'Never find us treating each other in such a manner,' he went on. 'There's no need to be afeared any more, chit. We'll take care of you. You're home now.'

———

We trudged along the forest paths and collected seven more cold and bewildered newcomers. Some had used brants, as I had the first time I'd come to Lharmell, not knowing what I was getting into but clambering aboard the giant bird just the same. Some had come in boats. Others had travelled with full-fledged harmings. The Turned greeted one another and then stood about assessing each other's contribution to the Lharmellin cause like we were so many cattle.

'Sorry bloody bunch.'

'Snivelling idiots, most o' them.'

'He'll do all right, that one there. Arms like tree trunks. He'll go well in the field. Not a fighter among the rest of them, though.'

'Just look at her,' said the woman, kicking dirt in my direction. 'What was our brother thinking what made her? Mind like a dull tack.'

This went on for a bit longer while us 'sorry bloody bunch' grew colder and colder.

Finally, the woman sighed. 'All right. Call down the birds. I'm hungry.'

A moment later eight black shapes appeared in the sky above the forest. A ripple of unease went through the un-Turned, even though most had already ridden on the giant birds. As they dived towards us I let rip with my loudest, most terrified shrieking, and got boxed about the ears. Several others cowered, hands over their heads. I followed suit, dropping to the ground, careful not to let any bare skin touch the dirt.

The harmings roared with laughter and yanked us up by the scruffs of our clothing.

'Quiet yourself, chit,' said the man who had collared me. 'Only a few birdies. They don't mean you any harm. Come on, you'll ride with me.' He looped an arm about my waist and carried me bodily to the waiting mounts. I took a deep breath, preparing to scream, but he cut me off. 'I don't like to, but if you scream in my ear I'm not above clouting you a good 'un.'

I reasoned I'd probably made a fair impression already. No one suspected I was the rebel harming who'd last year infiltrated a Turning and murdered their leader before their very eyes.

So I closed my mouth.

He lifted me onto the bird and climbed up after. 'Now, sit still, or you'll fall and break your damn silly legs.'

———

I had been surprised by the amount of leaf litter the previous evening and now I saw where it came from. The valley within the tors had, months earlier, been filled with evergreens. Now they were stripped and blackened. That was because of Rodden and me, and the acid storm the Lharmellins had called down after we'd slain their leader. It had killed the brant we'd been riding, separated us from Griffin, and nearly killed us, too.

From the air I saw the movements of bodies clothed in black and brown and grey, but it was difficult to tell numbers among the burned trees. The harmings set the birds down. I dismounted, the harming man holding tight to my wrist.

'What is your name?' I asked him, staring into the crowd. Hundreds, I thought, watching the milling bodies. Perhaps thousands.

'Gribben.'

I was tired of playing the frightened idiot. 'Let go of me, Gribben,' I said.

My tone startled him. He dropped my arm. Without a backwards look I marched into the crowd.

———

Someone handed me a cloak. I put it on and pulled up the hood. Then I stood very still.

I shouldn't try this. I might give myself away. But I had to know Griffin was safe. Breathing deep once, twice to steady my nerves, I sent a tendril of my mind eastwards, over the heads of the crowd. I was surrounded on all sides by harmings, Turned and otherwise. One slip and I would be dead.

There she is.

Griffin. Working hard for us. My heart swelled with pride. *Good girl*, I thought fiercely. The Turning place remained deserted. I felt Griffin fly from the copse into the cave, the leather cord tied around the lip of a sphere grasped in her talons. She hid the spheres behind rocks, on ledges – any place that would conceal them.

I drew away with care and came back to myself. I looked around. No one was paying me the slightest attention. I could do it! I could conceal myself from them.

I smelled blood and realised how hungry I was. I forced my way through the press of bodies until backs closed like a wall in front of me and I simply had to wait my turn. Finally a rough, unfired clay bowl was pressed into my hands. I tipped my head back and downed the scant mouthful. I handed back the bowl and shuffled off to the right with the rest. The amount was hardly sufficient but it soothed the dull ache of hunger that had been growing in my chest. It wasn't until the crowd had thinned that I noticed what a funny taste it had.

Horse, I thought. No, I could taste horses, but it wasn't horse blood. I ran my tongue over the roof of my mouth, trying to discern the flavour. Cattle? No, that wasn't right either. I tasted iron and fresh green grass and ... bread?

Farmer.

My hand flew to my mouth. Oh no. No, no, *no*.

What had I *done*? Of course it wasn't animal blood they were handing out. It was –

In the shadows cast by the rock face I saw them. Seven naked bodies strung up by their feet, arms dangling. Blood trickled over their wrists, dripping from their fingers and down over their chins. There were deep gashes in their necks, throats split ear to ear. I was close enough to see the shocked expressions in their eyes. Two of the bodies were small; children not yet into their tenth summers. Three were women. One was corpulent, the ropes cutting viciously into her ankles. I spotted the farmer, a man in his sixties, his hair greyed and his blue eyes clouded with age. All the bodies were streaked with dirt as if they had been dragged across the ground.

As I watched, a harming crouched before the shallow dishes laid out beneath the dripping bodies. She ladled blood into the earthenware bowls and brought them to the waiting crowd.

Horror and disgust was building up inside me, an uncontrollable wave that was about to burst forth and give me away. I tried to bite down on the feelings but they were too much. I couldn't look away. Any second, someone was going to hear.

A hand clamped on my shoulder and spun me round.

'Come away,' Rodden said. He reached for my hand.

We weren't supposed to be seen together. In all likelihood we were far more recognisable this way, after travelling so far together. I should have turned and marched in the other direction but my mind was churning and his hand holding mine was so warm. So comforting.

'I drank blood,' I whispered to him, voice shaking. 'It was –'

'Hush. I know. I saw.' His voice was sympathetic. I saw he wore the backpack that contained the master glass.

'I can't believe I was so stupid. I feel sick. I feel like I'm going to –'

We had only moved a few feet when it happened.

'Hey!' The exclamation was indignant, surprised. I looked up to see a man staring at us, frozen mid-stride, as if he couldn't quite believe what he was seeing.

The face was familiar. I dropped Rodden's hand, a guilty little gesture.

It was Orrik, changed since we'd last seen him on board the *Jessamine*, hurling us overboard. His hair was black and his eyes paler.

Rodden cursed.

Orrik had seen us kill harmings with his own

eyes. I looked around for somewhere for us to run. We were surrounded on all sides.

He drew his cutlass. 'The traitors!' he screamed.

I felt hundreds of pairs of eyes turn to look at us. Several more men drew their cutlasses and I recognised them as sailors from the *Jessamine*, too.

The crowd began to close in around us, their voices growing in pitch and volume as word spread.

I grasped Rodden's arm and started backing away, feeling for my knife. I could see Rodden was reaching for his, too. We edged closer, standing back-to-back, weapons drawn.

We should have realised the sailors might be here, and could recognise us. It seemed so unfair, to survive for this long only to be caught right before we could execute the final part of our plan. We'd travelled so far, been through so much to get here. And now it was over.

Rodden began to say something to me, but it was too late. Harmings leapt for us. I swiped viciously with my knife, catching one on the arm. It reeled back, the wound smoking.

They scrabbled at my clothing, tearing the cloak from my body. The knife was knocked from my hands. Ragged nails scratched at my skin. A hundred furious white-blue eyes danced around me. I opened my mouth to scream and a fist connected with my lower jaw. My teeth snapped painfully together and everything went black.

———

Rodden's breath, quick and fast. Cursing. The sounds of a beating. A cry of pain.

My arms ached. They were raised over my head and bound tightly at the wrists. Sharp rocks poked my spine. The ground beneath my feet was hard and just as uneven. I was stiff with cold and my head ached horribly. I opened my eyes and for a moment thought it was night. Then I saw the rocky ceiling above. All around.

The Turning place?

We were inside a smaller cave, perhaps an offshoot of the main cavern. Several feet from me, three figures danced in the lamplight. A man was at their feet, his white shirt grimed and bloodied. As I watched, one of the figures aimed a kick at his head and he fell backwards. He landed with a thud at my feet and lay there gasping for air.

'Rodden,' I croaked.

His eyes fluttered. Blood trickled over his face.

A figure loomed towards us. I recognised Orrik.

'The bitch is awake. Melf, where's that bottle the master gave us?'

'Why are you hurting him?' I cried as one of the sailors dragged him away from me. Pain flashed through my jaw. Orrik took a bottle from one of the others and yanked out the cork. His hand gripped my hair and jerked my head back. The bottle was pressed against my lips and a bitter liquid flooded my mouth. I knew the taste. Laudanum. Fingers pinched my nose and the angle of my head meant I had to swallow or drown in a mouthful of liquid.

I swallowed. Orrik forced the whole bottle down my throat and then flung the glass vessel against the wall of the cave. It exploded into bright blue shards. He turned back to Rodden.

The whole bottle. I knew little about the drug but had heard that large doses were ill-advised. Dangerous, even. I doubted that he meant to kill me but, intent or not, it could be the result.

More to the point, why was I chained to a wall, drugged and ignored while Rodden received the violent attention of a group of thugs? I recognised the others now as they again lay into Rodden with their boots and fists – they too were sailors from the *Jessamine*. I was the one who had killed the rabbits, not him. I was the one who had killed the Lharmellin leader. It didn't make any sense.

'Why are you hurting him?' I called. I begged them to stop. I cried out to Rodden to defend himself but he was fairly insensible and able to do little but protect his head with his arms. I saw bruises and cuts on the faces of the sailors, evidence that, at the beginning at least, Rodden had fought back.

After a while my arms stopped aching. My body felt light and a wave of warmth rolled up from the pit of my stomach. I still watched the scene before me but no longer had the energy or inclination to call out. Then another wave engulfed me and though I could have sworn my eyes were open, I could see nothing. Then they were closed and I saw too much. I felt cold, but too heavy to shiver. I was distantly aware of time passing. The lamplight was gone. Then it was back again. Rodden and the sailors disappeared.

How odd, I thought, that I could see all this with my eyes closed, but nothing with them open.

This didn't bother me overmuch. I hadn't a care in the world.

———

I awoke with a gasp to utter darkness. A bolt of terror hit me. I was blind! The drug had done something to my eyes. I closed them, thinking that perhaps they were still broken and doing things backwards. More blackness. I began to shiver, great, teeth-clacking shivers that made my bruised jaw ache. I stared hard around the alcove, blinking rapidly. A shaft of pale yellow light fell across the entranceway and everything else snapped into focus. My racing heart slowed. Not blind. Just cold and alone and in the dark. The stupefaction had passed and I was again subject to terror, fear and pain. Everything was back to normal.

A hollow ache in my chest indicated it had been several days since I had fed. I must have been unconscious for all that time. I had a sense of time passing, voices speaking around me. My arms, still tied above my head, ached. My fingers were cold and swollen and I was barely able to move them. I pulled weakly at the knots and the room began to spin. Leaning to the side, I retched bile, foul and bitter tasting. It reeked of laudanum. When the queasiness passed I straightened and looked around again.

There was a shape on the floor ten feet away. 'Rodden?' I whispered. There was no response. I searched for the thread between us but the laudanum had dulled everything. I couldn't feel the tors, but that might have been because they were sitting right on top of me. That thought brought on another wave of nausea and for a few minutes I concentrated my breathing so as not to not to be sick all over myself. When it passed I held my breath and strained forwards. I caught the sound of Rodden's shallow breath and sagged with relief.

I leaned back. So, Orrik was a harming. We hadn't thought of that, which made us very stupid as we both knew that the *Jessamine* hadn't made it to port. If I hadn't been so shaken by the sight of the dead humans strung up by their ankles then we might not have been recognised. I mentally kicked myself. What had I expected them to eat? This was Lharmell.

The sound of singing reached my ears, an inexpressibly sweet sound. The Lharmellins were chanting. Blood rushed to the surface of my skin, answering their call. The singing grew louder, the notes overlapping one another as they echoed off stone. Human voices joined the song – or rather, harming voices. The voices of those about to be Turned. I realised it was happening now. The Turning. Would we be forced to join them, or be thrown into the crowd and torn apart at the climax of the blood frenzy? I tried to imagine what would be worse. Once Turned, would I remember the things I had done this past year and loathe myself for having killed so many harmings? Worse, would I turn on the ones I loved? I imagined returning to the palace in Pergamia. Poisoning the wine at the high table with Lharmellin blood. The king a harming. My sister. Carmelina.

My mind fled from this. Far better to be dead than commit such deeds.

The backpack. Where could it be? Was there any possibility we would even be able to find it? Smashing the master glass with us inside the cave would be suicide but at least we would take many of them out with us. I wondered if I could bear to break it, knowing that Rodden and I would probably die too. I wondered if I would even be given the chance.

Footsteps. The entranceway grew brighter. A figure appeared holding a lamp and a bucket. It was a man, tall and sallow with forearms as thick as tree branches and roughened with sparse black hairs. Blue veins stood out on his lined face, though his movements betrayed no stiffness. He paused to gaze down at Rodden and the look of relish on his grizzled features made my blood run cold.

He placed the lamp on a ledge and dumped the contents of the bucket over Rodden. The water ran red with his blood. Rodden groaned, and struggled into a sitting position. There was dried blood on his top lip and chin and his face was a mess of bruises and swellings. The harming threw away the bucket and cut Rodden's bindings. He winced in pain and relief as they fell away.

'Are you okay?' I croaked.

Rodden's head snapped up. He saw me tied to the wall and his eyes widened. He turned to the harming. 'What is she doing here? This has nothing to do with her.'

The man gave a short, barking laugh. 'Come now. Are you very surprised?' His voice was gravelly with age.

I glanced between the two men. There was bitterness on Rodden's face.

'You know each other?' I asked.

'Oh, we're old friends,' the man rasped, turning to me with a smile. The teeth that hadn't yet dropped out of his head were black. His nose looked as if it had been broken several times. Puffy blue veins stood out all over his bald head. 'Won't you introduce us, my boy?'

His father? But his father was dead.

Rodden gave a heavy sigh. 'Zeraphina, this is Levin Servilock.'

EIGHTEEN

'It's you.' I spluttered the words into the silence that ensued. Rodden had his face pressed against his knees. Servilock stood there grinning and looking between us. This was the man who had given Rodden Lharmellin blood. Who had made him kill his family and the girl he loved. A man clever enough to run a harming training enclave right in the middle of a city. And now he was here, in Lharmell.

'You're the new leader, aren't you?' I asked. My mind raced. 'The way the harmings have changed their behaviour since we killed the Lharmellin leader – the way they seem more organised, more devious. That's because of you. I've heard about you,' I spat. 'You're a monster.'

He gave Rodden a vicious kick to the ribs, eliciting a yelp of pain. 'Say that again, girl.'

I bit back my next words.

'Very good.' He paced around Rodden, looking down at him. 'What a treat it is to have you both here. I knew my star pupil would return to me. I waited so long for him in Verapine, and then I thought, no. He won't come back to me here. He'll go to Lharmell. And it was here my real work began. I have galvanised the harmings into an inexorable force. Made them realise that they're not slaves. That we are the ones with the true power, for we retain our human cunning. We are free to move about the world.' He smiled his nasty smile. 'And here you are, my boy.' He looked up at me. 'I must thank you, by the way. In the confusion and sorrow that followed the death of the Lharmellin leader I was able to take control of everything. All harmings look to me now.'

'But do the Lharmellins? They don't want to sing for you, do they? They've let Amentia become warm again.'

His lip curled into a snarl. 'They'll comply. They'll see this is the right way. The Turnings continue. The ice will follow.' He produced a knife and looked down at Rodden. 'Now, down to business.'

My eyes widened. 'No!'

He raised an eyebrow. 'What, this?' he said, holding the weapon aloft. 'Oh, it's not for him, girl.'

Rodden started. 'No, you can't –' He was kicked again for his efforts and lay on the ground, gasping.

Servilock approached me, crouching down to scrutinise my face. He was so close I could smell his fetid breath. 'You're not as pretty as the other one. She was milk and honey, all softness.' His eyes roved over me. 'You, you're … pointy. As prickly as a kitten that can't sheathe its claws.'

He must have meant Ilona. Milk and honey. And I was pointy. Even now the comparison made my heart twist with jealousy. No wonder he didn't love me.

His eyes narrowed. 'But you love him. That's more than she did. Poor Rodden. I tried to tell him she was never going to marry him. He's got such terrible taste in women, you see. They're always landing him in trouble. Why, he wouldn't be here now if it wasn't for you. That's right, isn't it?' he rasped. 'Wasn't this all your idea?'

I seized upon his words. 'Yes, it was me. I'm the one who killed the leader. This was all my idea. Let Rodden go, please. Throw me to the harmings. Let them rip me apart if that's what you want. You've already done enough to Rodden.'

'Hmm,' he said, considering my words. 'Not a bad little speech.' He turned to Rodden. 'Your turn, my boy. Care to beg for her life?'

Rodden's face crumpled. 'I'm sorry, Zeraphina.' He seemed defeated.

'What, is that all? But then, you never begged for Ilona's life, either. It would have been strange if you had, though, since it was you who was killing her.'

Rodden was silent, and it frightened me. It was as if he'd already given up.

'Girl,' he said, 'you're looking at the future ruler of Lharmell. He will take my place once I am gone. He will be even greater than me. I trained him to be so. Under harming rule, Lharmell has flourished this last year. More harmings. Enclaves throughout the land. Under Rodden, it will thrive.'

'He'll never be like you,' I spat.

Servilock smiled at me – a pitying smile. 'We'd better get this started, don't you think?'

Rodden looked up in time to see Servilock drag the point of the knife across my chest.

He scored me from collarbone to opposite shoulder. He grinned as he did it, his yellowed eyes bright. I screamed and kicked out at him, drowning out Rodden's hollers of protest. My foot connected with the harming's ribs and the knife jerked away.

I writhed in my bindings. Blood soaked the front of my dress. How was this going to end? I couldn't see a way out, not when Rodden had already given up.

When my eyes stopped watering I noticed a dark shape in the corner, beyond where Rodden sat.

There it was. His backpack. It was out of my reach but Rodden could get to it easily. There was no way of telling him it was there, though, without alerting Servilock. But if I distracted Servilock it might give Rodden the chance to see it for himself.

'Did you see that Turning?' I asked, my voice shrill from pain.

Look up, you dolt, I urged Rodden. *Look around.* He was eyeing the knife in Servilock's grip and for a moment I wondered if he was thinking of a way to get it from him. But the misery and fear in his eyes made my hopes plummet. 'Did you see me kill your leader?'

'Don't provoke him, Zeraphina. It will only be worse for you,' Rodden said.

Stupid man. I wasn't trying to provoke him, I was trying to distract him.

Servilock grinned at Rodden. 'Ah, so you can feel it?'

'Feel *what*?' I asked.

Rodden nodded. 'Yes. Please, let her go. Once was enough. Don't make me do it again.'

'Nonsense. You'll enjoy yourself. Just like last time.'

Rodden squeezed his eyes shut. 'Make her – make her like –' He cut himself off.

'What, Turn her? And have a constant reminder of your betrayal? I don't think so.'

'No!' How could Rodden ask for such a thing? And what could he feel? Thanks to the laudanum I could feel nothing. I wondered dimly where Griffin could be, and hoped she hadn't been caught. What if the Lharmellins had discovered the yelbar gas and removed it? But if they had, surely Servilock would be gloating over our thwarted plan.

'Even afterwards, I'll remember,' Rodden said. 'Just like last time. But this time I won't run away. I'll kill you the first chance I get.'

Well, this was more like it. 'Don't drink anything, Rodden. No matter what he does to me.' *Not while the bag is there. We still have a chance.*

The singing beyond our alcove reached a crescendo. Rodden moaned. A shudder went through him and he collapsed in a heap.

'Rodden!'

'Foolish girl,' Servilock sneered.

'What have you done to him?'

Servilock gazed down at his former pupil writhing

about on the floor. From the Turning place came the first unearthly scream of the frenzy.

'No,' I whispered.

Servilock knelt down and stroked Rodden's black hair from his brow. 'It is done. I gave him the blood hours ago.'

No!' My screams were lost among the shrieking of the Turning ceremony. I pulled afresh at the ropes that bound my wrists but they did not give an inch. 'Get away from him.'

Servilock looked up, eyes flashing. 'He was never yours, girl. He was always mine. It was just a matter of time before he came back to me. Deep down, he knew I was here.'

'No, he didn't. He searched for you in Pol.'

Pleasure suffused his face. 'You see. My students never desert me. They are bound to me. They love me.'

'He wanted to kill you. He told me what you made him do to his family, to – that girl.'

A thousand voices rose in ecstasy. Rodden's back arched. There was a scream of a dying Lharmellin, sacrificed so the harming numbers could grow.

'He's going to be hungry when he wakes up. He hasn't fed in days.'

Rodden roared, the sound of an animal in pain.

'He won't hurt me.'

'That's where you're wrong.' Servilock pinned me with his icy stare. 'He's not your Rodden any more. He's becoming something else.'

The singing died away. Rodden stilled. He opened his eyes.

'There,' Servilock whispered.

I held my breath, waiting. He would know me. He had to know me.

Slowly, Rodden pulled himself upright. His nostrils flared.

'Rodden?'

His head turned in my direction. His irises were white, the pupils pinned. Unable to help myself, I shrank back. He looked terrifying. He looked *hungry.*

'It is messier when the blood is given before the ceremony,' Servilock said. 'But as you can see, it gets the job done.' He stood back. 'And it's only going to get messier.'

Rodden's eyes locked on the blood that trickled down my chest.

'It's me. Zeraphina,' I said.

He gathered his legs under his body.

'Rodden, it's *me.*'

At the same moment I started to say, too late, far

too late, 'Your pack, it's behind you,' he snarled and launched himself at me.

I would not scream because I refused to be afraid of him. This was Rodden. Rodden who'd bandaged my cuts. Who'd kissed my cheek and once, such a long time ago it seemed now, had given me the only kiss my lips had ever known. Rodden, who could never hurt me no matter how much he feared he might.

So why was it happening now?

His eyes were wide, the pupils tiny black dots in his pale irises. He snarled, his breath hot on my neck. The knife flashed. It sat at an odd angle in his hands, as if he was unaware of it being in his grasp. He grabbed at me – and the snarling died away. He enfolded me in a brutal embrace and he pressed himself against me, shuddering. Behind me the knife scraped against stone.

'My love,' he whispered. I felt dampness where he pressed his cheek against my own. 'My love.'

My heart swelled fit to burst. He had not Turned! He knew me. Somehow, some way, the blood had not driven him out of his body. 'Rodden. Oh, thank the stars.' Our tears mingled. His hand stroked my hair, the knife still in his grasp. His other hand trailed over the gash on my breast.

'Ilona,' he whispered.

I stiffened. Over Rodden's shoulder Servilock was grinning at me. I began to struggle. 'No. Rodden, it's me. Zeraphina.' I tried to push him away from me, needing to see his face, but he held me fast. 'Rodden, please.' I searched for the thread between us. The laudanum had begun to fade but I was sluggish and it kept slipping from my grasp. The man at the other end didn't feel right. He was still Rodden, but there was a sticky blackness to his insides that hadn't been there before, as if they had been coated with tar.

'Your bag,' I said desperately. 'It's behind you.'

Rodden pulled back slightly and saw the blood that now coated his fingers. They dug into my flesh and the blood flowed more freely. His white eyes bored into mine. I saw the flash of silver out of the corner of my eye. The knife.

'Rodden.' The word was a thin shriek. My voice seemed to make him pause, for I didn't feel the stab of the blade.

If he could remember Ilona from all those years ago then he could remember me. The hand that dug into my shoulder was the one that wore my silver ring. 'On your hand,' I gasped. 'Look at the ring on your hand.'

He tightened the grip on the knife and raised it over his head.

'Please,' I begged. 'Look at your hand.' I angled

my shoulder towards his face, trying to get him to see it. I could sense the struggle going on beneath the surface. Rodden was in there somewhere.

'Whose ring is that?' I asked, urgent, my voice a whisper so Servilock wouldn't overhear. 'Where did you get it? Please, you have to remember. Look,' I said, indicating my hands above me. 'I have the same one. Do you remember when I gave it to you on the battlements?'

We were both breathing hard. He didn't move, staring at me.

'*Say* something,' I pleaded.

His gaze shifted to my hands. Back at his. There was a flash of recognition in his eyes and the pupils dilated for just a moment.

Then the snarl returned.

I would not let myself be frightened. No matter how much he snarled, how shocking his eyes looked, how hungry he was, Rodden was still in there. And I was going to reach him. 'Listen, you stubborn, arrogant jerk,' I commanded, quelling the waver in my voice, 'for once in your life listen to what I'm saying and *remember who you are.*'

He opened his mouth as if to speak. I held my breath, certain he was going to say my name, and then –

He kissed me. My heart plummeted. He didn't know me. He still thought I was Ilona. Rodden would never kiss me like this. It was the kiss he'd given me in the ballroom in Pergamia. The kiss that was supposed to be the first, and the last. It had been a goodbye kiss, one to send me home. And now it was goodbye again. He must have kissed Ilona just like this. Just before he killed her. His arms encircled me, his hands holding me tight to his body. The hands that still held the knife. I kissed him back because it was the last thing I would ever do. He was gone. Servilock had won. The harmings had won. Tears leaked from the corners of my closed eyes. I still loved him. I would always love him, though always was almost over.

He broke the kiss. 'Zeraphina,' he breathed.

His knife cut through the ropes at my wrists and they fell away. Then he launched himself at the pack in the corner.

I don't know who was more shocked, me or Servilock. Rodden landed on the pack and I heard the crack of glass. A split second later a hundred glass balls shattered in unison.

Servilock stood agog, confused by what had just happened, not knowing what the breaking glass meant.

'Zeraphina,' Rodden said again, and my name on his lips invigorated me. The knife came skittering over the rock floor towards me. I grasped the hilt in my stiff fingers.

'You disobey me –' Servilock began. But then the screams started. A handful at first, confused and high, unlike those of the Turning frenzy. Screams of agony. Then the whole Turning place beyond our alcove erupted in shrieks.

Servilock staggered and braced himself against the cave wall.

'You can feel them dying, can't you?' said Rodden. 'They're all going to die. Every last one. And you as well.' He pulled a yelbar knife from his pack.

My hands were cold and swollen, but I brandished my knife and faced Servilock.

He looked between us, both free, both brandishing knives and ready to attack, as if unable to comprehend how it had happened. I could barely comprehend it myself. 'You have killed yourselves,' Servilock roared, and dashed out into the cave.

He was probably right. There was a chemical smell in the air that made me feel sick and dizzy. Rodden pulled off his cloak. 'We have to make it to the exit and seal it behind us, and we have to make it there blind. Can you run?'

'Yes, but I can't sense the direction. I was drugged –'

'Just run.' He pulled the cloak over our heads and grasped me about the waist. 'Deep breath,' he said. 'Let's go.'

We staggered into the Turning place. I could see nothing with the cloak over my head and my eyes squeezed shut, but I heard plenty. The Turning was in chaos. Bodies careened into us. The harmings seemed to be running about at random.

The yelbar gas stung my eyes. My head throbbed. I stumbled over the uneven ground, my lungs nearly bursting, but I didn't dare take a breath. Rodden tripped and fell, almost dragging me down too. I hauled on his arms and we were up and running again.

We were no longer jostled by the crowd. The passage should have been full of escaping harmings. Where were they? Were they too stupid to get away?

The air changed. Light forced its way through the thick cloth. Rodden threw it off us and, still running, we took great lungfuls of fresh air.

We stopped at the edge of the trees. I could see nothing moving. Overhead the clouds were heavy but did not threaten an acid storm.

'I must go back and seal the cave. Stay here and

call a brant.' He limped back, and I wondered how badly he was hurt.

I searched the sky for brants, and then remembered. Griffin. Where was my bird? It had been days. I tried to call her with my mind but I was still so foggy. Rodden would find her. He would be able to call a brant too. I turned back and ran to the cave.

A huge rock was being manoeuvred to block the entrance.

From the inside.

'*No!*' The scream tore through me. I doubled my speed and slammed into the rock. It didn't budge an inch. 'Rodden.' I pushed at it with all my strength. 'What are you doing? You can't stay in there. You'll die.' I scrabbled at the stone.

'Get away, Zeraphina.' I could hear him clearly despite the barrier between us. There were gaps where the rock didn't quite meet. 'You have to leave.'

'I'm not going anywhere without you. How could you trick me like this?'

'I'm sorry. You would never have let me go back in.'

'You're right about that. Come out here this instant.'

'I can't. It's over for me. I'm Turned.'

'You're not – you're fine. You came back.'

'It won't last. I can't resist the blood forever. I can already feel it changing me again. Which is why you must leave now.'

'But I love you,' I burst out.

His voice softened. 'I know you do. I love you too.'

Shock made me step back. I stared at the rock. 'Say my name,' I said. 'Say you know who I am.'

'I love you, Zeraphina.'

A great heaving sob took my voice away.

'From the moment I first heard you all the way off in Amentia, I've loved you. I couldn't keep myself away. That's why I stole your ring, so I would have a little piece of you everywhere I went. Why I arranged for your sister to marry Amis. To draw you closer, even though I knew it was wrong. I couldn't believe there was someone else like me. Someone whose insides felt like my own. You always believed in me, even after you knew the truth. But deep down I knew that it would have to end this way. I've done some terrible things. Happiness was never meant to be mine.'

My voice shook with unshed tears. 'But why do you only say this now? Why couldn't you have told me before, when you could have held me? How can I tell you that I love you with this rock between us?

Please, come out so I can tell you, or let me come in because I don't want to leave without you, no matter where you go. Do you hear? Take me with you.'

The yelbar gas would be spreading. It wouldn't be long before it reached him.

'We could run away,' I went on desperately. 'We could go to the Jarbin. Be with Uwin and Oilif. She ran away, and look at them. They are so happy together. That could be us.'

'You know it can't. I tried so hard to make this end differently. But look what we have achieved. I think we have killed every Turned harming in Lharmell. All but one. The last one has to die as well. I'm going back down the passage now, and you must find a brant and fly home. Don't let all this be for nothing.'

'No, Rodden. Don't go, not yet.' I thought frantically for a way to delay him. 'You can't leave me yet.'

But he was drawing away. I could feel it. The laudanum had faded just enough and I felt the thread between us. I tugged on it hard. As hard as I could, knowing it would hurt him, and not caring. He faltered. He was already so weak from the beating. But he continued down the passage.

And then something happened. Something like wildfire racing through a dry forest. I heard a distant cry. Orange poison raced down the thread towards me and exploded in my chest. I reeled backwards, falling to my knees and retching. Tears ran down my face and pattered on the dry leaves.

No.

I sent out clumsy thought-fingers, feeling for him.

'Rodden,' I called, pressing my face to the gaps in the rock.

It couldn't have been him. That cry had been another harming. He was still just behind the rock, waiting for me to leave so he could hide himself away in Verapine. Kill the last of the harmings without putting me in danger.

I hunted for the thread, I searched for it further and further down the passage.

But it wasn't there. He was gone.

I screamed and the sky, only just beginning to lighten, darkened again into night. An eagle's cry rent the air; my eagle. She shrieked again and again, each call sounding closer.

The clouds boiled with the power of my anguish. Bolts of lightning ripped through the heavens and thunder rumbled over the land. The sky opened, and sheets of freezing rain poured from the clouds as if they would drown all beneath them.

ACKNOWLEDGEMENTS

Thank you to all my friends and family who read *Blood Storm* through its various drafts, inspired me, and supported me beyond anything I expected. Your encouragement and enthusiasm make me so very happy. Especially the 'kisses for your brain'. And my apologies to those whom I gave nightmares!

The team at Random House Australia have been a joy to work with, again. Thank you so much Kimberley for your editing and insight; Zoe for your excitement; and Astred for the cover. THE COVER. Wow. I am one lucky author. And thanks of course to Sarana and Dorothy for all your marketing and publicity work.

I have to give a shout out to my beautiful cover girl, Ana Gremard, who not only embodies the spirit of Zeraphina effortlessly, but is model and photographer in one.

I can't imagine what it was like to write before there were blogs and Twitter, but I'm so grateful that there are now. Thank you to the Aussie blogosphere (and beyond) for getting behind *Blood Song*. Your support has been amazing.

And thank you of course to Ginger Clark, who's always got my back.

ABOUT THE AUTHOR

Rhiannon Hart remembers writing before she could read, puzzling over the strange squiggles in *Jeremiah and the Dark Woods* by Janet and Alan Ahlberg and putting her own words in their places. Her first love was Jareth the Goblin King at the tender age of eight. She wrote fan fiction in high school but she'd never admit to it out loud, so don't ask. When she's not reading or writing she is belly dancing, chasing after other people's cats, or putting the pedal to the floor at her sewing machine. She grew up in north-western Australia and currently resides in Melbourne, where she works in marketing. Rhiannon has been published in the *Australian Book Review*, *Magpies*, *Viewpoint* and mamamia.com.au and blogs at rhiannon-hart.blogspot.com. Rhiannon is currently working on the Third Book of Lharmell.

Did you miss

BLOOD SONG

THE FIRST BOOK OF LHARMELL

Read on for a sample

ONE

I was thinking of blood again so I went to practise my archery. That's what I always did when I thought I was going to kill something. I hit the bullseye every time and nothing had died yet, so at least I had that going for me.

I didn't know any other sixteen-year-old girls but the ones in my books didn't obsessively fire arrows because they felt the urge to bite someone. They worried about suitors and ribbons and things. Then again, a few got fed to dragons, so I seemed to have it better than some.

There was still an hour before sundown but the forest around me was blackening into an early twilight. The light barely mattered; I could practise well into the night if I wanted to, still firing perfect shots.

Leap was curled up on my discarded cloak. His eyes were slitted and he watched me, purring when I glanced at him. Far above us Griffin was hovering over the clearing, golden wings spread against a steely sky.

My feet were tangled in the long, unkempt grass. The grounds of the Amentine palace were once the most magnificent in all southern Brivora. Now, they have fallen into disrepair. As the wealth of the House of Amentia trickled away over many generations, so too did the magnificence of the palace. The gardens were weedy and overgrown. The forest had reclaimed the land, and uncut saplings had become towering oaks. Ivy had crept inexorably up the steep castle walls, reaching far above my head to touch the windowsill of my lofty bedroom.

By the time my mother took the crown as queen, the disorder was complete. It would take huge sums of money to repair not only the gardens to their former magnificence, but also the crumbling castle, the spreading mould and unfashionable décor – money we didn't have. It was easier for my mother simply to shut up the unusable parts of the keep. So this was what she did.

I preferred it in the grounds where there were still tracts of scraggy grass and I could set up my archery range, the forest enveloping me on four sides.

The world had all but forgotten our existence, but I found I did not mind so much. I liked my solitude. If given the choice, I would prefer to stay that way forever.

But we wouldn't. Lilith was to be married. And sometime soon, all too soon, it would be my turn for a husband. As Second Daughter I would have to make my home with my husband in his kingdom, wherever that should be.

I grimaced, and swiped another arrow from my quiver. My skin crawled at the thought of someone touching me.

Lilith, on the other hand, had always detested our home for its chilly and ramshackle nature, and was looking forward to her marriage to Prince Lester and life as the future Queen of Varlint. Amentia was hers by inheritance but I doubted she would rule it from its rightful seat. Rather she would reign by proxy from Varlint. Perhaps Amentia had seen its last queen.

I notched the arrow, which I had fletched myself with Griffin's golden feathers, and aimed at the target thirty feet away. I drew back on the taut string, my eyes narrowing, seeing nothing but the ringed red circle.

Before I could fire I was distracted by the urgent drumming of hoof beats approaching rapidly. I tried to shut out the noise but the horse's scream as it was pulled to a sudden halt made me start.

'Drat.' I lowered my bow and waited, ears cocked towards the keep.

Silence.

I raised my bow and drew back on the string. I had the red dot in my sights again when voices reached my ears. I couldn't make out the words but the speakers were agitated. Again I lowered my bow, preferring to wait until the interruption ceased. I glanced at Leap; he was tucked into a tight ball, his short silvery fur fluffed out against the cold. His purr rumbled deep in his chest, and he flexed his claws luxuriously.

I was raising my bow for the third time when a cry rang out. It was sharp and defiant, the noise evaporating quickly in the brittle air.

Lilith.

'Oh, blast it all!' I cried, hurling my bow to the ground, where it bounced harmlessly in the long grass. My concentration was ruined so I bent to unstring the bow. There was no point practising any more today. I would have words with my sister when I got inside. She had no respect for –

I noticed that Leap had lifted his head and his ears were pricked in the direction of the castle. His pupils dilated and he raised himself into a crouch.

My breath caught. Something was wrong.